The ROAD HOME

Books by Beverly Lewis

The Road Home
The Proving • The Ebb Tide
The Wish • The Atonement
The Photograph • The Love Letters
The River

HOME TO HICKORY HOLLOW

The Fiddler • The Bridesmaid
The Guardian • The Secret Keeper
The Last Bride

THE ROSE TRILOGY

The Thorn • The Judgment
The Mercy

ABRAM'S DAUGHTERS

The Covenant • The Betrayal
The Sacrifice • The Prodigal
The Revelation

THE HERITAGE
OF LANCASTER COUNTY

The Shunning • The Confession
The Reckoning

ANNIE'S PEOPLE

The Preacher's Daughter
The Englisher • The Brethren

THE COURTSHIP
OF NELLIE FISHER

The Parting • The Forbidden
The Longing

SEASONS OF GRACE

The Secret • The Missing
The Telling

The Postcard • The Crossroad

The Redemption of Sarah Cain
Sanctuary (with David Lewis)
Child of Mine (with David Lewis)
The Sunroom • October Song
Beverly Lewis Amish Romance
Collection

Amish Prayers
The Beverly Lewis Amish
Heritage Cookbook
The Beverly Lewis Amish
Coloring Book

www.beverlylewis.com

The ROAD HOME

BEVERLY LEWIS

BETHANYHOUSE
a division of Baker Publishing Group
Minneapolis, Minnesota

© 2018 by Beverly M. Lewis, Inc.

Published by Bethany House Publishers
11400 Hampshire Avenue South
Bloomington, Minnesota 55438
www.bethanyhouse.com

Bethany House Publishers is a division of
Baker Publishing Group, Grand Rapids, Michigan

Printed in the United States of America

Library of Congress Cataloging-in-Publication Data
Names: Lewis, Beverly, author.
Title: The road home / Beverly Lewis.
Description: Minneapolis, Minnesota : Bethany House, a division of Baker
    Publishing Group, [2018]
Identifiers: LCCN 2017050531 | ISBN 9780764219672 (softcover) | ISBN
    9780764219924 (hardcover : acid-free paper) | ISBN 9780764219931 (large-print
    : softcover)
Subjects: LCSH: Amish—Fiction. | GSAFD: Christian fiction. | Love stories.
Classification: LCC PS3562.E9383 R63 2018 | DDC 813/.54—dc23
LC record available at https://lccn.loc.gov/2017050531

Scripture quotations are from the King James Version of the Bible.

Cover design by Dan Thornberg, Design Source Creative Services
Art direction by Paul Higdon

18 19 20 21 22 23 24   7 6 5 4 3 2 1

To
Paul and Diane Cucciniella,
my longtime reader-friends
and fellow bookworms!

Pray, and let God worry.

—Martin Luther

Prologue

AUGUST 29, 1977

If you're anything like me, you want to plan ahead. Not too far, but enough to feel prepared. Or at least somewhat settled.

I felt that way while stepping out the back door with my little brother Chris on his way to his first day of school at the one-room Amish schoolhouse of Centreville, Michigan. Carrying a shiny red apple for his teacher to show her respect, Chris was *gut* and ready. I'd taught him to count to fifty in English and drilled him in the alphabet, too.

Chris glanced up at me with his big blue eyes, and I almost leaned down to hug him. He was so adorable in the new school clothes I'd made for him—a pale blue shirt and black trousers—and his thin black suspenders and new straw hat. From the time he was nearly two, I had sewn his clothes, seamstress that I was. After having ten children, *Mamma* was plumb tuckered out, so she had assigned most of Chris's care to me once he was weaned.

This day, though, things were about to change. And right quick, too, as our four school-age brothers would burst out of the house at any moment now. Chris would walk to school with them,

7

swinging his little lunch pail in rhythm with theirs, moving ever so quickly into the world of boys and, eventually, young men.

Out near our mailbox, Chris stopped briefly to greet one of *Dawdi* Schwartz's peacocks, which had come strutting out onto the dirt road toward us. Then, of all things, if the bird didn't spread its colorful feathers and just stand there while Chris grinned at him. Dawdi and *Mammi* Schwartz lived in an addition built onto our uncle Matthew's farmhouse. With only two bedrooms, it was small, but the sitting room was oversized, unusual for most *Dawdi Hauses*. Best of all, it was less than a quarter mile from us and a short distance from the three-year-old Amish schoolhouse.

"Mammi Schwartz will prob'ly wave to you on the way home from school," I told Chris. "On nice days, she might even come out and offer a treat."

"I like *your* snacks best, Lena," he said in *Deitsch*, anticipation shining on his little face.

I patted his slim shoulder as he mentioned the gathering we'd had last evening at the house. Like usual, I'd helped Mamma with the big feast, even though my sister Emma did most of the everyday cooking. Mamma's kitchen was always filled with people and delicious food.

Chris licked his lips. "Your chocolate cake made me want more than one slice."

"I noticed that." I grinned at him. "But no one paid any mind since it was *Dat's* birthday."

"And the start of school for *me*," Chris said with a dramatic nod of his head.

At just that moment, here came Hans Bontrager in his father's buckboard, his brown bangs peeping out from beneath his wide-brimmed straw hat.

"Hullo, Lena Rose!" Hans slowed his beautiful chestnut-colored horse. "Where are ya goin' this fine August mornin'?"

I blushed, and little Chris must've noticed, because his eyes started blinking right quick. "Oh, just sayin' good-bye to *mei Bruder.*"

"A new scholar?" Hans smiled as he studied Chris.

"*Jah,*" I said. "And eager for book learnin'."

Hans glanced behind me, where four more of Chris's and my brothers were coming our way now, laughing and talking. "He might as well join the rest of the *Kinner,* ain't?"

I nodded. "This day couldn't come soon enough for him."

"*Gut* thing they finally allowed Amish schools around here, ain't so?"

I wholeheartedly agreed. Like Hans, I'd had to attend public school. How Dat had despised sending us older kids off to the world thataway! Why, some of the men in nearby Elkhart County, Indiana, had been put in jail for keeping their school-age children home. It had been an awful time for many Old Order families.

Hans picked up the driving lines. "Well, I'll see ya at the deacon's house for Ping-Pong come Saturday night," he said before clicking his tongue to signal his horse forward.

Once Hans was out of earshot, Chris said quietly, "He must like ya, Lena Rose."

I smiled down at his earnest face. It had long been my hope that Hans and I might court one day, and now that we were an official couple after two months of dating, my dream had come true.

"Ya comin', Chris?" asked our brother Timothy.

I brushed a stray bit of milkweed fluff from Chris's hat. "Have yourself a *wunnerbaar-gut* day," I said, proud as a Mamma to see him off.

He turned and gave me the dearest smile. "See ya after school," he called in return. Twice more he looked back, waving each time as though I might disappear from sight.

Standing there, I watched Chris fall into step with our brothers Timothy and Benjamin, ages eight and nine, and the twins—Mose and Sam—ten and a half. All of them hugged the side of the road, bobbing along as they picked up their pace.

Ach, the moment was bittersweet. Even so, I was happy for Chris, and I marveled at how much he'd grown since the days when I steadied him while he learned to walk, or put a small spoon in his dimpled right hand to teach him to eat his applesauce.

Like any doting big sister, I trusted that he'd do well now that he, too, was one of the big kids.

Walking back toward the house, I looked over my shoulder at Chris once more before heading inside.

Today, Mamma had entrusted Emma and me with making sure the younger children were cleaned up and ready for school on time. She'd hated having to miss seeing Chris off herself, but early this morning she had gone to Middlebury, Indiana, to substitute teach at an Amish-Mennonite school not far from the RV factory where Dat worked as a supervisor in the cabinetry department. Naturally, I'd promised to tell her all about Chris's morning once she and Dat arrived home this afternoon. Oh, I could hardly wait to share Chris's joy with her . . . despite my own mixed feelings.

Mamma will understand. She's been through this ten times now!

─ᴄ᷇ ᷄ᴄ─

In the kitchen, seventeen-year-old Emma was making an attempt to hurry along our younger sisters, Liz, turning fourteen in October, and Verena, twelve, both dallying as they were known to do. "Yous don't wanna be late on the first day, do ya?" Emma said as she motioned them toward the back door. "Time's a-wastin'!"

"Pay close attention to the teacher," I said as they poked along, jabbering in *Deitsch* as if in a world of their own. "If you're late, you might have to wash all the chalkboards after school!"

At my warning, they scurried along.

"You sound like Mamma," said Emma, who turned her attention back to the four apple pies she was making for tonight's supper—two for the twelve of us, and two for our close neighbors, Elmer and Polly Neuenschwander. Although our amiable neighbors were Old Order Amish like we were, they gave all of us children gifts every year at Christmastime. And because of that, Mamma had made pies and fresh-baked bread to take over to them for all these many years.

I sat down at the table and sighed. "I was glad to see Chris head off for school. But honestly, I feel a twinge of sadness, too."

"Aw . . . well, he's been itchin' to start." Emma pushed one pie after another into the old black wood stove.

"*Jah*, and I'll get more work done without my little shadow, ain't?"

Emma was more interested in baking than in looking after a younger sibling. In fact, I'd often hinted that she would do well to run a bakery somewhere and skip marriage. She would just roll her brown eyes at me and laugh. Truth was, every courting-age young woman round these parts was keen on getting hitched up with a fine Amish boy, settling down, and having babies.

"Maybe it's time to turn the pages of your own life, sister . . . with Hans." Emma came over to sit beside me on the long wooden bench, flour on the tip of her nose.

I agreed, thinking how exciting it was to be his girl. "He said he'd see me at Ping-Pong Saturday night," I said.

Emma eyed me for a moment. "He *told* ya . . . didn't ask?"

I wasn't sure how to take her seeming concern. "*Puh!* We have an understanding now."

"Well, surely he's polite and still invites you on dates."

"Now and then, *jah*." I was so new at all this courtship business, I really didn't know what was considered acceptable. I was
surprised Emma already had opinions on such things.

"I've seen him wink at ya during Singings." Emma's eyes locked
with mine. "I s'pose Mamma has an idea you're seein' someone."

"Not just yet, but I'll tell her soon. Still . . . ain't like I'll be
wed by this November."

"*Nee*, yous need time to get well acquainted." Emma put her
arms around me. "I'm happy for ya, if you think he's the one."

"You'll be the first to know when I'm engaged," I assured her,
filled with hope.

"And I'll hold ya to it," Emma said as she went to check on
her pies.

CHAPTER

1

Centreville, Michigan, was situated on the Prairie River. It was a close-knit town, and Lena loved it for just that reason. Everyone knew each other by first name . . . and also minded everyone else's business, which was either good or bad, depending on who you were or what you'd done. There were always amusing stories floating around on the grapevine: which sixteen-year-old fellow had raced a train in his new open carriage at the railroad crossing in nearby Wasepi, or which young woman had sewn the hem of her dress too short. Or even which Amish farmer had sneaked off to listen to his portable transistor radio when Hank Aaron beat Babe Ruth's home run record.

Aside from ordinary gossip like that, there was no one more caring and generous than the People up and down those southern Michigan back roads. These were the folk Lena Rose had known all of her eighteen-and-a-half years, and her heart was tightly wound around her hometown and the family she loved so dearly.

That hot late-August afternoon seemed to drag on like never before as she helped Emma put up peaches. Lena caught herself looking at the day clock, wondering what new things six-year-old Chris was learning.

She remembered again her own school days, when she and other Amish children were required to attend public schools. *How far we've come*, Lena thought, glad Chris got the chance to do his learning amongst the People. She fastened the lid on the last jar of peaches and put it in the canner, thinking ahead to what she might prepare as an after-school snack for her younger siblings.

"Goat cheese and crackers, and sliced apples," she murmured to herself.

Emma glanced at her. "*Ach*, delicious," she said. "But it's too soon after the noon meal for a snack, ain't?" she teased.

The two of them discussed what they planned to make for supper, wanting to have the food ready to serve and the table set when Mamma arrived with Dat. "No need to have her lift a finger today," Lena said, eager to see to it that everything was just so for their hardworking mother.

"Are we sure there won't be any extra mouths to feed tonight?" Emma asked.

"I hardly think so, considering all the family was together yesterday." Lena recalled last evening's wonderful-good time with Dawdi and Mammi Schwartz.

Pouring some coffee, she thought ahead to hearing Chris tell about his first day. Surely he would be as full of stories and fun as ever. She remembered last Sunday, when she'd driven Dat's second family carriage to Preaching service—they regularly had to use two buggies to fit all twelve of them. After settling herself into the driver's seat that morning, Lena had watched Chris race across the driveway and hop right in next to her, excited to talk about his plans with cousins that afternoon.

My sweet little brother, she thought, taking a tentative sip from her steaming mug.

At that very moment, their house cat leaped lightly down

from her favorite spot on the sunny windowsill near the entrance to the utility room. She stretched long and leisurely, mouth wide.

"Your food dish is full," Emma told the cat, pointing over to the corner, "in case you're hungry *again*."

"Our Tubby Tabby," Lena said, laughing softly. "All she does is eat and sleep."

"Dat says if we all ate as often as she does, we'd be as round as full moons." Emma smiled.

They continued their work in the kitchen until they were startled by several loud raps on the frame of the screen door. Lena and Emma turned in unison to see two policemen standing on the porch.

A myriad of worries bloomed in Lena's head—had something happened to one of the children at school? To little Chris?

Emma coaxed Lena to go to the door, where she was so nervous she could scarcely answer sensibly when the officers asked if this was the residence of Jacob and Elizabeth Schwartz.

"*Jah*, 'tis," she managed to eke out.

The kind-looking older policeman asked if they might step inside for a moment, his jaw set solemnly. And even before they suggested the two young women sit down, Lena Rose sensed something dreadful, felt it clear down in her bones.

"There's no good way to say this." The younger officer looked at his feet for a moment before revealing that Dat and Mamma had been in a terrible road accident. "It happened earlier this afternoon in Indiana . . . on the outskirts of Middlebury," he said, his voice low.

Holding her breath, Lena waited for more information. *Are they in the hospital?*

Behind her, her sister whispered, "Will Dat and Mamma be all right?"

The policemen's expressions remained grim, and the two men exchanged glances.

"I'm awful sorry," the younger officer said then.

She couldn't bear to hear what followed.

"No one in the passenger van survived."

Lena tried to process what this meant. Mamma and Dat were both strong and in perfect health. How could her precious parents be gone? *Gone all too suddenly to Glory.*

"They never knew what happened." The older officer said this as if to reassure them, but Lena felt a wave of despair descend as the awful words lingered in the air.

After the policemen left, Lena Rose held Emma in her arms for the longest time, too stunned to cry herself. *How can this be?* she kept asking herself, trapped in a state of disbelief. She could scarcely take a breath, shocked to think that their parents had died, along with other Amish passengers from the nearby town of Sturgis.

Only hours before, Mamma had kissed all of them good-bye before getting into the large van with Dat—their usual routine. Lena had hugged Mamma extra close. Who would have imagined that it would be the last she'd see her and Dat alive—the last time they would say "*Ich liebe dich*" to each other?

Somehow, Lena and Emma managed to get themselves out of the house. They searched first in the barn for their fifteen-year-old brother, Wilbur. Not finding him there or in the stable, where the market wagon was missing, they trudged across their father's wide pasture to Deacon Joe Miller's adjoining farm. *We must talk to him before the younger children return home,* Lena Rose thought as the train whistle blew in the distance. Her heart ached at the very idea of telling them the dire news.

Fortunately, the middle-aged deacon was home, so Lena

informed him of what the police had said only a mere half hour earlier. Stone-faced and shaken, the dear man vowed to undertake the job of getting the word out that Jacob and Elizabeth Schwartz had perished . . . and that their ten children were suddenly orphans.

"What'll happen to us?" Emma asked later as she and Lena waited in their Mamma's kitchen for the rest of their siblings to return from school. The minutes seemed to stretch into hours. Wilbur had returned from the Truckenmiller hardware store in town and was out in the barn with Uncle Noah, their father's eldest brother, who had pulled up in his buggy shortly after receiving word from the deacon. And Mammi Schwartz, a good many aunts, and Clara Yoder, their nearby preacher's wife, as well as a host of other womenfolk, including English neighbors, had arrived to take over making supper and other chores.

When the younger children hurried into the house, with confusion on their faces at all the activity and the sight of so many buggies parked in the side yard, Lena went with Emma and Wilbur to sit with all of them in the front room. "This is the hardest thing I'll ever have to say, my dear brothers and sisters," she said softly, struggling to get the words out as she told them what had befallen their Dat and Mamma.

The school-age boys wore deep frowns as they turned to look at one another, mirroring the shock and horror of their older siblings. Wilbur put his arm around the twins, and Lena and Emma reached for Verena and Liz as the girls wept. Yet it was young Chris who took it hardest. The poor boy slipped between his sisters and crawled into Lena's lap like a toddler, crying as she held him, his shoulders shaking. It wasn't long before the rest of the children formed a sort of circle around them, hands clasped. *They all depend on me,* Lena thought, wishing she were stronger. How would she tend to them when her own heart was in tatters?

After the family picked at their supper amidst an atmosphere of leaden sadness, Dawdi and Mammi Schwartz lingered with them at the table, and Deacon Miller opened his *Biewel* and began to read. Then all heads bowed at the table for a silent prayer before Lena Rose and Emma helped Mammi ready the younger children for bedtime.

In the midst of her own distress, Lena fleetingly wondered if it might be possible for them to stay together in their parents' farmhouse. But the question loomed much too big in her mind for such a day. "I'll do whatever it takes to keep us together," Lena told Emma later, determined to be courageous for her siblings' sake.

"I know ya will," Emma said, tears flowing freely as she sat on the edge of the bed.

But truly, Lena had no inkling what the future held.

2

By the time the sun had set that day, Lena Rose felt completely immersed in the reality of their enormous loss. This heart-rending sorrow was too much for anyone to bear, even a young woman taught to accept whatever came her way as being from the hand of the Lord. The sovereignty of God was the way of peace and not strife, Dat had always said. The People did not shake their fists toward heaven, questioning the hitches along life's path. But in spite of her acceptance, Lena could not understand how this could possibly be part of God's plan.

In the few days before the funeral, Uncle Noah came regularly to look in on them with his wife, Mary, both of them doing what they could to comfort the children, even spending the nights there. Mercifully, the ministerial brethren had suggested a joint service to spare the family the difficulty of facing such an ordeal twice.

Once the burials were behind them, Lena knew life must somehow go on for her and her siblings. She was busily redding up the front room the day after the funeral when she glanced up to see all her brothers and sisters shuffling into the large room.

"We'd like to talk to ya, Lena Rose," Emma said softly. "Just our family."

Their faces were grim, though little Chris looked the most forlorn.

Wilbur got right to the point. "What's going to happen now? Do ya know? Can we stay put here . . . with you overseein' us, maybe?"

Lena sighed, her heart going out to them. "I'm working things out with Uncle Noah as best I can, but I can't say for sure."

Liz's and Verena's expressions registered worry.

"Why can't we keep on livin' here?" Liz asked. "It's our home . . . where we were born."

"*Jah*, we wanna stay with *you*," Mose echoed as his twin nodded. Their solemn eyes focused on Lena.

"We'd obey whatever you said," Chris pledged.

"With no fussin' or talkin' back," Benjamin added.

"We promise," Timothy said.

Emma nodded her head and pressed her lips together as if trying not to cry. "We belong together."

"You're absolutely right," Lena said, recalling the earnest conversations she'd had with various relatives these past few days. "But the bishop thinks I'm too young to keep the house and farm going. There are just so many responsibilities." Lena wished she were better equipped to handle such a challenge. "I'm doing all I can, though, and I can promise each of you that *Gott* will watch over us, no matter where we end up," she said, trying hard to make herself believe the words.

Emma sighed and looked dejected. "I can't just *hope* we'll stay together, Lena Rose. I need to know it!"

"Oh, sister." Lena pulled her near, understanding exactly what she meant.

—◌ ◌—

After evening prayers, while Emma and Wilbur had the younger children wash up for bed, Lena Rose sat down at the kitchen table with Uncle Noah and Aunt Mary, not certain what to expect. The deacon had appointed Noah to locate a home for them, preferably with relatives.

"I know you've been hopin' to keep all of yous together here in your father's home, but it's just not feasible," Uncle Noah said, confirming Lena's fears.

"Would ya at least give me a chance to try? I'd do everything within my power."

Uncle Noah shook his head. "I'm mighty sorry, Lena Rose," he said. "I truly am. But the brethren and the People are in agreement. It's too much to ask."

Lena Rose knew better than to argue with her father's elder brother, but something in her wanted to continue to fight. She traced her finger along a groove in the table Dat had built soon after he married Mamma. "I was afraid of this," she admitted. "And honestly, I can't think of anyone in Centreville who's able to care for all ten of us. But I can't bear to see us separated."

Uncle Noah regarded her kindly. "I wish I could locate a family, but with this many *Kinner* . . . it just isn't gonna happen. Not even with close kinfolk."

Suppressing her heartache, Lena considered the few uncles and aunts who were in any position to take in more than one or two of them, what with the number of available bedrooms or the advanced age of the relatives themselves. She knew he was right.

"At the very least, the twins ought to stay together," she urged.

"Keepin' Mose and Sam together does make *gut* sense," Uncle Noah agreed, his wrinkled hand gripping the coffee cup while his usually jovial wife looked on sadly across the kitchen table. "If we could, Mary and I would open our home, but with just the one bedroom, there's no room for even one extra in our *Dawdi Haus*." Uncle Noah stroked his long graying beard.

Lena Rose assured him that she did not expect that. Even so, she would continue to pray for a single family to step forward, unlikely as that was.

"The Neuenschwanders just up the road might have room for three of the boys. Maybe the twins and Benjamin could go there," Uncle Noah suggested, brow furrowed, "since they're close in age."

"But Benjamin and Timothy are so fond of each other. I don't think the two of them should be separated, either," Lena said, shaking her head. "*Ach*, I really dislike splitting up *any* of us, let alone having some go outside the family."

Uncle Noah ran his thick fingers through his beard. "'Tis not ideal, I know."

Truth was, Lena felt overwhelmed by the weight of it all . . . and the news of their enormous loss was still only days old. She wished with all of her heart that she knew what her parents would want for them. As relatively young as Dat and Mamma were, they'd never discussed anything of the sort. But unexpected things sometimes happened, and Dat had always taught them to trust in their heavenly Father. "*He alone knows what's best*," dear Dat had often said.

"We really oughta call it a night," Aunt Mary said as she leaned forward at the table, her blue eyes filled with tears. "Let you get some much-needed rest, Lena Rose."

I don't see how, Lena thought miserably.

"Meanwhile, we'll look to *Gott* for help, as we do each day." Uncle Noah pushed his chair back.

Aunt Mary quietly picked up their coffee cups and carried them to the sink.

Lena was relieved her aunt and uncle were staying with them again tonight. On top of her ongoing sorrow, she felt panicked about the likelihood of not being able to keep the family together, of disappointing her brothers and sisters. The sense of utter helplessness was almost paralyzing.

Going upstairs after her uncle and aunt headed for bed, Lena tried not to think about the dilemma her beloved family was facing, let alone their treasured house being sold at auction to the highest bidder. *We're losing everything.* But at least the house wouldn't be put up for sale till they were all settled with new families.

Must we split up, O Lord? she prayed. *Isn't there another way?*

Tiptoeing from one bedroom to another, Lena looked in on her cherished siblings, covering them with the lightweight summer quilts Mamma had made through the years. She couldn't bear to think of being apart from any of them. How could they endure such a thing, especially now?

At Wilbur's bedside, she clasped her brother's strong hand, his bedsheet twisted like a rope around him. "You can't sleep, *jah?*" she whispered.

He lifted his head and nodded. "Who can?" Wilbur pushed his free hand through his light brown hair. "I overheard ya talkin' downstairs."

Lena nodded without elaborating.

Sighing, Wilbur said, "If only I was older . . . then maybe we could stay together, ain't?"

"*Gott* sees our hearts. . . . I know He cares for us." She gripped his hand all the more tightly.

Wilbur's breath seemed to catch in his throat. "No matter what, we'll always be a close family, *jah?*"

"For certain." She patted his hand and remembered the time one of their bantam hens had pecked the back of her hand while they were collecting eggs. Eight-year-old Wilbur, bless his heart, had wiped the blood off with his blue paisley kerchief. Even though he was three years younger than she, Wilbur was always finding little ways to look after her. *Dat and Mamma were both so pleased with him. . . .*

Not wanting to break down in front of her brother, Lena left the room quietly.

She made her way back to the youngest boys' room and walked to Chris's bed. Leaning down to gently touch his forehead, tears welled up as she remembered his heartbroken reaction to their parents' passing. He'd clung to her like he had as a tiny boy when frightened by thunder and lightning.

Satisfied that Chris was asleep, Lena made her way to the room she shared with Emma at the far end of the hall, next to Liz and Verena's room. *Dear Lord in heaven, please comfort our broken hearts again this night,* Lena prayed. She couldn't let her dismay at the accident keep her from praying.

The oil lantern was still lit on Emma's side of the bed, where her sister sat in her white cotton nightgown reading her *Biewel*. When she looked up, Lena saw her tear-stained face and went to sit beside her.

"Has anything been decided yet?" Emma asked softly, her blond braids already out of her daily bun for the night.

Lena sighed, her mind foggy with grief. "Our hope is in the Lord. We must keep prayin' for a family to take us in. *All* of us."

"Oh, Lena . . ." Emma frowned and looked terribly worried. "Who could offer such a thing?"

Lena Rose didn't want to tell her dear sister that, aside from a miracle, they would be scattered to the winds.

"I've been thinkin'," Emma said, her voice husky with emotion, "I'd like to help you and the womenfolk sort through Mamma's and Dat's things tomorrow. Could I?"

"Are ya sure, sister?"

Emma blinked and nodded. "Won't be easy, but I really want to."

Gently, Lena pulled her sister near. "Doing it together will make it less painful. *Denki*."

Thus far, Lena Rose had done her best to grieve privately; she had to be strong for her brothers and sisters. *Dear Lord, may it be so,* she prayed as she removed her black *Kapp* and unpinned her own heavy braids. She thought of all the many times Mamma had gently brushed and braided her hair when she was little. *How I miss you and Dat already*, Lena thought, tears falling.

⸺◌ ◌⸺

The deacon dropped by a few days later on his way to help the neighbors dig potatoes with other menfolk from the church district. He proposed that Lena Rose and Uncle Noah go with him to the front room to talk. There, her uncle shared that he'd heard from one of his English neighbors that they were interested in opening their door to a few of the children. "But I turned them down," he said. "Didn't seem right, really."

Deacon Miller then went on to name a nearby family that had offered a place for Emma, Liz, and Verena just yesterday. "They're real fine Amish folk with other children similar in age. Your sisters will be well looked after. And another home just up the road from them has space for Wilbur."

So it's done. A chill swept through Lena. *We are to be separated.*

"There is also one particular couple who could really use *your* help, Lena." Deacon's expression turned serious. "Harley Stoltzfus is your father's second cousin, and his wife, Mimi, is a seamstress like you. They replied to my telegram and indicated they'd be glad to pay ya for your work . . . and happy for your companionship for Mimi, too."

Harley . . . and Mimi? Lena had heard her father talk of these relatives—Dat had met Harley at a wedding many years ago. *But they live in Pennsylvania!*

Uncle Noah raised his eyebrows and nodded. "It would be a *gut* situation for ya, Lena. And maybe you could send some of the money ya earn to help with your younger siblings—for clothing and whatnot."

This was the worst possible thing Lena could think of. Oh, how she despised the idea of leaving Centreville!

"Your father kept in close contact with Harley through the years," her uncle continued. "He was mighty fond of him."

Lena shook her head. "But they live out east." Truly, Harley and Mimi Stoltzfus might as well have been on the other side of the world.

"That's the difficult part," the deacon agreed slowly, eyes serious.

"It's entirely up to you," Uncle Noah assured her. "But you'd have a place to stay for the time being—just a few months or so—and then surely something here will open up for you."

"Only a short time, then?"

"*Jah*, that's my guess . . . and your Dat would be in favor of Harley and Mimi's invitation, to be sure," Uncle Noah added. "Your room and board would be free there, too—another benefit."

Even though he'd said it was her choice to make, she could tell that her uncle thought it was a good idea.

"Besides, as unlikely as it may seem, you might come to enjoy your time there. Lancaster County is beautiful, with many *gut* folk."

How can I possibly enjoy anything ever again? she thought, wanting only to be with her brothers and sisters.

Yet as challenging as this was, Lena knew she had to set a good example for her siblings and be courageous. She needed to consider this option, no matter how discouraged she felt.

Their discussion continued, and in the end, they put their heads together to decide where all of her brothers and sisters would live, Chris included. Lena gave a great sigh and straightened her shoulders. There remained just one more decision to make.

If I do go to Pennsylvania, I'll be home soon, she reasoned, recalling Uncle Noah's words.

3

Two weeks later, Lena Rose found herself on a bus heading to Pennsylvania. Though she knew she would never send it, she passed the time by writing a long letter to Emma, express-ing how heartsick she was at leaving, even though she expected to see them all again at Christmas. *But that's three long months away. . . .* Writing out the sad words also helped her release the intense grief she felt at the sudden loss of Dat and Mamma. The memory of the policemen coming into the farmhouse with the devastating news continued to plague her nightly dreams, shat-tering her life anew.

She recalled now her last encounter with Hans, who'd dropped by to see her as she helped pack up the house for auction. Her beau had worn such disappointment on his handsome face when she told of her plans to go to Pennsylvania for a few months to help her relatives with sewing work.

"Where else can I go?" she'd said woefully. There was simply no one in Centreville able to take her in. Lena had even tried to rent a place with several other young women her age, but without ready employment, that had turned out to be a dead end.

Hans had been silent as she shared about her thwarted attempts to stay in Michigan, not suggesting she check with any of his own relatives. Considering how he seemed to care for her, she wondered why.

Yet as they were about to part ways, Hans had reached for her hand and asked if he could keep in close touch with her by mail. "I'd like to continue courtin' you long-distance till you return," he'd said, his usual bright smile somewhat faded. "I'd hate to lose ya, Lena Rose."

Her heart had been soothed, hearing him say it so fervently, and she'd nodded, her eyes searching his.

"You'll write back, *jah?*" he had asked.

"Of course!" she was quick to reply. Truly, it was a relief to know he would be awaiting her return.

As the sun began to rise, Lena Rose leaned now against the cool pane of the bus window and gazed out at the familiar landscape of her life. *I'm leaving my family and everything I know behind.* She sighed, trying to keep her composure.

—⁓ ⁓—

After the bus arrived in downtown Lancaster, Lena got a taxi and instructed the driver to take her to West Eby Road. After stepping into the back seat, she closed her eyes, weary from the long, confining bus ride and her heavy heart.

At the appointed address in Leacock Township, she admired the white frame farmhouse with ivy laced about its stone foundation. The place was well kept, with a rather large *Dawdi Haus* attached to the east side of the main house. It looked as though both houses had been newly painted, and a darling little potting shed nearby was sheltered on one side by a tall silver maple. What Lena could see of the lawn had been freshly mown, and the side near the driveway neatly edged. On the long front porch were several pieces of brown wicker furniture—two rockers and other chairs.

Suddenly, it seemed as if months had passed since Lena Rose had helped her siblings get packed and moved in with their new families. She swallowed the hard lump in her throat. Uncle Noah and Aunt Mary had been so kind as to suggest that Lena and her sisters choose favorite pieces of furniture to set aside for their hope chests, which Uncle Noah had stored for all of them. Lena Rose had also encouraged each of the children to choose something smaller of their parents' personal possessions to take with them, letting her brothers and sisters make their choices first. Afterward, she had selected a handful of colorful postcards of Holmes County, Ohio, which Dat had written to Mamma from afar one summer while they were courting.

Lena paid the driver as she got out of the cab, glad to finally have arrived. Yet young Chris was constantly on her mind, and she wondered how he was doing. Did he still wish the Neuenschwanders might have had room for him, too, with his close-in-age brothers? He'd whispered this to her the day before she'd said her farewell, his lower lip trembling. *Dear boy!*

Alas, other than herself, Chris and Wilbur were the only ones who had been placed in a home without other siblings. She hoped Chris would slowly adjust to life with Dawdi and Mammi Schwartz, who'd also agreed to take Tabby, the family's beloved cat. Chris was a lively boy, so their grandparents' being up in years concerned Lena, but the way things had worked out, there was no better option, and she was thankful that Chris was with people he loved and had always spent so much time with. Mammi Schwartz had promised to write to Lena at least once a week, and it would be heartening to have those updates.

Scenes of her other siblings together with their new families played out in Lena's mind as she carried her suitcases up the driveway to her own new residence, trying to be brave. Lena thought of the difficult good-byes said there to the deacon and his dear wife and the others who came for Lena's own send-off.

"Nothing will be the same without you here," Emma had tearfully admitted that day.

Lena thought of all the upcoming fall activities she would miss. All the milestones. And silently, she recited her brothers' and sisters' names to God, asking for divine comfort.

Just then, a large black German shepherd came running toward her, wagging its tail. "Someone's here to greet me," she murmured. "Aren't you a friendly one."

The dog accompanied her as Lena made her way around toward the side yard, where she spotted a picturesque bench made from willow branches near a large tree and a rose garden. She paused a moment, set down her suitcases, and went over to touch the bench, feeling the contours of its wood and eyeing the seat cushion.

A peaceful spot, she thought.

Then, as she was about to approach the window-paned back door, she heard a man's voice. Turning, she saw the man who had to be her father's cousin, Harley Stoltzfus, waving and calling her name as he hurried toward her. He closely resembled her dear father, though an older version of him.

"Willkumm, Lena Rose," Harley said, extending his hand. "I see you've met Blackie." He nodded to indicate the dog and then picked up her things. "Mimi and I have been lookin' forward to your arrival. You have no idea how glad we are to see ya."

"Denki, it's kind of yous to make a place for me," Lena said, following him through the door as he opened it and stepped aside. It was hard not to stare at the man. The set of Harley's brown eyes and the shape of his mouth were so similar to Dat's. Even the lines near his eyes fanned out in the same way, as though he smiled a lot.

"Mimi, lookee who's here!" Harley called as they entered the outer room, where shoes and boots were lined up on the floor under a row of jackets and sweaters hung from a wooden panel of hooks.

In the kitchen, Lena Rose noticed the highly polished black cookstove, exactly like her mother's back home. Whatever was cooking inside smelled delicious.

"Mimi must be busy in her sewing room," Harley said just moments before a woman came into the kitchen through a narrow doorway. "Lena's arrived," he said, touching Lena's arm lightly as he made introductions.

"Hullo," Mimi said, her voice lilting up at the end of the word. She looked a bit flushed as she pushed a stray hair away from her round face. "We prayed for traveling mercies. Thank our dear Lord you made it safely."

Lena stepped forward to politely embrace her. "I couldn't be more grateful."

"Well, dear, it's our honor to have you with us."

The woman's warm demeanor was soothing, and Lena felt welcomed like close family, rather than merely a second cousin once removed.

"Ada, our older married daughter just up the way, came and redded up the house real *gut*—cleaned like we were hosting Preachin'," Mimi said, face still aglow. "You'll see her over here helpin' out once a week."

"Mimi's too busy sewing to bother keepin' house," Harley said, a twinkle in his eyes.

"'Tis true, actually," Mimi said, giving her husband a good-natured look. "But remember, Lena Rose, I don't expect ya to do a speck of cleaning, either. And you'll have spare time away from sewin' on Saturdays, as well as Sundays."

"I'm glad to do what I can, though," Lena said, truly meaning it.

Mimi explained that Harley's uncle, Solomon Stoltzfus, lived in the *Dawdi Haus* next door, as did their youngest son, Eli, who had recently turned twenty and just moved out of the main house. "The two of them often come over for the noon meal, as well as supper. Not all the time, mind you, but whenever they're tired of peanut butter and jelly sandwiches." At this, she smiled.

Harley chuckled. "Mimi's a fine cook, and they know it," he added, winking at his stout wife.

Lena couldn't help recalling how Mamma had enjoyed having extras at their large table. With family and friends surrounding them, those meals had been the best of times.

"Let's get ya settled before we have supper," Mimi said, offering to show Lena her room upstairs. "You'll be down the hall from us in our younger daughter's old room. Tessa moved south of here, near Bart Township, when she married nearly two years ago. . . ." The way Mimi's voice trailed off caught Lena's attention, but she just listened. It would take some doing to get herself established here with a strange new family. Such a jolt, really, after living her whole life in one farmhouse, where the creak of every floorboard was familiar.

Thankfully, it'll only be for a few months. . . .

───～⌒ ⌒～───

When Harley and Eli came in for the evening meal, Eli sat at the table with Lena, as cordial and welcoming as his parents. Like many other Amish farmers in the area, Harley relied on the help of his youngest son and a number of farmhands to run the large dairy operation.

Eli reached for two snickerdoodle cookies that Mimi had said she'd baked that morning. "It won't take long an' you'll feel right at home here," he said.

Aware that his countenance reflected only compassion, Lena

took his words to heart despite her own doubts. Mostly, Eli's comment brought a sense of relief.

"I must try to count my blessings," she whispered.

—ᘓ ᘒ—

That night, as Lena prepared for bed, she prayed again for her brothers and sisters, as well as for her parents' siblings, knowing that her uncles and aunts were also grieved by the unexpected loss. And she asked the Lord to remember the families that had taken her siblings in, grateful for the big hearts of the People in the Centreville church district.

When Cousin Mimi Stoltzfus knocked gently on the bedroom door, offering to pray for her, Lena struggled to hold back her emotion in the soft light of Mimi's lantern.

Mimi stayed a bit longer to sit on the edge of the bed and talk quietly with Lena. "If there's anything at all ya need," Mimi said, "ya mustn't hesitate to ask." Then she began to sweetly quote a psalm. "'The LORD is nigh unto them that are of a broken heart. . . .'"

"*Denki*," Lena said, having never considered the hope offered in that verse.

Mimi squeezed Lena's hand. "Harley and I will keep you and your brothers and sisters in our prayers. We'll do everything we can to help you feel comfortable here."

"You're so kind." Lena felt truly cared for in this house.

"Now, you just try an' rest, all right?" Mimi rose and tiptoed out of the room.

Lena drew a slow, deep breath and almost wished the kindly woman had kissed her cheek, like Mamma always had when Lena was little. Sighing, she let her tears fall onto the plump feather pillow.

—ᘓ ᘒ—

At the first rays of sunlight the next morning, Lena slipped out of bed and went to the window. The view of acres of hay and corn fields, and the expanse of pastureland to accommodate the large Holstein herd there, was a bit different from that in Centreville, where her father's house had overlooked a vast pumpkin patch and fruit farm. The similarities, though, reminded her of home, and it was jarring to realize yet again that so many miles separated her from her siblings.

Lena noticed Mimi's rustic bench as she stood at the window, wrapped in sunlight. The pretty rose trellises that surrounded it made the area almost like an outdoor room, and Mimi, as poised and pleasant a woman as Lena had ever known, had shared about her time spent praying on that well-worn bench there beneath the trees. *"Those prayers have brought great blessings to my life, and answers from God's unfailing hand,"* Mimi had told Lena shortly after her arrival yesterday. *"I miss that spot in the deep of winter,"* the lovely woman had added.

According to Mimi, her prayers were not so much about pleading, but more a time to be still in God's presence. *"I like to give Him thanks in my own quiet way,"* Mimi had explained.

Lena had never heard of such a prayer bench, though the idea of sitting somewhere so tranquil to beseech her heavenly Father had appeal now that she considered the notion. As for herself, Lena knew the thing that would bring her the greatest joy would be to eventually return home. Surely the deacon or Uncle Noah would locate a place for her to work and live right quick.

Till then, I'll be content to devour Hans's letters! she thought, eagerly anticipating the arrival of the first one. Lena dressed for the day, recalling Uncle Noah's obvious relief when she'd agreed to accept Harley and Mimi's invitation here, where so many things were unfamiliar, from the closed style of family buggies to even the dialect of Pennsylvania Dutch. The cut and colors of Lena's

Plain dresses and aprons would surely stand out amongst those of the Leacock Township womenfolk, as well. And the hair bun beneath her black head covering with tiny pleats in back was wound of tight braids—far different from Mimi's smooth bun worn under a white, heart-shaped *Kapp*. *Will they think I'm fancy?* she wondered.

Yet despite a natural desire to fit in, Lena thought it wasteful not to wear her customary dresses, capes, and aprons, as well as the *Kapp* of her church district. In all truth, it wouldn't matter much, since she wasn't going to be in Lancaster County for too awful long.

May the time here pass swiftly, Lord.

CHAPTER

4

The following morning, after the breakfast dishes were washed and dried and placed back in the cupboard, Cousin Mimi motioned Lena Rose into the sewing room to offer her the job of pinning on patterns for a dress, cape, and apron while Mimi did some of the customers' alterations.

Being given free room and board, and getting paid for her help with sewing and mending, seemed nearly too good to be true.

"It's a privilege to work alongside ya," Lena said as she reached for the pincushion, then unfolded the unfamiliar pattern onto the royal blue fabric. She smoothed it out and began to pin it in place.

The room set aside for Mimi's sewing had three large windows, two on the side facing the backyard, and one facing the *Dawdi Haus*. It was furnished practically, with a long table for laying out patterns, a tall, skinny spool chest, and a freestanding cupboard stained to match. In addition, a treadle sewing machine sat along the back wall beneath a multicolored, quilted wall hanging that looked to be an antique.

"Has Eli invited you to attend the next Singing with the other courting-age youth?" Mimi asked, breaking the silence. Her rosy-cheeked face shone there at the treadle sewing machine, where she sat threading the bobbin.

Lena cringed inwardly, thinking it was much too soon after her parents' funeral to start attending community gatherings other than Preaching. "Eli and I haven't talked about that. We're just gettin' acquainted, really."

"Well, I know you'd be welcomed by *die Youngie*," Mimi said, giving her a compassionate smile.

Lena thought now of Hans. "Honestly, it's nice of you to consider me, but I'll be more comfortable stayin' home."

"Whenever you decide to go is fine," Mimi said, her glasses sliding down her nose as she squinted over the top of them. "I just thought you might want to spend some time with people your own age." She smiled. "I don't need a mirror to know that I'm a bit long in the tooth!" Then she laughed.

Lena shook her head and smiled in return. "Well, let me be your mirror. You seem plenty young enough to be good company for me."

"Well now." Mimi's face reddened. "Such a kind thing to say."

Lena nodded. "I mean it. And I'd like to say how much I appreciate you and Cousin Harley opening your door to me. Eli too."

Mimi nodded and returned her gaze to her sewing machine, where she began to make a long seam, her stubby fingers carefully guiding the bobbing needle as her feet pedaled below, creating a homey humming sound.

The minutes ticked slowly by as Lena and Mimi worked. Despite the Stoltzfuses' kindness, Lena's parents' passing was heavy on her heart, and she wondered how she would adjust to so many things. In all truth, Lena Rose was glad for the quiet job that sewing afforded. Here lately, she felt best when alone with her thoughts; the grief at never seeing Dat or Mamma again was so sharp most of the time—nearly crushing.

She tried to imagine her brothers and sisters sitting down to a kitchen table other than Mamma's. Or falling asleep in beds other than their own. Quickly, she brushed away a tear and hoped that Mimi hadn't noticed.

It wasn't lost on Lena that her coming to Lancaster County had turned Harley and Mimi's own household somewhat topsy-turvy. In the days before Lena's arrival, their son Eli had moved to the upstairs bedroom of the *Dawdi Haus*, where Harley's uncle Solomon had his bedroom on the first floor. Mimi had been quick to explain to Lena that it wasn't a hardship for Eli, up as he was before dawn every day for the milking. Eli liked feeling a bit more independent, yet he remained only a few steps away, ready for good fellowship or a round of Dutch Blitz from time to time in the evening.

Yesterday, Lena had met Eli's very blond sweetheart-girl, Lydia Smucker, who'd dropped by late in the afternoon with baked goods for Mimi. Lena had been impressed by the young woman's exceptional friendliness—as kindhearted as Mimi. Lydia had even invited Lena to go for a walk with her sometime, so they could get to know each other better. Encouraged by the connection, Lena had thanked her, grateful for such a caring new acquaintance.

Even so, she still questioned how this move could be God's will for her.

Presently, Lena Rose reached for the large pinking shears, thinking that if she ever *did* decide to go to a Singing here, it would be to sit with Lydia, who reminded her of dearest Emma. Besides young Chris, it was Emma she missed most, though her closest sister had vowed to write each week about her latest news and each of the other children. *My lifeline to home . . .*

Wilbur had also promised to write, though she expected his

letters would focus on what he was doing to help his host family on the farm rather than be filled with sentiment.

Mimi's chair gave a squeak as she leaned forward, and Lena glanced her way and noticed the woman's lips moving. Was she praying?

Or perhaps Mimi was simply talking to herself while she worked. It wasn't any of Lena's concern, but praying aloud, even in a whisper, was something her parents had never done. But then, there were a few spiritual practices Lena was discovering here that were rather new to her. For one thing, at supper last evening, Eli and Harley had discussed the daily reading in a devotional book they both owned. Dat and Mamma, on the other hand, had always only read the Good Book for devotional time or for family reading—Dat had said it was *"more than enough."*

Like an unexpected wave falling over her, Lena was filled with a longing to see little Chris and the rest of them. At least she had her Saturdays off from sewing so she could write to her siblings. That and attending Preaching on Sundays would help to occupy her thoughts with other things.

She tried to push away her sorrow and focus on cutting along the dress pattern lines with Mimi's sharp scissors, but she found herself asking God to heal her siblings' broken hearts and her own. *I'll write a letter to Mammi Schwartz to read to Chris,* she thought, missing him terribly.

─ා ල─

Hungry as a horse, Harley Stoltzfus smelled the bacon cooking in the kitchen that Saturday as he removed his black work boots in the utility room and hung his straw hat on its designated peg. He had gotten up at three-thirty to check on Jennie, one of his mares. The animal struggled with arthritis, and Harley had made a point of going out to rub liniment on her joints twice a day, treating her like a family member. He took special care when grooming her, too, and talked to the gentle horse when no one was around, as had been the case this morning before Eli came out to the barn when the farmhands arrived for the milking.

As they were finishing up, Preacher Elam King had dropped by to see if Harley wanted to go deer hunting next Friday, the first day of bow-hunting season. Tall, lanky Elam King was one of the two preachers in the district and lived just three farms down from the Stoltzfus homestead. For as long as Harley could remember, the man of God had always been neighborly, even years before Elam was chosen by divine lot to help shepherd the flock of People overseen by their bishop, Amos Lapp.

Harley would have been hesitant about leaving Mimi alone all day if Lena Rose hadn't come to stay. After their younger daughter, Tessa, married outside their church district and moved with her husband, Emmanuel Beiler, down near Bart Township, Mimi had missed her something awful, close as they had always been. *Till Manny started courtin' Tessa, anyway.*

Mimi had also missed having someone to help her share the workload. Harley had watched her struggle these past two years without Tessa, and his concern had been great enough that he'd prayed for the Lord to lead his wife through this challenging time. Some of Harley's best praying for Mimi and their family took place when he was lying in bed, when the rest of the world was sound asleep and his heart was still and the cares of life could be set aside. In those moments, he believed he was in touch with something powerful—*Someone* who heard his prayers.

And then, all these months later, it had suddenly come up that Jacob and Elizabeth Schwartz's children were in need of a home. Even though Harley and Jacob had been brought up states apart, it was hard to think of his cousin being gone. For many years now, Harley and Jacob had enjoyed keeping in touch through letters.

So it had been easy for Harley to open his heart to Lena Rose, orphan that she was. And he felt a powerful responsibility to Jacob to look after her for the time being. *She needs space to grieve and get back on her feet.*

Harley turned on the faucet in the utility room and waited for the water to warm before soaping up his hands and forearms. He couldn't help wondering if Lena might be the answer to his prayers for Mimi, too. *A daily companion for my wife.* And the extra money the two women would bring in, even after Lena's weekly pay, would be another added blessing.

Lena Rose is surely an answer from heaven. No matter the situation with Tessa, Mimi does seem more content again, Harley thought now as he reached to dry his hands on a towel. It was for that reason that he had agreed to go deer hunting with the preacher next week. He would let Mimi know so that she could plan accordingly when it came to meals. *Lord willing, I'll get us a nice buck.*

Harley caught another whiff of the frying bacon, which drew him like a magnet into the kitchen.

—◌ ◌—

Three weeks later, on a lonely October evening, Lena went out to walk through Harley's pastureland, knowing the dairy cattle were already in the barn for the night. She had taken her flashlight, shining the circle of light on the dirt road as she headed for the field lanes where the mules pulled the hay baler and other farm equipment. All the while, she recalled Mammi Schwartz's recent letters, in which Chris had eagerly dictated messages for Lena Rose. *So sweet,* she thought as she recalled the precious letters. By now, she nearly had them memorized. But one thing nagged at her: *It sounds like he's beginning to think I'm not coming home.*

Lena wished for all the world that her grandparents could take him to one of the English neighbors and dial her up someplace on a telephone. *Oh, to hear his little voice again!*

Alas, with no *Englischers* that she knew of near Harley and Mimi's farmhouse, the whole notion would take some doing.

I'll try to arrange something by mail with Emma, decided Lena, knowing her sister could surely line up a phone call. *And in the meantime, I'll locate an* Englischer *family here on West Eby Road,* she thought, determined to keep her plan between herself and Emma for now.

The stillness of the night closed in around her, and Lena wondered whether she ought to pray about something so minor. *Cousin Mimi likely would. She talks to God about practically everything. . . .*

5

It was a bright and sunny morning, the first Saturday in November, when Lena got up the nerve to ask Cousin Harley if she could take the family buggy for an errand, intending to place her phone call to Chris. While Lena had only had occasion to make a few calls during her lifetime, she felt that talking to her youngest brother, who still couldn't write a letter of his own, was important enough not to wait till she saw him at Christmas. Both Mammi Schwartz and Emma had written a number of times about the struggle young Chris was having adjusting to life without his parents and siblings. *Maybe hearing directly from you will help him settle in better,* Emma had suggested when she had written to set up the details.

Thankfully, Lena had managed to locate a Mennonite neighbor willing to allow her to place the long-distance phone call from their home, provided she covered the cost. Deb Grant had been quick to accommodate when she learned from Lena of her dilemma while at the local general store.

The phone rang just twice before she heard Emma's voice on the line. "Hullo . . . *Schweschder?*"

"*Jah*, 'tis Lena Rose callin'. *Denki* ever so much for helpin' make this possible."

"Oh, it's so *gut* to hear your voice again!" Emma said. "Chris is right here, all smiles, tryin' to be patient. So I'll let him talk to ya. Then I want to get back on to update you 'bout some things, all right?"

"Sure," Lena said, eager to talk to her little brother.

She could hear whispering from Emma as her sister handed the phone to Chris.

"Hullo?" His small voice sounded wispy, like he was unsure of himself, this being the first time he'd ever talked into a phone.

"*Wie geht's*, Chris? I've missed ya, dear *Bruder!*"

"*Ach*, Lena Rose, when're ya comin' home?" he asked mournfully.

"Well, just as soon as I can find some work there and a place to stay." Hearing him ask made her all the more homesick for him . . . and the rest of her family there. It stirred up such a longing to tousle his hair and smile into his blue eyes.

"I'll give ya my room at Dawdi Schwartz's, if ya want."

"Aw . . . but where would you sleep, Chris?"

"I wouldn't mind the floor."

"Well, you need your rest, though. You're a growin' boy—sprouting up real fast, from what Mammi says." Lena was touched by his generous offer but knew that if it were really an option, it would have come up before she left Centreville. "And . . . you can be sure that the deacon and Emma are keeping an eye out for somethin'."

"I just wish you could come home tomorrow," he said, his voice cracking.

"I wish that, too. But Christmas isn't so far away, and we'll get to spend time together then."

There was no answer to that, only the sound of sniffling, and the next thing Lena knew, Emma was on the line apologizing. *Oh dear,* thought Lena Rose, worried the phone call might have made things worse.

"Just wanted you to know I've been talking to our kinfolk here, and so far no one has good-paying work for you," Emma was saying.

"I've been writing to Deacon Miller, and some of our relatives, too," Lena Rose confided. "And still nothing has turned up."

"Please don't give up, sister . . . all of us want you home as soon as possible. We'll get ya here."

"Well, at least I'll see all of you at Christmastime."

"That'll be *wunnerbaar!*" Emma exclaimed.

"It certainly will. And I think Hans will be glad, too."

"Does he write often?" asked Emma. "Not that it's any of my business."

"To tell the truth, he's not much for letters, but when he does write, it's real nice to hear from him."

"Courtin' by mail can't be much fun," Emma said.

"True, but it's the best we can do right now. And if he loves me . . ." Lena's voice trailed off.

"Well, *jah,* but do ya love *him?*"

Lena felt a little surprised at this and gave a light laugh. "I'm going to marry him one day," she declared in answer. "And live near all of you there in Centreville."

They talked a bit more about how their other siblings were faring, then said their good-byes, not wanting to test the kindness of the Grants by running up the phone bill beyond Lena's ability to pay it.

When the call was over, Lena stood there looking at the phone, wondering why things had to be so difficult.

I feel so bad for Chris, she thought. *Maybe I shouldn't have called.* She offered Deb Grant cash on the spot, but the cheerful woman refused, saying she wanted Lena to feel free to call home at another time. "We can figure out what you owe then, if you'd like."

Ever so thankful, Lena shook the woman's hand and quietly left the house, feeling all in.

_ᴄ‿ᴄ_

The early weeks since Lena's arrival had been busy ones—going to market and running errands with Harley and Mimi, but mostly trying to fulfill a mountain of customers' orders.

Each evening around sunset, Lena observed Cousin Mimi go around and lower the dark green window shades in the large sewing room just off the kitchen, like she was tucking the place in for the night. Little habits like this made Lena remember the way her Mamma had done things, and she found herself having to redirect her thoughts right quick, lest tears come. She was trying to be content assisting Cousin Mimi with the many custom sewing and mending orders they received each week. The work was satisfying enough, and Lena looked forward to mailing most of her earnings to Uncle Noah to distribute amongst the families looking after her youngest siblings.

It's the least I can do. . . .

_ᴄ‿ᴄ_

With only one week left before Thanksgiving, the weather shifted abruptly to steadily cold temperatures and snow. But despite the blustery weather, Cousin Harley had gone hunting again, this time with his son Eli, both of them in hopes of getting a nice plump turkey. Lena took notice of the heavy snow as she and Mimi rose to stretch their legs in the sewing room, going to look out one of the windows, standing close enough to see their breath fog the windowpanes. "*'Early snows are always a welcome sight,*' my father used to say," Lena said softly, reminiscing aloud.

"Not sure I can say I feel thataway. We've had snow here as early as late October," Mimi said, glancing at Lena and smiling.

Lena shrugged. "Maybe Dat found it easier to spot a turkey flying against a snowy landscape." She thought of Cousin Harley's bow-hunting trip back in September—he'd had no deer to show for his full day out shivering in the cold woods.

Now Mimi nodded absently, still staring out at the thick flakes falling ever so fast, the air filled with white.

"If this keeps up, it'll stick to the road like whipped cream." Lena's mind was hundreds of miles away, in her beloved Centreville. Was snow falling there, too? She recalled one very gray December sky on her way home from Murk's Village Store with Mamma. She'd watched the white flakes flutter down against a backdrop of stark tree trunks along the road. In just a short time, the snow had thickened so much that the trees were nearly invisible. Mamma had not fretted, though, only gone silent, and Lena had known she was praying.

Little Chris had stayed home with Dat that particular day, Lena recalled, and she couldn't help but wonder if Chris might not be staring out the schoolhouse windows this very minute, thinking how easy it would be to catch snowflakes on his tongue at morning recess. Lena had saved the drawing he'd made for her after their phone conversation—a wonderful little pencil drawing of two pumpkins, one of them partially colored in with an orange crayon. Mammi had written *For Lena* near the bottom of the page. He'd printed his full name below it, the letters sloping downhill to the right. Everything about the drawing made Lena smile and miss her little brother.

She let herself daydream of Hans, too, thinking fondly of his occasional letters, and especially his latest, in yesterday afternoon's mail. Oh, to have had the time to sit down immediately and write back, but Cousin Mimi's orders were accumulating—perhaps because winter was upon them and customers were in need of coats and some mending of outer garments, too. There had been a surge of new requests in just the past few days.

I'll stay up late tonight, Lena Rose mused, wishing she dared tell Hans of her deepest, most cherished hopes and dreams. Dreams of their life together as husband and wife. *How soon before he'll hint at marriage?* she wondered.

She chided herself to be content—a mere two months had passed since her coming to Leacock Township, although it seemed longer.

She thought back to former Thanksgiving Days, recalling all the wondrous aromas of baking foods—turkey and stuffing and fresh rolls. And oh, the pies—mincemeat, pecan, and pumpkin!

Still musing, Lena spotted a gray enclosed carriage turn onto the lane. Recognizing Eli's sweetheart-girl and her mother, Fannie, Lena snapped out of her daydream. "We have company," she told Mimi, who'd already sat down and returned to work without Lena's realizing it.

"Might be more customers," Mimi said, sounding hopeful.

"Looks like it's Fannie and Lydia Smucker," Lena replied. "I'll get the door."

"Invite them in out of the cold, won't ya?" Mimi's voice was sweet.

Lena waited till the two women were coming up the back porch steps to greet them, both of them wearing royal blue dresses with matching blue capes and aprons beneath their short black coats, as well as for-good black shoes. *They must be going somewhere in town,* Lena thought as she opened the door and welcomed them in as Mimi had urged. "*Willkumm.* Your order is ready," she said graciously. "Please follow me."

"You sound so professional," Lydia teased, giving her a smile. "Remember, we're your friends, *jah?*"

"Of course," Lena said, laughing softly as she motioned to them. "Won't yous come with me? How's that?"

"Much better." Lydia grinned as they walked through the utility room into the kitchen, then on toward the sewing room.

Lydia's way of teasing reminded Lena of Emma, but she brushed that aside and ushered them into the large room. There, Mimi looked up and stopped her work at the treadle machine.

"Nice surprise, seein' yous," Mimi said, getting up immediately and offering to take Fannie's and Lydia's coats.

"*Ach*, we can't stay this time," Fannie said, round roses on her cheeks. "'Tis real cold out, and who knows how much snow we'll get. We'd best not tarry."

Lydia looked more than a little disappointed as she followed Lena Rose over to the small counter, where she removed her wallet from her coat pocket. She waited till Lena tallied up the amount due and gave her cash for the full payment.

"I'll write up your receipt," Lena said, reaching for the pad.

"Ain't necessary," Lydia said with a glance over her shoulder. Then, in a rather conspiratorial manner, she lowered her voice and said, "You must know by now that I wish you'd come to the youth activities. Why not try the Singing after Thanksgiving?"

At the thought of going, Lena felt stressed. But looking into Lydia's eyes just now, she had a strong feeling that Lydia would understand her reasons for staying away, yet Lena Rose was nearly tempted to agree, if only for the sake of friendship.

"I can't thank you enough for askin'," Lena said. "But . . ."

Lydia touched Lena's hand. "Then why not join in the fun?" Lydia glanced her mother's way, her expression indicating that she didn't want anyone to wonder what they were discussing. "Won't ya at least think 'bout it?"

As of yet, Lena really hadn't contemplated mingling with the youth there, not when she was grieving. Even so, she was wondering what the months ahead were going to look like if she didn't get to return home soon. Despite Uncle Noah's assurance that she would be gone for but a few months, there had been no word about anything more than a Christmas *visit*. "It's nice to be invited, but I shouldn't go." She almost added *this time* but thought better of it. "It's just too soon."

Lydia nodded sympathetically. "I'm here for you if ya want to talk," she said as her mother called to her. "Everyone needs a friend."

Because Lena was so surprised, even impressed, by Lydia's keen interest in befriending her, she felt a little melancholy when Lydia and Fannie said their good-byes and headed back outdoors to their waiting horse and carriage.

6

The morning before Thanksgiving, the muffled sound of hunters' guns echoed in the distance and awakened Lena Rose. She rolled over and switched on the flashlight on the lamp table next to the bed and squinted across the room at Chris's drawing, propped up on the dresser. She'd put it there so she could see it first thing each morning, and it was the last thing she saw before she blew out the lantern each night. Mammi Schwartz's recent letter was filled with specifics about Chris's activities, including school and the outdoor chores he did with Dawdi.

She wished to highest heaven the dear boy could write his own thoughts in a letter. And while she'd purposed in her heart to keep the phone call mum, at breakfast that morning Lena decided to tell Mimi about her conversation with Chris early that month. His emotional response had been troubling.

Mimi frowned and looked startled at the news, there in her seat to the right of the head chair, vacant today because of Harley's determination to be successful this hunting trip. "Guess things must be different in Michigan. Our church ordinance doesn't allow phone calls for any reason 'cept an emergency."

"Honestly, I thought it *was* an emergency," Lena said. "Chris and I are very close. . . . I helped Mamma raise him from when he was a toddler, ya know. He's been having a real hard time with the distance between us." Then, softening her tone, Lena told Mimi about the undertow of concern she'd sensed in Mammi Schwartz's letters, as well as direct comments from Emma. "That's the only reason I went ahead and did it."

Mimi was very quiet for a moment, her hazel eyes serious. "Still doesn't seem wise to me. I hope he wasn't all the more homesick, just hearin' your voice."

Lena recalled how Chris had given the phone to Emma. "I'm afraid he was," she admitted.

"Well, bless his heart." Mimi looked sad.

"I never wanted to upset him." Lena sighed. "It's partly my fault for doting on him too much. And the rest of my siblings are old enough to cope much better than Chris." Lena's voice broke so that she had to stop talking.

"*Ach*, dear. Your parents' passing is heavy on your heart. I'm sorry you've had to endure so much at your age."

"Nothin' is gained by feeling sorry for myself, though."

"'Tis true, but give yourself ample time to grieve." Mimi then began to recount the sudden loss of her grandmother when Mimi was only eleven. "I loved her dearly . . . stayed several summers with her and my Dawdi, helpin' pick raspberries as big as your eyes. And when snap and snow peas came on, we'd sit and shell peas on the porch together for hours. We talked a lot 'bout love and life in general." She sighed. "I'll never forget my shock when *Mamm* told me she was gone. Just didn't seem possible."

Lena blinked away tears as she listened, touched by Mimi's story.

Mimi's round shoulders rose and fell. "I know only a fraction of what you must be goin' through, Lena Rose. But I do care that you're grieving so."

Looking at her just then—the gentle smile crinkling the corners of Mimi's eyes—Lena could see love and earnest caring. Somewhere during the past two months, dear Mimi had become her friend.

—⟡ ⟡—

Harley arrived back from hunting in the Welsh Mountains with a few hours to spare before suppertime. He'd had the foresight to line up extra help for the afternoon milking, since he hadn't known just when he and Eli and Arden Mast, Eli's friend, might return. But now that he was home earlier than planned, Harley had time to clean the turkey he'd shot. Arden had gotten one, as well, with Eli determined to get one on the next hunting trip.

Harley stopped to give Blackie a good neck scratching, then hurried across the side yard and into the house to announce to Mimi that they would have fresh wild turkey for their noontime dinner tomorrow. She smiled near like an angel and dropped everything then and there to set two large pots on the black wood stove to boil the water for dipping the turkeys in before plucking their feathers.

Harley got a few split logs for her from the bin and slid them into the belly of the stove. "Was starting to think I'd lost my aim," he remarked, referring to having missed getting a deer back in September and to the unsuccessful trip last week, too. "Guess I'm a better shot with a gun than a bow."

"You're a fine shot, dear." Mimi chuckled, bright-eyed. "Should I set extra places for supper? I'm makin' plenty of meatball stew and corn bread, just in case."

"Sounds *wunnerbaar-gut.*"

She smiled over her shoulder at him. "Maybe your uncle Solomon would like to eat with us, too."

"I'm guessin' so," Harley said. "Soon as we dress the birds, I'll get washed up."

We'll have us a real nice Thanksgiving, Harley thought, grateful to have Lena Rose around to enjoy the holiday with them. *Truth is, Mimi and I are both more content with Lena Rose here,* he thought. Their lives had fallen into a mundane rut after Tessa up and moved away with her husband, and Lena had a way of bringing life and a sort of hopefulness back into this house even though she was in mourning for her parents. *Such a change from Tessa's final months here.*

Yet Harley much preferred to count his blessings. It was one way to keep from thinking too much about how son-in-law Manny Beiler had made it clear at an auction last week that he and Tessa and their infant son would be celebrating Thanksgiving with Manny's parents this year. *Second year in a row.*

Like her older sister Ada, Tessa had always been close to Mimi. But Tessa's quick courtship with Manny—and his being from another church district—had been a concern to Harley and Mimi, and this had put a strain on their relationship with her. In the end, Tessa had been more anxious to leave home than either he or Mimi had expected, leaving Mimi high and dry with work when Tessa accepted Manny's proposal after a whirlwind courtship. And since their wedding, Manny had said scarcely more than a dozen words at a time to Harley—not that there had been much opportunity, with the young couple keeping to themselves most of the time.

Now that the sacred knot had been tied, Harley was on his guard not to let his disappointment turn to resentment. The only thing to do was make the best of being Manny's father-in-law, challenging as it was.

⟿ ⟿

"Let's use the floral-rimmed plates for supper, Lena," Mimi said from the sink after Lena had put her pan of corn bread into the oven. "We're havin' company."

Pleased for the opportunity to set a pretty table, Lena agreed and headed into the next room, where the spacious dining buffet and hutch stored oodles of dishes for family gatherings. Two comfortable reading chairs were on the other side of the room, a large wicker magazine basket between them.

Now that she'd had time to ponder it, Lena wished she hadn't brought up the telephone call to Mimi. She hadn't meant to disappoint her hostess. Fortunately, while Mimi had been surprised at Lena's indulgent phone call, she seemed inclined to overlook it this time.

Once the table was set, Lena removed her half apron and went to the back door to look out through the window. Harley and his son Eli were crouched with another young man—tall and robust, and as blond as she'd ever seen—dressing the turkeys. She remembered the last time she'd eaten wild turkey and let her mind drift back to the memory of her father's exuberance over bagging two big birds. Her brother Wilbur and Dat had always been the biggest eaters, and Lena caught herself smiling, missing her long talks with her oldest brother, especially. Like the time he'd asked Lena's opinion about a particular teenage girl who would soon be old enough to start attending Singings—just as Wilbur himself would be.

Emma, in turn, had always valued level-headed Wilbur for advice, especially where it involved the fellows at Sunday night Singings. Being the oldest boy, Wilbur was also the brother who dropped her and Emma off at youth activities, making it possible for them to go out riding later with a young man if asked.

"Have ya had a chance to meet many of *die Youngie* in the district?" Mimi's question interrupted Lena's memories.

Lena pressed her lips together. "Well, *jah* . . . some at Preaching services."

"Hope you don't feel ya have to sit at home on the weekends for my sake," Mimi added.

"You sound like Lydia Smucker." Lena laughed and glanced toward the back door window. "Did Eli or his friend manage to get a turkey?" she asked absently.

"Not Eli, not this time." Mimi caught Lena's eye. "But you could ask his friend Arden 'bout it when they come in for supper."

"Oh, I'd rather let the menfolk do the talkin'," Lena said, turning back to glance out again. Harley was removing his protective gloves, and Eli and the tall blond fellow looked to be heading over to the *Dawdi Haus. Are they going for Harley's uncle Solomon?* she wondered.

As was often the case, her mind again wandered back to Centreville. What she wouldn't give to lay eyes on Chris and her other siblings again.

Christmas can't come soon enough!

As Lena had guessed, here came Eli and his friend with Harley's uncle Solomon, one on each side of the older man to steady him as he limped along with his cane, his gray head shaking slightly with palsy. Eli's blond friend caught Lena's eye and gave her a smile before going over to pull out a chair for Solomon at the table, holding the man's cane while he slowly lowered himself and sat with a sigh.

"*Denki.*" Uncle Solomon nodded his balding head as he looked up and motioned for the young man to sit in the chair next to him. "Have you two met?" Solomon asked, squinting over his dark-rimmed spectacles at Lena, then again at Eli's friend.

"Hullo," Lena said quickly to eliminate the embarrassment.

"Arden Mast, this here's Lena Rose Schwartz from Michigan."

Solomon pointed his trembling finger at her, a smile on his bearded face. "She's helpin' Mimi keep her head above water in the sewin' room. Ain't that right?" He glanced at Mimi, who was carrying a large white tureen filled with the meatball stew.

"Lena's a fine seamstress, for sure," Mimi said as she set the tureen down near where she would be sitting, to the left of Lena Rose.

"*Ach*, don't know about that," Lena said softly.

"Well . . . if Mimi says so, I know it's true," Arden remarked, his voice strong and confident as he smiled at her again. "Real nice to meet you, Lena Rose. I hear ya met my cousin Lydia Smucker. She's had some nice things to say about you." He looked at her as if he wanted to say more, then seemed to decide against it.

After the silent table blessing, and all through the meal, Arden engaged Lena Rose and the rest of the family in interesting conversation.

Later, when Arden passed the platter of moist and delicious golden corn bread to Solomon—the corn bread she'd baked—he held the platter steady while the older man chose a generous square. It was yet another small gesture of kindness from Arden, and it did not go unnoticed by Lena Rose.

Lena poured another cup of coffee for Cousin Harley, enjoying the peace of the morning with him and Mimi the day after Thanksgiving. Just the three of them were there in the kitchen for second breakfast, which was more substantial than the coffee and doughnuts Harley and the farmhands had grabbed on their way to the barn before four o'clock that morning.

Mimi was over at the kitchen counter, putting the toasted bread on a plate, when she asked, "Lena, would ya mind delivering Cora Ruth Ebersol's new coat to her? I think she'd really appreciate it." Lena had set the sleeves into a coat for the Amishwoman who was too busy to sew for herself.

"Not at all," Lena replied. "I really feel for her. Five little ones in just seven years of marriage!" Lena remembered how taxed her own mother had been.

"And twins for her youngest." Mimi came to the table with the toast. "But you know what havin' multiples in the house is like, *jah*?"

Lena nodded. "What one doesn't think of, the other certainly does."

Mimi glanced at Harley. "We wanted twin boys back when we were younger. Still, we're real thankful for six healthy singles."

Harley nodded his head. "Now the grandbabies are comin' on fast—nearly a new one every year."

Lena went to the fridge to get a bottle of orange juice. "That must be *wunnerbaar.*"

"Nothin' like it."

"'Tis a blessing, for certain." Mimi took her seat to Harley's right and fanned herself with her hankie. She kept it up for more than a minute, puffing air out through her lips.

Harley studied her but said nothing, his eyebrows raised as if to acknowledge that Mimi was overheated. Lena finished pouring the juice into their glasses, then went to sit next to Mimi while Harley asked the silent blessing.

When the prayer was finished, Harley quietly cleared his throat and raised his head.

"Amen," Lena said before remembering that no one said amen aloud following grace here in Lancaster County. She'd forgotten yesterday, too, at Mimi's Thanksgiving dinner, when it had just been her and Solomon, along with Harley and Mimi, of course. Eli had gone to Lydia's parents' home at their invitation, and the married children were either hosting their in-laws and families or were celebrating the holiday with extended family. It still wondered Lena why none of them had come to enjoy Mimi's delicious spread—the turkey was as delicious as she'd ever tasted. It struck her as odd, but Mimi hadn't seemed to mind, so that was all that mattered. *Perhaps they're all planning to come for Christmas,* Lena thought, looking forward to being with her own close-knit family on that day.

Harley suggested just then that it would be all right for Lena Rose to take the family carriage and the best driving horse over to Cora Ruth's place. "You can stay a while, too, if you'd like to visit," he added with a quick smile, "unless Mimi needs you back right quick."

"Well, there's plenty-a sewing waitin'," Mimi acknowledged, "but I agree—take your time, Lena. Even though Cora Ruth's mother lives with her, I daresay she loves havin' someone else to talk to who's older than five."

Lena nodded. "I'll deliver the coat, then." Honestly, she looked forward to getting out of the house, since she primarily kept busy in Mimi's sewing room during the week. Sometimes Ada or Tessa or one of Mimi's daughters-in-law would stop by for a visit, and there were occasional trips to market, too. Sundays, on the other hand, were a pleasant change of pace and scenery, because Lena had always loved to gather with people of like faith, even if this community of believers dressed differently and their church ordinance wasn't quite like Lena's back home.

In thinking ahead to attending Preaching this Sunday, the possibility of another encounter with genial Lydia Smucker crossed Lena's mind. She hadn't forgotten Lydia's eagerness to have her join the youth at a Sunday Singing.

Lena thought back to her recent letter to Hans, having stayed up later than usual to pen it. Writing to him, and to her brothers and sisters, helped her make sense of this life she was living so far removed from all of them—an unexpected source of strength, the act of picking up a pen and writing. Hopefully, with snow on the ground and the outdoor work winding down, Hans's letters might start coming more frequently.

—⚬৲ ৴⚬—

Lena Rose held the driving lines carefully, feeling the sway of the mare's trot as they went over the snow-packed roads.

A surprising number of folk were out and about as Lena drove up Stumptown Road, past the historic gristmill complex—Mascot

Roller Mills. Most of the carriages were moving in the opposite direction, and Lena assumed they were headed for a quilting bee or a Sisters Day somewhere. *Oh, to have more free time to do something different like that,* she thought.

It wasn't that she begrudged her sewing routine. Not at all, considering how much Mimi needed the help. But Mimi seemed content to be nearly homebound, and the Stoltzfus house just seemed so quiet, if not almost empty, compared to Dat's house filled with ten children growing up together. *Is Mimi depressed about Tessa moving so far away?*

At the Ebersols' turnoff, Lena noticed a little white stone springhouse out near the road, and a slight grade leading over to the farmhouse with its double *Dawdi Hauses.* She didn't know who lived in the smallest of the houses, unless that was Rebekah's. Mimi hadn't told her much regarding Cora Ruth's widowed mother, only that Cora Ruth had nearly more than she could manage most days. "*'Tis a blessing Rebekah's there,*" Mimi had said.

Cora Ruth had an uncertain look on her face when she saw Lena Rose at the back door bringing the new black coat, but she welcomed her inside while holding one of the infant twins. Close by, one of the older children was rocking a wooden cradle with her foot.

"*Kumme* in an' have some coffee, won't ya?" Cora Ruth said, then closed the door.

"*Denki,* sounds nice." Lena followed her to the large kitchen table, where two little towheaded boys were sitting and playing with wind-up ducks and other miniature animal toys. Seeing them made her think of Chris when he was that age.

Pretty soon, Rebekah came in, her gray hair all done up perfectly in a tight hair bun like Cora Ruth's, looking perkier than Lena expected for a woman Mimi had described as in her mid-sixties.

"What made ya think to deliver the coat?" Cora Ruth asked Lena Rose, handing Rebekah the sleeping baby in her arms.

"Mimi thought it might help ya."

"Ain't that nice?" Rebekah said. She bent to kiss the top of the baby girl's silky head and went to sit on the rocking chair close to the wood stove. "I was awful sorry to hear of your Dat and Mamma's passing," she said, looking serious just then.

Lena nodded, offering a small smile.

"How are ya managing over at Harley and Mimi's?" Rebekah asked.

Lena was quick to say how wonderful the couple had been to her.

"Oh, they'd do anything for ya," Cora Ruth agreed.

"That's true," Lena said with a glance at the two young boys, so happy and well-mannered as they played together at the end of the table. She supposed they were about two and four, if she wasn't mistaken. But she reminded herself that she was primarily there to spend time with Cora Ruth, though she was also interested in getting to know Rebekah better.

When Cora Ruth brought over mugs of coffee and set them on the table, she asked Lena if she'd had a chance to read the recent weekly periodical, *The Budget*. "There's something right funny in the column for your hometown."

"Oh?"

"Here, let's see if I can find it," Cora Ruth said, reaching for the paper and thumbing through. "Here 'tis." She folded the outer pages back and placed the section from the Amish scribe in Centreville in front of her, tapping the spot.

Silently, Lena read about a three-legged biddy chicken hatched by one of Deacon Joe Miller's hens. Lena had to smile, wondering if Emma or Hans might write her about this. She thought of how Dat and Mamma had been close friends with Deacon Miller. "I'd sure like to see a picture of that chicken." She slid the paper over to Rebekah. "Here, maybe you'd like to read it, too."

Rebekah glanced down at the page, then up right quick, frowning a bit. "Would you mind readin' it to me?"

Cora Ruth shook her head. "Oh, Mamm . . . it's all right."

"Well, since it ain't in *Deitsch* . . . chust go ahead an' read it to me, if ya don't mind." Rebekah's voice had taken on an irritable edge.

Lena Rose had encountered another older woman back in Centreville who was also hesitant about reading, especially out loud. But Lena did as Rebekah requested and read the account of the three-legged chicken. Rebekah barely cracked a smile, instead looking down at the baby snuggled against her.

"It's mighty strange, I daresay," Cora Ruth said of the chicken and reached to take *The Budget* back. "I'm sure Melvin'll get a kick out of it."

"*Puh!* He has better things to do." Rebekah sighed loudly and looked out the kitchen window, an indecipherable expression on her face.

Cora Ruth gave an apologetic shrug to Lena.

"Looks like it could turn out to be a milder day," Lena said, trying to lighten things up.

"Well, it'll be a good while, I 'spect, till it's *really* mild again," Rebekah said, looking Cora Ruth's way. "Though I've never been round here when things thaw out."

"You're just visiting, then?" Lena asked Rebekah.

Rebekah glanced at Cora Ruth again. "Well, not exactly . . . not anymore."

Oddly, Cora Ruth called loudly to Emily just then, interrupting the flow of conversation.

Rebekah abruptly changed the subject. "Lena Rose, did ya know there's a cookie-baking frolic happening today?"

"So *that's* where all the womenfolk were goin'. On the way here, I saw plenty-a buggies headin' in the same direction." Lena still felt awkward at the way both women had avoided answering her question about Rebekah.

"*Jah*, it's the annual party down yonder at the bishop's house," Cora Ruth said, jumping back into the conversation. "His wife, Patricia, likes to get a head start on Christmas. They bake lots of cookies ahead of time, then freeze them—just oodles, with all those women workin' together."

"Mamma never really had much hope of freezin' any cookies at our house," Lena said, smiling. "There were so many of us."

"Ain't it cheaper to bake them by the dozens?" Rebekah asked, seemingly more relaxed now. She shifted the baby onto her shoulder and got her *Kapp* string stuck.

"One of our neighbors once joked to Mamma whether havin' *children* might be cheaper by the dozen." Lena smiled. "But there were only ten of us."

"Close enough, ain't?" Rebekah said with a chuckle.

Lena nodded. "I doubt my father would've agreed that *more* of us were any cheaper," she said. "Things were tight much of the time till Dat began workin' at the RV factory, but Mamma always did her best to make ends meet. She started substitute teachin' the last few years, after I finished eighth grade. Before that, there were plenty of hand-me-downs in our house."

Lena explained that she was the firstborn, and that her sister Emma had always ended up with Lena's clothes, especially when they were small. "Quite a few of my baby clothes made it all the way to Liz and Verena. After that, there weren't any more girls."

"So, four girls and six boys, then?" Cora Ruth asked, turning to pick up the twin who had stirred and was now crying in the cradle.

"*Jah*, including a set of twins—both boys."

"Well, what do ya know? Our twins are girls," Cora Ruth said. "Cora and Constance—ain't that sweet?"

"It is," Lena said, noticing the darling twins were not identical. One had hair and the other was quite bald.

"Did your Mamma have much help with all of yous early on?" Cora Ruth asked, rocking back and forth with the crying baby and occasionally making soft shushing sounds.

"Oh, even when I was a youngster, she had my help before and after school—and in the summertime, too," Lena assured her. "And Dat's parents lived neighbors to us. So there were extra hands, for certain."

Cora Ruth nodded and sighed. "A true godsend." She looked Rebekah's way just then, smiling at her. "The Lord God provides."

Lena agreed.

"If circumstances hadn't been, well, what they were when Mamm came here ten months ago . . ." Cora Ruth sighed heavily. "*Ach,* I'm just glad she came then and stayed on with us. Thank the dear Lord, too, that she was here when the twins were born."

"Now, Cora Ruth, no need to dig that all up." Rebekah's voice sounded tense again. "Just let it be."

Lena couldn't help once more noticing the strange tone between Rebekah and Cora Ruth. *What's so secretive about a widowed mother coming for an extended visit with her married daughter and family? Unless,* thought Lena, *Rebekah came to stay before her husband died . . . but why would she do that?*

After finishing her coffee, Cora Ruth had all the children greet Lena and then asked if Lena might come by sometime again. "If orders slow down for Mimi, of course."

"That'd be real nice," Rebekah put in, surprising Lena. "Why not drop by next Wednesday? Cora Ruth's got a doctor appointment, and I could use some help with the children."

"I'll see if Mimi can spare me for a while."

Rebekah perked up like she hadn't yet this entire visit, but Cora Ruth suddenly looked ill at ease.

On the ride home, Lena wondered why no one had mentioned whether Rebekah had initially come to visit to help Cora Ruth with the older children, before the twins' birth. Pondering this, and Cora Ruth's attempt to say something that Rebekah clearly rebuffed, Lena was downright curious. Was there another, more scandalous reason? But she didn't want to think such a thing, nor would she ask Mimi about it. *"Ain't becoming of ya,"* Mamma would have said.

Still, Lena couldn't help but wonder.

8

Harley turned up the collar on his black work coat against the afternoon chill, mighty thankful to already have accomplished a fair amount of work. He'd updated all the breeding records before going around the herd for several hours with his longtime vet, Roy Griffin, who'd come to test for TB and brucellosis. The work of a dairyman was nearly endless, but dairy farming was in Harley's blood and clear back in the family tree on both sides of his and Mimi's lineage.

Roy mentioned that he'd just come from the Mast dairy farm, where he'd seen Harley's good friend Abram Mast. "Are you and Abram thinking of quitting farming anytime soon? Thought you might know his plans, close friends that you are," Roy added.

Harley let out a chortle. "Oh, we've been kickin' that idea around quite a lot for a couple of years now. Runnin' a dairy farm ain't somethin' any man oughta do for too many years—it has a way of wearing out the body real *gut*."

They talked a while longer about the toil involved, even with able farmhands. Then Roy said out of the blue that he'd seen Arden Mast down at the general store the other day. "Right during afternoon milking, too. Seemed strange."

Now, Harley knew full well that Roy Griffin had himself a gossiping mind-set, and he never really knew what would spring from the man's mouth. He expected that Roy wasn't done with the matter yet, and he was right.

Roy said he'd struck up a conversation with Arden, discussing the dairy business and how he must be chomping at the bit to be a partner with his father. "But, between you and me, Arden looked less than enthused. In fact, Arden gave me the uneasiest look when I asked why he wasn't home for milking. It made me wonder if he and the old man were at odds."

"*Nee*, can't imagine that," Harley said now, uncomfortable with this sort of speculation. "Them two's as close as any father and son round here, I'm sure ya know."

"Oh, I don't know why I said anything," Roy said, swinging his long arms as he headed toward his parked truck. "Guess I wondered if you'd heard something about it." He stopped walking and turned.

"Not a word," Harley said.

They waved and parted ways, and after Roy left, Harley wondered why he seemed so interested in Abram and Arden's business, unless maybe he was just nosy about every farmer. Harley shook his head. *Who knows what he might be saying about me.*

Just then, Harley saw the postal truck coming up the road. Not usually the one to get the mail, he decided to surprise Lena Rose for a change, since she typically got it these days. So he made his way down the drive to the mailbox, where he found a handful of bills, a circle letter for Mimi, and two envelopes addressed to Lena Rose, both with a Michigan postmark. Harley slipped the latter in with the rest of the mail and walked back toward the house, trying to resist being as snoopy as Roy.

But as he passed the front porch, a wave of curiosity hit him, and he looked to see if the handwriting was the same on both envelopes to Lena. Lo and behold, it was. He also couldn't help noticing the name *Mr. Hans Bontrager* on the first line of the return address.

What do you know? Lena must have a beau. . . .

—◌ ◌—

"How was Cora Ruth today?" Mimi looked up from hemming a dress as Lena returned and took her place in the sewing room. "Glad for her new coat?"

"Oh, you should've seen her. She was so pleased."

"Well, bless your heart for doin' that." Mimi set down the rose-colored garment meant for a little girl. "And you must've had a nice visit, too."

Lena shared about her time over there. "The children were so well-behaved they hardly made a peep. Well, except for one of the twins, who was fussy," Lena told Mimi. "After Cora Ruth, Rebekah, and I had coffee, Cora Ruth introduced me to each of them. I even held one of the babies—such cute, tiny girls they are."

"I'm glad ya had a nice time."

"It was fun bein' around the children," Lena said, not wanting to admit how much she missed a lively house full of antics and merrymaking. "Rebekah asked if I could lend her a hand next Wednesday, when Cora Ruth goes for a checkup at the doctor's. Would that be all right?"

"If you want to, sure."

Mimi seemed anxious to get back to her hand sewing, not saying more about the Ebersols or Rebekah.

And as Lena worked, she knew it was just as well, lest her own curiosity rise up again.

—◌ ◌—

Lena Rose curled up with Hans's pretty card and the letter in her room, having waited till now to sit down to relish his words after a long, busy day. She felt cozy and peaceful, surrounded by the lantern's light and Mimi's warm handmade quilt—a Log Cabin pattern done in tans, blues, and browns.

The card was an attractive "I miss you" card with a farmland scene of Centreville, which stirred up more longings for home.

She smiled as she began to read the letter—his way of writing was such that she could practically hear him talking. It made her antsy to see him again.

Partway down the page, following his usual friendly greeting, Hans had written a little about the current weather there and what sort of winter *The Old Farmer's Almanac* was forecasting. *He's always put stock in that almanac,* she thought, chuckling to herself.

Hans also told what he had been doing since he last wrote. And then she read these words:

> *I realize this is something we discussed before you left, but it still bothers me, Lena. I'm discouraged about the distance between us, and every day I wish it had worked out for you to stay here, like you'd hoped.*
>
> *Honestly, a long-distance courtship is harder than I thought.*
> *At least it's almost December. I'm really looking forward to seeing you at Christmas. What a good time we'll have together!*

She rolled over and sighed. Thinking of seeing Hans again, and the visit to her hometown, made Lena wish she had some photographs of Hans and her family all lined up across the dresser mirror. Even so, she knew better than to desire such forbidden things, and having photos might stir up even more yearning, now that she thought of it.

The small parcel of postcards she'd chosen as her remembrance of Dat and Mamma was still tucked away in a far corner of her locked suitcase, beneath the bed. She could have taken them out and read them by now, but Lena was hesitant, afraid she might hear her father's words in her head as she read what would no doubt be his loving declarations to sweet Mamma while they were courting. She was not at all ready for that.

Lena outened the lantern and climbed into bed for the night; she could see the full moon's radiance glowing through the shade. Frankly, she understood her beau's frustration and felt the same way.

If only a family back home could take me in and I could get a paying job, she thought. *Then things would be all right.*

Tired, Lena Rose said her silent bedtime prayers and added one for divine wisdom. What more could she do?

Hans cares dearly for me, she thought, trying to quell her disappointment that things weren't moving faster.

But after more minutes passed, she gave up on falling asleep, got up, and started walking down the hall to stand at the window. There, she stared at the big, round moon as it shone over nearby farmhouses and barns, as well as the barren fields below. *I've got to see my beau,* she thought, tears welling up.

CHAPTER

9

That last Saturday of November dawned cold yet sunny, and Lena rose early to write a thoughtful reply to yesterday's letter from Hans. After penning her thoughts, she set the letter aside and brushed her long hair—Emma had always called it "dishwater blond" in jest—and wound it up in a braidless bun, the way Mimi and Lydia wore theirs. After that, she dressed and headed downstairs to help Mimi make breakfast, still wanting to write to her siblings, too. There would be plenty of time to do that and mail all the letters after the dishes were washed and put away.

After Lena and the Stoltzfuses, including Solomon and Eli, had enjoyed a generous meal of fried eggs and scrapple, potatoes, and plenty of coffee, they stayed around for Bible reading before Harley and Eli returned to the barn. The verse Harley had repeated after breakfast continued to echo in Lena's mind. *"Trust in the LORD with all thine heart; and lean not unto thine own understanding."* He had gone on to read a few other verses similar to this command from their heavenly Father. Lena appreciated Harley's observations and pondered them while she tended to the dishes as Mimi sewed.

It was as Lena dried the coffeepot that a passenger van pulled into the driveway, coming to a stop near the back door.

Lena noticed it first; then Mimi came and looked out the window.

"Well, goodness' sake, this must be Tessa!" Mimi exclaimed.

Lena Rose couldn't help but take note of the dear woman's delight. This was one of nearly a half-dozen visits from Harley and Mimi's younger daughter that had taken place since Lena's arrival, something Mimi had pointed out, telling Lena that they'd rarely seen Tessa before Lena came.

"I can't wait to hold my little Joey!" Mimi remarked as she headed directly to the back door to greet her four-month-old grandson and Tessa.

Lena hung back as she had the other times they'd visited. It had been somewhat awkward since the very first time Tessa had stopped by, especially when Mimi mentioned that Lena was working alongside her in the sewing room and was nicely situated in Tessa's former bedroom. At the time, Lena had felt a twinge of guilt at Tessa's injured expression. That and Tessa's cool demeanor toward her communicated that Tessa perhaps viewed her as a rival who was trying to take her place. Truth be known, Lena felt just terrible about it.

"Hullo, Mamm," Tessa said as she came up the porch steps in her black coat and outer bonnet, a scarf around her neck and Joey in her arms.

Mimi welcomed her inside with a kiss on the cheek. "*Kumme* in, dear. It's awful cold to be out with the little one."

Tessa handed the bundled baby to Mimi, who leaned close to his tiny face and began to make over him.

Lena Rose joined her, curious to see how much Joey had grown in just a couple of weeks.

"He's prob'ly hungry again," Tessa said as she hung up her coat. "And I nursed him before we left the house."

"Well, he's a growin' boy. Ain't ya, sweetie?" Mimi cooed and walked the length of the kitchen with Joey, then back toward Tessa and Lena. "Are ya spendin' the day, then?" Mimi asked, hope in her eyes.

Tessa removed her black outer bonnet and placed it on a wooden peg next to her coat. "We'll just see how Joey does."

"He'll be fine," Mimi replied. "Just fine."

She'd love for them to stay into the afternoon, thought Lena Rose, her heart going out to the woman.

"There's plenty of food for the noon meal," Lena said, hoping to pave the way. "It's really no trouble."

"No trouble a'tall," Mimi echoed.

For a moment, Tessa's eyes locked with Lena's. Then at last she nodded, agreeing to stay for the meal as she sat down in the nearby rocking chair.

"I'd be happy to hold the baby later while you eat," Lena offered.

"Oh, he'll prob'ly sleep through dinner," Tessa said hastily.

Lena nodded, and Mimi gave Lena a thoughtful glance, but Tessa quickly changed the topic, saying that three of the milk cows her husband was in charge of had escaped from the barnyard yesterday morning.

"Did Manny manage to round 'em up?" Mimi asked, cuddling the baby as she sat on the long wooden bench.

"He did, but it took a few hours, and by then their udders were awfully full. It was terrible, really." Tessa shook her head. "Oh, Mamm, Manny despises workin' as a farmhand. He just isn't a dairyman, and to top it off, there's been mastitis in the herd—bacteria in the milk are makin' it impossible to pass inspection. *Ach*, there've been all kinds of troubles lately." She stared out the nearby window. "Manny's even talked 'bout quitting his job and doing something else. In fact, he's thinking of partnering with a would-be cabinetmaker up here—a younger fella he met through Eli."

"You'd move back to Leacock Township?" There was a look of expectancy on Mimi's round face.

"Honestly, I don't know. But I feel cut off from everyone I grew up with," she said softly. Going silent for a time, her gaze shifted to Lena, who held her breath, thinking this was just what Mimi needed to hear.

Mimi raised Joey so she could kiss his tiny face. "Well, it'd be *wunnerbaar-gut* to have yous closer."

"Believe me, Manny's not happy workin' for his uncle, so no one can talk him into stayin' put doin' what he's doing now. But as to whether or not we'll move here . . . well, there's a catch, I'm afraid." Tessa glanced up at the ceiling, then down quickly at her hands in her lap. "Manny worries that his potential partner's father might oppose the plan, since . . . well, Abram Mast just assumes Arden'll take over the farm in a year or so." The light had gone out of Tessa's pretty blue eyes, and she untied her black neck scarf and slid it off.

Arden? Lena thought, surprised to hear his name in this conversation. *He doesn't want to go on with his father's farm?*

"Well, running a dairy farm's exhausting work," Mimi said, shifting Joey in her arms. "I know that for truth, and so do you, dear."

Tessa nodded emphatically. "I remember helpin' Dat and my brothers till they left home to marry," she said. "I was never so thrilled as when Dat hired farmhands." She paused a moment. "Sometimes I really wonder what Eli's thinking, stayin' round here and getting up at four every morning all year long."

"Undoubtedly, he'll take over the operation someday. And I say bless him for that." Mimi smiled.

"Better Eli than Manny," Tessa said. She reached to rub the back of her neck. "Eli seems better suited for it than Aaron, Caleb, or Will, don't you think?"

Mimi nodded. "Eli enjoys bein' around the cows . . . he's cut from the same cloth as your father."

Tessa glanced at Lena Rose. "It's nice you don't have to be out there before the crack of dawn."

"Oh, I would if necessary . . . but I'm content to work indoors with your Mamm." Lena looked over at Mimi. Lena had said something similar about Mimi the first time she'd met Tessa in late September.

"We're a *gut* team," Mimi said of Lena, then smiled down at the baby, making little sounds with her lips.

This made Lena Rose feel good, but she worried what Tessa might be thinking, since Lena had taken her former place in Mimi's business.

But Tessa's mind was clearly elsewhere. "You have a way with your grandson, Mamm," Tessa said, observing her mother with the baby.

"*Ach*, I'd spoil him if I could. Wouldn't I, darlin'?" she cooed at the infant.

Tessa seemed to sigh and looked toward the farmland calendar on the wall, staring at it for a moment. "Arden Mast wants to present his and Manny's plan to Abram the day after Christmas."

"Sounds like they've thought this through," Mimi said.

"For sure. But Manny's holdin' his breath and moving forward cautiously, in case the whole thing ends up fallin' apart." Tessa reached for Joey when he started to cry.

"What'll happen if Abram disapproves?" Mimi asked.

Tessa shrugged and opened the bodice of her dress to nurse her son. "I really don't know."

Rising, Mimi went to boil water for tea.

Meanwhile, Lena got up to fetch the teacups and saucers from the corner china closet, finding it very interesting to think that Arden Mast wanted to do something other than dairy farm. She remembered the day before Thanksgiving, when Eli had brought Arden along to supper after their hunting trip. *Arden doesn't seem like a fellow who'd want to swim against the current,* she thought. *Or disappoint his father . . .*

⸺ ☙ ❧ ⸺

Whether it was due to Lydia's friendly urging or to Lena's loneliness, on Sunday evening at twilight, Lena found herself being driven by her cousin Eli to the Singing, where quite a few open black buggies and several enclosed family carriages were already lined up in the side yard adjacent to the two-story barn. Eli took care of the horse while Lena made her way up the ramp to the barn's haymow, glad she'd worn her warm snow boots. The air was frosty, and she wondered if someone might build a bonfire outside.

For now, her mission was to look for Lydia, who had vowed to be waiting for her near the entrance to the hayloft. So, wanting to appear as confident as possible, Lena Rose headed right to the upper level of the bank barn and heaved open the wooden door.

True to her word, Lydia was standing nearby, still wearing her black coat and outer bonnet. Her mittened hands peeked out from her coat sleeves. "You're here, Lena. I'm so glad you came!"

"Been waitin' long?" Lena asked, noticing how cleanly swept the wide wood planks were, the hay piled high on either side of the barn, and the hay baler parked off to one corner. The hosting family had certainly gone to a lot of trouble.

"Only a few minutes," Lydia said. "I was talking to some of my cousins about the Christmas Eve school play. I hope you can go, too," Lydia added. "Harley and Mimi enjoy seeing their grandchildren give their recitations each year."

Suddenly, Lena's heart was far away—this would be young Chris's first time in the school Christmas program in their own community. "I've been hopin' to return home by Christmas," she told Lydia. "Or at least a visit."

"Can't imagine bein' gone so long from family," Lydia said, then went on to talk about how the Leacock Amish schoolteacher was older than some. "She's close to thirty, I've heard. And word has it she's teachin' the children *speaking* parts for the Nativity scene. I've wondered if she might bring in some lambs, maybe, and some camels, too." Lydia laughed. "Just kidding . . . that'd be much too fancy, ain't?"

Lena was glad to have someone so interesting to talk with while they waited for the rest of *die Youngie* to arrive.

Three girls not far from them were talking quite animatedly about the coming holiday, saying what they were going to help their mothers make for the Christmas feast: candied fruit, pineapple coconut pie, chocolate macaroons, and sour cream chocolate cookies.

Lena's mouth watered at the delicious options. She recalled all the splendid Christmas Eve afternoons she, Mamma, and Emma had spent in their large yet cozy kitchen baking their favorite holiday pies—cherry, pecan, and elderberry custard—and sand tarts, thin as dimes—and fresh loaves of bread. Wilbur or one of the younger boys would sneak in and put his fingers in the bowl of cookie dough when Mamma wasn't looking. Lena knew, and so did Emma, but they would shrug it off, remembering when they, too, were little and doing the snitching.

Then, on Christmas, after they had all eaten their fill at noon, Dat would get an enormous grin on his handsome face and tell the older children to help Mamma get the younger ones all bundled up and ready, and out he'd go to the stable, bringing around the hay wagon. Those wagon rides along the snowy road north of Centreville to the red covered bridge had been one of the high points of every winter, all of them clustered together to keep warm. They had laughed and sung Christmas carols, then stopped in at neighbors' to deliver cookies or popcorn balls and to sing "Joy to the World" and "Away in a Manger." She had loved just being together, the twelve of them, enjoying their holiday traditions.

Cherishing the memories, Lena refused to dwell on her losses. There was much to look forward to, she told herself, holding her breath for Hans to come through with a plan for their time together. *Surely he will.*

"Are you all right?" Lydia asked, pulling her out of her reverie.

"Oh *jah*, sorry . . . just thinkin' about home."

Lydia nodded sympathetically.

Across one side of the hayloft, the young men stood in groups of five or six, wearing their black felt hats and black for-good clothes from church earlier. Lena didn't attempt to see where her cousin Eli was just now; instead, she turned to look toward the clusters of young women dressed in pretty plum-colored dresses and matching capes and aprons, others in different colored dresses with aprons from the same colored fabric. Lena had worn her best mourning dress, a black dress and matching apron without the cape, in the style of the Centreville womenfolk, which stood out amidst the others as she and Lydia moved toward the rest of the courting-age girls, some already seated on one side of a long table. Fewer fellows were seated on the other side, as more were still milling about and talking.

A couple of young men walked across to greet Lena.

"Join us anytime," one very tall young man told her, offering a firm handshake and saying his name was Andrew Blank. "Don't hesitate, okay?"

Lydia introduced Lena to Andrew's blushing friend, John Glick, who was caught between a smile and puckering frown, revealing his apparent shyness.

"Nice to meet you both," Lena said, pleased with the warm reception but also hoping none of the young men would get the wrong idea about her reason for coming.

The farmer hosting the evening blew into the pitch pipe to start the Singing, and Lena followed Lydia to the table to sit down, trying to be discreet about being the new girl.

"See? You're causin' a real stir already," Lydia said, glowing.

Rather embarrassed, Lena began to join in song with the others, surrounded by her budding friends.

During the time for refreshments, Lydia excused herself when Eli came over to talk with her, which was all right with Lena, who decided to take her hot cocoa to the corner and just observe. She felt more comfortable there, and besides, it wasn't the first time Lena had ever leaned against the side of a barn feeling this shy, like John Glick had seemed. Lena felt a bit sorry for him, remembering how it felt to like someone, or be attracted to them, and be nearly tongue-tied, like she had been when first going to Singings in Michigan.

Sipping her cocoa, she relished the chance to simply watch the pairing up, and was all the more eager to see Hans at Christmas.

"Are ya holdin' up the wall?"

She had been so deep in thought, Lena hadn't even seen Arden Mast come over. "Sorry?"

Playing along, Arden gave the wall a little push. "Looks like it'll prob'ly stay up without your help."

Lena laughed. "Actually . . . I was just thinking."

Arden smiled, his deep dimples showing. "I tend to think too hard sometimes, too." He glanced over his shoulder at Eli and Lydia, who were still talking together. Eli was eating a doughnut, and Lydia was reaching into a small bag of popcorn. "Looks like

Lydia found someone else to talk to." Arden smiled at Lena again. "I'm glad she did."

Lena hardly knew how to react.

"I s'pose Eli gave you a ride over," Arden said.

"*Jah.*"

He paused, glancing up at the barn rafters for a second, then back at her. "I s'pose you'll need a ride home, too."

"With Eli, I'm guessin'."

"Well, he's taking Lydia home . . . and me, as well." Arden explained that his buggy was on the blink. "So I hope you won't mind ridin' with the three of us."

Lena saw that she had managed to get herself in a jam. "Well, I guess since Eli's my ride home, too, I have no choice but to go," she answered.

"We'll see that you get home in one piece," Arden said.

Looking at him, she realized he was teasing her. "*Des gut,* then."

Later, after the last gospel song was finished, Lydia whispered to Lena, "I hope ya won't mind doublin' up, just for the fun of it. Okay?"

"Doubling up?" *Goodness!* she thought, certainly seeing the downside of being too secretive with Lydia.

"Arden and you, and Eli and me," Lydia said, clearly trying not to smile.

So word had already gotten to Lydia from Eli about Arden's riding with them. *It's my fault for not telling Lydia about Hans,* Lena scolded herself as she and Lydia made their way across the barn to get their coats and scarves. *They might be in cahoots,* she thought as she spotted Eli and Arden waiting for her and Lydia over near the sliding barn door.

10

Bitter cold as it was now with light snow falling, Lena hoped Eli would have the sense to take the others directly home after the Singing. Lydia had gotten into the front seat of the carriage with Eli's help, sitting next to him now as he picked up the driving lines. This left Lena awkwardly with Arden in the second seat of Cousin Harley's enclosed family buggy, which Eli had borrowed for the evening.

"So now that you've been here awhile, what do you think?" Arden's voice broke the stillness as they moved forward, the horse's hooves sounding like soft rhythmic thumps against the snow-packed road.

"It's pretty," Lena replied, aware that Eli and Lydia were whispering to each other. *Though not any prettier than Centreville,* she thought, glad for her warm scarf and mittens.

"What have you seen so far?" Arden continued to make small talk, his gloved hands resting atop the heavy buggy blanket he'd carefully draped over Lena . . . then himself.

She mentioned the nearby gristmill, the general store, and the various farmhouses where Preaching services had been held. "Oh, and the farm market, of course."

"Have ya been to Root's or the Green Dragon yet?"

"We've talked about goin' lately, but Mimi's sewing and mending took up autumn's finer days," Lena said, feeling strange knowing from Tessa about Arden's hope of opening a cabinetmaking shop. *What sort of fellow leaves his father in the lurch?*

"Well, I think you'd enjoy it if you could find the time," Arden replied. "The Saturday-night auctions at Green Dragon are a lot of fun, as maybe you've heard from Harley."

She listened, then mentioned there were markets in Michigan's Amish country, too. "Maybe you aren't aware of that," she said softly, wanting him to know she hadn't come from the sticks.

"I've never been out of this state, actually," Arden said as he leaned up to look out the front window at blinking car lights ahead.

"Wonder what's happening up yonder," Eli said, leaning to the side to see better.

"I hope no one's broken down in this cold," Lydia said, sounding worried.

"Might've run out of gas," Eli remarked. He sat back in the seat as they approached the car. "What do ya say we stop and offer some help, Arden?"

"Sure."

"I'll slow up and have a look-see at who's behind the wheel," Eli said, putting on the buggy brake. "See if I know 'em."

As they approached, all of them looked at the car parked on the shoulder. The interior lights were on, and a man and woman were studying a map.

"Looks like they're just lost," Eli said.

"*Jah,* so keep goin'," Arden advised.

"They've got a map . . . they'll be fine," Eli told Lydia, then slipped his arm around her. "Are ya warm enough?" he asked.

"*Jah,*" Lydia answered before suggesting they all go to her house for hot coffee. "I'm sure Mamma left out some cookies and sweet bread."

"All right with you, Arden?" asked Eli over his shoulder.

Arden paused. "What do ya think, Lena Rose?"

"We could play Dutch Blitz," Lydia said quickly, without turning around, appearing quite cozy up there next to Eli.

At first thought, Lena didn't think she ought to, considering it would look like the four of them were double-dating. On the other hand, she didn't want to spoil the evening for Lydia and Eli. "If we're not out too late, I guess," she agreed reluctantly.

Eli glanced back at them. "Don't worry, Lena, we won't meet the rooster's crowing comin' and goin'. My father's entrusting your welfare to me."

"Then I say she's in *gut* hands," Arden said.

It was as if Harley had taken his son aside regarding Lena's first outing here. The idea made her feel warm inside. *Not every young woman has such attentive relatives,* she thought, hoping with all of her heart that the families that had taken in her brothers and sisters were equally as caring.

When they arrived at Lydia's, it was soon apparent that her parents had retired for the night, leaving on the kitchen gas lamp that hung low over the gleaming wood table, where plates of goodies were laid out, covered with plastic wrap. There was a note, too, in the prettiest handwriting: *Enjoy the treats!*

In Centreville, Lena knew of fellows who took their sweethearts back to their homes to play games or talk. Some even spent the night in the spare room, or stayed the whole weekend if it was a Saturday evening. She didn't know anything at all about Lancaster County courting traditions, but she trusted Eli's judgment.

"Who'd like some coffee?" Lydia asked, going to the woodbin and picking up some logs for the cookstove. Eli went over and coaxed the smoldering embers into a flame for her while Arden took off his coat and black felt hat, then politely offered to help Lena with her coat.

"*Denki*," she said, again feeling a bit awkward. Thankfully, Arden hadn't asked her any more personal questions.

Why isn't he already courting someone, pleasant and engaging as he seems to be? she wondered. Eli undoubtedly knew, as they were close friends, but Lena wouldn't inquire for fear of giving the wrong impression. She certainly did not want that!

Eli lingered with Lydia while she brewed some decaf coffee, which led to Arden taking a seat at the table. Lydia suggested he sample her mother's baked goods, and Arden seemed happy to do so.

Not knowing what else to do while Lydia happily soaked up Eli's attention near the stove, Lena pulled out the long bench on the opposite side of the table from Arden and sat. "Which one's your favorite?" she asked, indicating the variety of goodies.

"Definitely the chocolate squares. They taste like my Mamm's."

"I thought it'd be the chocolate chip cookies," Lena said, filling up the time till Lydia came over and joined her, hopefully. "My brother Wilbur is a big fan of those. I used to bake them all the time with my mother and my sister Emma."

"Cookies are fine—don't get me wrong," Arden replied, looking spiffy in his blue shirt and black suspenders. His blond hair was shiny clean, and his striking blue-green eyes narrowed a little when he smiled, which was often. Arden just seemed to be a very happy sort—considerate and even-keeled. "My sisters like to bake, too. All three of them," he added. "How many sisters do you have?"

"Three, also—Emma, Liz, and Verena." She paused, waiting for the next question sure to come: "*And how many brothers?*"

"And Eli says you have a bunch of brothers."

She nodded, smiling now. "Six, *jah*." It was hard to talk about her siblings in terms of mere numbers when they were each truly unique . . . and ever so much fun. "How many brothers do you have?" she asked.

"Two are married, and one is two years older than me," he said. "I'm the last of the litter."

The one who typically takes over the family farm, she thought, studying him. She couldn't tell by his expression if he was a man who would break his word, but if it was true what Tessa had said, Arden was moving in a different direction than his father was expecting. She didn't want to judge him since she didn't know all the details—and it wasn't her place to know, anyway. From her limited experiences with Arden, it was just real hard to see anything but honesty in him.

"So tell me . . . what's it like in Michigan?" he asked, his voice low as he folded his hands on the table. "If I'm not oversteppin'."

"I don't mind," she said and began to share some of the differences, even mentioning the fact that some of the Swiss Amish had open buggies all year round. "Can you imagine that?"

"And Michigan's mighty cold, ain't?"

"Cold's not the way I'd describe it. More like freezin' to the bone."

"So they must have some way of heating their buggies."

"Well, I know of some folk over on the thumb of Michigan that have natural gas heaters in their buggies. Real dangerous, my father always thought."

Arden shook his head. "Is it worth the risk?"

"And of course we use buggy blankets like you do here, with woolen cloth and quilted batting . . . a necessity, especially for older folk and little children."

Arden smiled, his gaze lingering on her as if something humorous had struck him. But he said nothing at first.

"What?" she finally asked.

Arden shrugged. "Your accent . . . I like it."

She had to smile.

"It's interesting." And the way he said it, she thought he'd rather have said it was cute.

They talked further about Lena's hometown, and Arden asked about the type of farming there.

"Well, it's not like here, where farmers tend to pick one kind of crop or livestock. We have many jack-of-all-trades farmers . . . some have ten cows and ten sows, two steers or so, and a few hundred laying hens," she said.

"Reminds me of an old farmer I know from round here, but he's retired now. A good sense of humor, but lonely as a cloud now his wife's gone. He doesn't live too far from Harley and Mimi, actually."

"Oh?"

"*Jah*, not sure if you've had a chance to meet James Zook, but he's as entertainin' as the winter is long."

"Hmm," she murmured. "I've heard Harley mention him occasionally."

Lydia and Eli finally got themselves over to the table and brought the tray of mugs, steaming with hot coffee. Lena had lost track of time while talking with Arden, but she wouldn't have said she minded or regretted the minutes spent getting to know her new friend.

Even so, the evening made her miss Hans all the more, knowing she would have preferred to spend the time with him. *I wonder what he's doing tonight.*

But considering no date had been established yet for her eventual return home, Lena didn't think it would hurt to make a few friends here. *If only to help pass the time.*

CHAPTER

11

The following Wednesday after breakfast, Lena rode with Cousin Harley for the planned visit with Rebekah Petersheim and her grandchildren, thankful for the lift since the roads were slick with a layer of ice, and now snow was falling again.

"When would ya like me to pick you up?" Harley asked, holding the reins taut.

"Oh, in a couple hours."

Harley glanced her way and nodded. "I'll come in time to fetch ya for the noon meal."

"*Denki.*" Lena nodded.

"Think nothin' of it. We're just glad you have it in your heart to help Cora Ruth some."

Recalling how her Mamma, especially, had always instructed her that others come first, Lena Rose smiled. So much about life and God's grace, too, had been gleaned from her parents—they'd spent time instilling the importance of serving others into her and her younger siblings.

At Melvin Ebersol's lane, Harley directed the horse to turn in, going all the way up to the back walkway before getting out to help Lena Rose from the carriage. He held on to her as they crept over the ice to the back door, as well, taking such good care, and Lena was grateful for Harley's fatherly way with her. "*Denki*, I'll see ya in two hours, then," she told him.

"Have yourself a *gut* time." He smiled.

The door opened, and there was Cora Ruth's oldest child, five-year-old Emily Ann, smiling up at her.

"Mammi's upstairs with the babies," the sweet little girl said in *Deitsch*, her hair all rumpled like it needed brushing.

"That's all right, honey-girl. *Denki* for letting me in."

Emily Ann closed the door behind her and showed Lena where to hang her outer clothing and bonnet. Then Lena followed her into the warm and spacious kitchen, where she went over to see what Abe and Bennie were doing in the corner on the floor. Their heads were practically touching as they played with wooden Lincoln Logs.

"We're building a barn," four-year-old Abe said, looking up at her with a serious look on his freckled face.

Two-and-a-half-year-old Bennie held up several pieces in his chubby fist, showing Lena a drooly smile.

She gently patted Bennie's silky blond bangs and said maybe they'd grow up to be master builders someday. "If ya keep practicin'," she added, remembering how Chris loved to build with Lincoln Logs, too.

Just then, Emily Ann came with a book and sat down on the floor near her little brothers. "This is my library book," she said, big blue eyes wide. "I like this story."

"You must've read it before," Lena said, taking a seat on the floor right beside her.

"*Jah*, Mamma reads it to me." The little girl sighed loudly. "I asked Mammi Petersheim to, but she's busy with the twins."

Lena well knew the familiar story of *Henner's Lydia*, about a little Amish girl who got very distracted while trying to make a hooked mat before going to market. It was a book Lena's mother had read to her and Emma when they were little.

It wasn't long before Rebekah joined them, and seeing Lena there on the floor with the children, she tilted her head and grinned. "Yous look so cozy, but there *are* chairs to sit on." She motioned for Lena and Emily Ann to go with her into the nearby sitting room, which they did.

"Won't ya read the story to me now, Mammi?" Emily asked, climbing onto her grandmother's lap. Emily opened to the first page. "It's the best book ever."

"Oh *jah*, 'tis." Rebekah looked at Lena, clearly uncomfortable.

"Please, Mammi?" Emily Ann persisted.

Rebekah kissed Emily's forehead and sighed. "I'm all in, dearie. Best be lettin' Lena Rose read it to ya."

But Emily stayed on Rebekah's lap, just turning the pages slowly, pointing out the characters to her Mammi while trying to tell the story in *Deitsch* in her own way.

Rebekah glanced away at one point, blinking back tears, Lena was ever so sure, and her heart went out to the woman.

So Lena offered to read the book to Emily Ann. Happily, the little girl hurried over and stood beside Lena, leaning against her arm during the story. *Like Chris used to.*

When the book was finished, Emily Ann went back to the kitchen to play with her brothers. Rebekah turned to look out the window, then down at the floor. Finally, sighing loudly, she twiddled her thumbs, avoiding Lena's gaze.

Lena hesitated as the silence seemed to pull the air out of the room. But soon, from out in the kitchen, came the sound of Emily Ann's exuberant giggles.

Proceeding with caution, Lena ventured ahead, hoping for the best. "My younger brother Benjamin used to have trouble reading English, so he would practice by reading out loud to Mamma," Lena said.

Suddenly, Rebekah's eyes were intent on her, as though following every word.

"I watched him with Mamma . . . the way she was able to help and encourage him. Mamma was a substitute teacher at a Mennonite school before she died."

"She helped your brother, ya say?"

Lena nodded and was about to tell Rebekah more when Emily Ann burst into the room and asked to show her grandmother a block tower she'd made. "Right quick . . . before it falls down!"

Lena smiled as Rebekah allowed herself to be led to the kitchen doorway, but the woman glanced back. "I'd like to hear more 'bout your brother's troubles reading English."

"I'll be happy to tell ya," Lena said, and Rebekah brightened.

Later, while the children were occupied at the kitchen table with a morning snack of orange slices and raisins, Rebekah sat next to Lena, her words hushed to a whisper. "I . . . 'spect you noticed . . . my hesitation to read."

"I'd be thrilled to help, if I can," Lena said gently in English, so the children wouldn't understand.

"Ain't sure anyone can, to tell the truth." Rebekah looked away and shook her head slowly, as though embarrassed. "Not like I didn't do my best to learn back when."

Lena put her hand on Rebekah's arm. "Well, you already know how to read, *jah*?"

Rebekah nodded. "It's English that throws me."

"It's not easy learnin' English when *Deitsch* is your first language. I can understand that."

Rebekah smiled now. "Teachin' must run in your family."

"Well, I learned everything from Mamma." Lena glanced across the kitchen at the children. "And I believe I can help ya."

"How . . . where would we go 'bout this?" Rebekah asked. "It'd be embarrassing if my grandchildren knew. . . ."

"Maybe Mimi wouldn't mind if you came by once a week over there—maybe on a Friday afternoon, once I'm done sewin'. But I'll check with her first."

Rebekah's face lit up. "*Jah*, that'd be perfect. Cora Ruth can manage without me for an hour or so."

Lena hoped this might be a way to make a difference for Rebekah, given that she seemed bereft of friends.

———

When Cousin Harley came for Lena, he offered his arm, as the weather had gotten even worse. She wondered how slowgoing it might be for Cora Ruth as she returned from the doctor's, and mentioned this to Harley.

"Well, I saw her and the horse and carriage headed this way," he replied.

"Maybe we should help her inside."

"I thought of that," Harley said, getting into the carriage warmed by hot bricks. They waited until they spotted Cora Ruth make the turn into the lane.

When Cora Ruth brought the horse and buggy to a stop, Harley walked gingerly over to help her down from the carriage and lead her inside. Then he returned to Cora Ruth's horse and carriage and began to unhitch the mare while Lena remained in the Stoltzfus buggy under the heavy woolen blanket.

Harley made quick work of it and soon was guiding the horse to the stable, then parked the buggy in the carriage shed.

By the time they arrived home, Uncle Solomon and Eli were

already eating with Mimi, who looked relieved when she saw Lena Rose. "Harley's out getting unhitched," Lena told her.

Eli jumped right up from the table. "I'll go out an' help."

"We were prayin' for yous to get home safely," Solomon said, his right hand shaking as he reached for his water glass.

"Indeed we were," Mimi admitted, still looking pleased they were home safely.

"We sure needed it." Lena went on to say that Harley had seen to it that Cora Ruth also got into the house safe and sound. "And he took care of her horse, too."

"That's my Harley, always lookin' out for others." Mimi smiled.

"How we treat folk matters," Dat always said, Lena thought, going back to the utility room to hang up her black bonnet and coat before making a beeline to the sink to wash her hands.

Mimi went to the table and poured hot coffee for both Lena Rose and Harley, topping off Solomon's mug as well.

Solomon thanked Mimi and glanced toward the back door as it opened and in walked Harley and Eli. Solomon waved them over. *"Kumme esse* while it's still hot."

Harley removed his hat and his boots, dropping them to the utility room floor. Then he wandered into the kitchen. "The mules are real jumpy," he said, pulling pieces of ice out of his beard. "Must be more bad weather comin'."

Lena looked out the window before she took her seat at the table, observing thousands of giant flakes. "Looks like we might get snowed in," she said.

"If so, we could definitely catch up on all the mending and whatnot," Mimi suggested as she waited for her husband to go and wash up in the utility room.

"No matter how severe the weather," Eli said, "the cows still have to be milked."

Soon, Harley returned and joined them, bowing his head for the mealtime prayer.

Given what she'd experienced at the Ebersols' today, Lena felt compelled to add another thank-you heavenward, and not just for the delicious spread before them—buttered noodles, fried chicken, and green beans with onion and ham bits—but for the amazing opportunity to assist a woman up in years with her reading.

Hans will be interested to hear about this, she thought later while serving dessert with Mimi.

But it was the recent memory of her and Arden Mast riding home from Singing with Eli and Lydia that made Lena Rose resist the smile that threatened as they all enjoyed Mimi's pumpkin pie. *No sense in drawing attention to myself over that!*

CHAPTER

12

That evening alone with Mimi, while they washed the supper dishes, Lena shared about Rebekah's difficulty reading
English. "Would ya mind if she came over once a week for a while
. . . so we can work together without her grandchildren around?"

"That's fine—and what a kind gesture, I daresay." Mimi was
nodding, her expression thoughtful. "I had no idea Cora Ruth's
Mamm struggled thataway."

"Prob'ly doesn't want it known."

"*Nee* . . . the poor woman's been through enough here lately.
Through the wringer and then some." Mimi stopped right there,
saying no more about Rebekah, which made Lena all the more
curious yet again. *What does Mimi know?*

—꘎ ꘎—

The very next afternoon, Lena Rose headed out to Gordonville
Book Store in the carriage with Mimi at the reins. Lena talked
about the kind of book she wanted to get for the first session with
Rebekah Petersheim tomorrow, during the Ebersol twins' nap time.

Mimi said very little as they rode along, the roadways mercifully mostly clear of snow. The prediction of being snowed in had never come to pass.

"Truth be told, I tried to put myself in Rebekah's shoes. And I couldn't stop thinkin' how it would be if I was her age and *my* granddaughter asked to be read to," Lena said. "I'd feel so frustrated . . . probably a little embarrassed, too."

Mimi slowly bobbed her head. "Never thought of it thataway." She looked at Lena, giving her a kindly smile. "It's hard to understand how it could happen, really. Of course, Rebekah went to school back when we were all attending public schools along with *Englischers*. Maybe she got lost in the shuffle somehow." Hands still on the driving lines, Mimi glanced over at Lena. "But since your Mamma was a schoolteacher, I'm sure you'll do fine with Rebekah."

Lena dipped her head, self-conscious. "I think she and I have some things in common." She paused, wanting to be careful how she phrased this. "I doubt Rebekah's made many connections here outside of Cora Ruth and the children."

Mimi was quiet for a moment. "It's true Rebekah's endured some distressing circumstances this past year." Mimi sighed but kept her eyes on the road. "She still needs our prayers."

This struck Lena's heart. "Cora Ruth mentioned that Rebekah was a big help with the little ones."

"Oh, I'm sure of that."

Lena Rose nodded. "Although Emily Ann's a great help for a five-year-old."

"Not all little girls are, but I know you were, Lena. Your father even wrote to Harley about how you and Emma helped your Mamma."

Lena blushed but thought it was sweet to know that Dat had shared such things about their lives out in Michigan.

"'Tis real *gut* for Rebekah to be with Cora Ruth and Melvin," added Mimi.

Pondering what had been said just now, Lena wondered if maybe she was supposed to have discovered Rebekah's difficulties in reading. And if so, perhaps it was the Lord who had prompted her to tutor the woman. *If I dare to think that way.*

In the bookstore parking lot, Mimi tied Barney, their more reliable road horse, to the hitching post, and the two women headed toward the entrance. A flash of sunlight on the window momentarily blinded Lena, and she heard a plane fly low overhead.

Inside, Lena perused the beginning readers while Mimi went to look at cookbooks "for fun," she said over her shoulder.

They had only been browsing a few minutes when the bell jingled over the door as another customer came in. Lena didn't bother to look up, engrossed in the choices before her, even though most of the books were obviously for young children.

"Hullo, Lena Rose."

A bit startled, she turned and saw Arden Mast. "I wasn't expectin' to see you today."

He smiled. "You never know where I'll show up." He winked.

"Lookin' for something to read?" she asked.

Arden shrugged and looked a little sheepish. "Well . . . I do enjoy bookstores, and I *have* bought quite a few books here. But . . ."

"Don't they have what you're lookin' for?" She almost asked if it was a book on starting up a cabinetmaking shop.

He shrugged, a suspicious twinkle in his eye. "Actually . . . I noticed Harley's horse parked outside and wondered if . . . well, it might be you, out and about."

"Are ya followin' me?" She tried not to smile.

"*Nee.*" He shook his head, seemingly flustered. "Not at all. I just happened to be headed this way."

She narrowed her eyes, pressing further with her little joke. "You're *sure* about that? Seems like quite a coincidence." She gazed at him with mock seriousness.

He must have caught the glint in her expression and returned her smile. "You *are* quite the kidder, ain't?"

Lena laughed, and Arden joined in, nodding as if pleased with their witty banter. Then he lowered his voice. "What I'd really like is to get to know ya better . . . sometime over coffee, maybe?"

She was flattered that he would ask and felt guilty for not being forthright earlier, no matter how much she'd enjoyed their bantering. "I'm sorry, Arden," she said softly, wanting to be honest. "I should've said somethin' sooner. You see, I have a beau back home."

Arden's face dropped a little, but he managed to salvage his smile. "Well, I'm sorry, too."

"It's my fault, really." She'd considered telling Lydia last Sunday night but hadn't even done that. And besides, like Lydia had pointed out, Lena *had* needed a ride home in the cold.

An uncomfortable moment passed between them. Then Arden stepped closer to look at the book in Lena's hand. "So . . . are ya hopin' to teach school here?"

"Not school, *nee*." She thought it best not to mention Rebekah's plight to anyone beyond Mimi.

He nodded, then another awkward moment followed. Thankfully, Arden didn't press her further. "Well, I'd better get goin'. Have a *wunnerbaar-gut* day, Lena Rose," he said, not sounding as disheartened as she'd feared. "Hopefully we can be friends."

"For sure," she said.

He grinned. "Oh, and I promise to quit following ya all over kingdom come!"

She laughed again.

"So long." Arden walked toward the door and left with a turn and wave to her, a pleasant look on his handsome face.

I did the right thing, Lena thought, returning her attention to the books.

Toward the bottom shelf, she was pleased to discover a set of old-fashioned *McGuffey Readers*, the first two of which she decided to purchase. *These will be perfect!*

_⸙ ⸙_

Harley noticed Melvin Ebersol's road horse pulling into the driveway late the following afternoon, bringing Rebekah Petersheim to her first lesson with Lena Rose.

Who would've pictured this? he thought, recalling Mimi's and his lengthy discussion about Rebekah's unusual situation. *Leaving her husband behind in New Wilmington, Pennsylvania, last year before his death . . .*

"*What Lena Rose doesn't know won't hurt anything,*" Mimi had assured him when they talked in the privacy of their bedroom about opening their home for the weekly instruction.

Harley had eventually agreed—the lessons wouldn't last forever. *Especially if Rebekah catches on quick,* he thought now, wondering how she'd failed to learn to read English, at least not well enough to read it aloud. Perhaps her teachers had given up on her . . . or she hadn't put her mind to it. But then, Harley didn't know the whole story. He chastised himself for thinking this way. *No use in idle speculation.*

Peering out the stable window, Solomon's dog, Blackie, at his side, Harley was glad to have sprinkled salt along the walkway so that the woman's footing was sure. Harley took notice of Rebekah's determined stride as she made her way toward the house, dressed all in black.

She looks mighty eager. . . .

_⸙ ⸙_

"*Willkumm*, Rebekah," Lena said as she opened the back door with a smile, excited about this first lesson. She waited for

Rebekah to remove her coat, scarf, and black outer bonnet, then hung them up in the utility room.

"Still can't believe you wanna do this," Rebekah said, following Lena into the kitchen.

"I'm lookin' forward to us working together." Lena added that Mimi was upstairs for a while and wouldn't be able to hear them, wanting Rebekah to feel completely relaxed and not worried that she would have an eavesdropper. "The front room's all ours." Lena led the way and suggested Rebekah sit in a chair where the light came in from the window behind her.

"The more sunlight, the better," Rebekah said with a smile.

Before they got started, Lena asked if Rebekah would like some coffee or hot cocoa.

"*Denki*, but *nee* . . . I'm all set."

"And I'm ready, too," Lena said, giving *McGuffey's Pictorial Eclectic Primer* to Rebekah, apologizing for its somewhat childish bent.

Rebekah studied the book's cover. "This looks like the first reader I had in school, many years ago."

Lena perked up her ears. "Starting with something easy like this will give you confidence," she told her.

But Rebekah seemed intent on talking about other things. "Alas, my Mamm was sickly back when I was a schoolgirl, and I was the only daughter still at home after a whole slew of brothers, so I missed a lot of school. It fell to me to help Mamm."

Lena listened, intrigued.

"And I was mighty shy, too. Nearly afraid to speak even when the teacher would have me read aloud in a group with the other pupils in my grade."

Lena was getting a better picture of things. "Did ya ever tell anyone? Your Mamm, maybe? Or the teacher?"

"*Nee*. After a time, I got better at mingling in with the other readers, movin' my mouth when they would read, knowin' that even when I could sound out the words, I couldn't keep up." Rebekah sighed. "By the time I was older, I was needed more at home, so I went from the schoolhouse to my mother's kitchen, helpin' every which way I could."

Lena sensed her frustration.

"My own children, as they were growin' up, prob'ly thought I wasn't interested in reading to them, so it's been an embarrassment, to be sure," Rebekah told her.

"Well, you're here now."

Rebekah's smile at that was sheer pleasure to Lena.

"Let's get started," Lena said, eager to see how challenging this would be. She asked Rebekah to read the first line from the page she'd selected. Rebekah went slowly, stumbling over a few of the words but doing fine with the simplest ones. After that, Lena asked her to read it several more times, and on the fourth time, she read along with Rebekah, this time slightly faster. They repeated that approach with each new line. At last, Rebekah had to stop for a moment. "No one's ever taken time to do this with me." She sighed audibly. "I really want this to work."

They read together for a full hour, sounding out the more difficult words together as they came up. As she prepared to leave, Rebekah looked at Lena, tears springing up in her eyes. "I never dreamed I'd have the chance to learn to read English better."

"Let's make that your goal," Lena said, not wanting to promise the sun and the moon. At the same time, she certainly did not want to throw a damper on the woman's enthusiasm, either.

Later, when the postal truck arrived, Lena quickly pulled on her coat and scarf and scurried out to the road, anxious to see if there were any letters from home. What was it about the landscape of home that stirred up her heart and captured her mind? It was so much easier now to appreciate the life she'd once had.

She let out a joyful *jah* when she saw several letters from Michigan—all of her siblings had written—and so had Mammi Schwartz.

And there were *two* from Hans!

Oh, she could scarcely wait to see him over Christmas. They were making plans by mail to attend a couple of youth-related activities during the holiday, as well as spend some time with Hans's family.

So very soon!

CHAPTER

13

That evening, Lena and Mimi sat in companionable silence in the small sitting room between the kitchen and the large front room, working on a thousand-piece jigsaw puzzle of a snowy farmland scene. Harley had left the house to help his eldest son, Aaron, with an equipment repair.

After a time, Mimi moved to the comfortable chair and began her knitting while Lena continued to find pieces that fit along the puzzle's border. Mimi's knitting needles flew as she worked, the clicking pattern a familiar rhythm as Lena worked on the puzzle, making good progress even on her own, considering she was used to doing these big puzzles with her brothers and sisters.

Later, feeling homesick, Lena went to sit across from Mimi and leisurely reread her letters, relishing the recent one from Mammi, a portion of it dictated to her by Chris. *I can't wait to see you at Christmas, Lena Rose. I miss you!* The words warmed her heart and caused a lump in her throat. The letter continued with Chris telling about his part in the school's Christmas Eve play. *I'm going to be a shepherd boy in the manger scene,* Mammi had written for him. *Dawdi's letting me use one of his canes for my staff. I'm mighty glad you'll be here to see the play!*

She reread the letter from Wilbur, too. He'd written that she'd be surprised at how much the younger boys were growing in her absence. *Especially the twins and Chris.*

Mimi's lips were pursed tightly as she concentrated on the next row of knitting. "It won't be long now and you'll be home for Christmas, Lena Rose."

"*Jah*, in about three weeks," Lena said, wondering how soon to purchase a bus ticket. And Hans was planning to meet her at the bus depot. Oh, she could scarcely wait!

She went over to add another piece to the puzzle, then gazed out the nearby window at the gray sky, a contrast to the white landscape below. The prayer bench and rose trellises were now solidly covered in snow. *Where does Mimi go to pray on such wintry days?* she wondered.

Lena glanced at Mimi. "Do ya miss your prayer bench this time of year?"

"Oh, s'pose I do, but a person can pray most anywhere, really." Mimi's eyes searched hers. "Why do you ask, dear?"

"It's such a special spot, is all."

Mimi set down her needles and studied her. "Is somethin' else on your mind?"

"Well, I've been thinking a lot about my visit home. I hope it won't be an inconvenience to you, considering all the sewing that'll pile up."

"I'll manage—likely wouldn't be doing much sewing over Christmas, anyway." Mimi paused. "And we'll look forward to your return."

"I hope that's all right, since nothing's turned up yet back home."

"I've been praying 'bout that, too," Mimi said softly. "I know how much you love your family and long to be there with them."

"*Jah*, ever so much." Lena paused, then hastened to add, "But I've enjoyed spending time with you and Harley, too, Mimi."

Truth be told, the words felt weak on her lips. *I've enjoyed it here, but I want to go home. To stay.*

Suddenly, she felt ungrateful. Yet Mimi didn't seem to notice her drop in spirit, going on now about her plans for Christmas dinner, telling which family members were coming after Preaching service that day, since the celebration fell on a Sunday.

Yet all the while, in the back of Lena's mind, she still felt guilty.

—⁓ ⁓—

One week later, Lena was busy with some mending for Cora Ruth Ebersol's neighbor, the elderly widower whom Arden Mast had described that night after Singing as a good-humored man.

Mimi mentioned that Cora Ruth had referred the gentleman to Mimi's sewing business several years ago, after his wife died. "Between you and me, I think he needs himself a wife again," Mimi said casually. "Someone to look after him." But as she continued to talk about the old widower, it seemed clear that the man was still quite married in his heart to his beloved wife.

"Sounds like a love for a lifetime," Lena murmured, picking up her needle and thread.

"Sorry?" Mimi glanced at her.

"Oh, I was thinkin' about what you just said." Lena raised the trousers she was reinforcing to examine the hem. "Do most married couples feel so strongly about their spouses after so many years together, do ya think? It wonders me."

"Well, Harley and I haven't been married nearly as long as ol' James Zook and his wife were, but I believe I'll feel that way, too, when I'm old and gray." Mimi sighed. "Sure isn't somethin' I want to ponder too hard just yet, losin' my beloved Harley."

"*Nee*," Lena whispered, thinking just then of her father's post-cards to Mamma, still tucked away in the suitcase upstairs. *I should read them*, she thought, especially missing her parents this close to Christmas. *Surely I'm up for it now.*

—◌ ◌—

While Mimi and Lena Rose worked in the sewing room, Harley went two miles up the road to help neighbor Calvin Grant finish up the remodel on his kitchen. It was a rare thing for Harley to be able to volunteer his time, but given that the fields lay dormant, he was more than willing. His paid farmhands would cover the afternoon milking.

Arden Mast had been doing the bulk of the remodel work with help from Manny Beiler, although Harley wasn't altogether sure when the two men had made much of an acquaintance or how this had fallen into place. Odd, really, since Arden should be plenty busy with the Mast family dairy operation. *That's between him and Abram*, Harley reminded himself as he placed the last of the trim pieces near the spacious pantry, something Calvin's wife had requested, the pantry being the initial reason for the whole redo.

From his corner on the opposite side of the kitchen, Harley could hear Arden telling Manny something about planning to "lay it all out to Dat once the holidays are past."

Harley did not know what to make of this but knew better than to eavesdrop further, so he struck up a conversation with Calvin, who immediately brought up the topic of Lena Rose. "My wife says she's a real fine seamstress," Calvin said from where he worked right behind Harley.

"That she is."

"Word has it Lena can do most anything with scissors, a needle, and thread."

Harley glanced over his shoulder and saw that Arden and

Manny had moved farther away, their heads together now as they chewed the fat while working.

"Your wife must be enjoying the company," Calvin added. "What with Tessa married and living a distance away."

"*Jah* . . . and we're havin' fun mastering jigsaw puzzles during the evenings with Lena. That and table games, too." Harley wasn't about to say anything about the blues Mimi had experienced after so suddenly losing her younger daughter to marriage. "Lena's a real help to Mimi, and the People in our church district have opened their arms to her." He thought especially of Lydia Smucker.

"The local young people are planning to use my pond out back on the day after Christmas for a skating party. Lots going on with the Amish youth."

"Second Christmas," Harley said, realizing Lena Rose would be home in Michigan.

"My wife and I are supplying the popcorn and hot cocoa afterward." Calvin went on to mention that someone had recently cut several round holes into the pond where the youth had skated other winters. "Sounds like Preacher Elam's teenage son has taken a keen interest in ice fishing."

"Not such a *gut* idea for a skating pond, that's for certain." Harley had to laugh. Here he was getting the scoop from his Yankee neighbor, of all things.

⸻ ꙮ ꙮ ⸻

Lena stopped to rub her neck and shoulders, sore from hours of mending. She looked forward to Rebekah Petersheim's arrival and the second lesson. But when Rebekah appeared at the back door with red, swollen eyes, Lena's heart dropped. Glad that Mimi had stayed put in the sewing room, Lena welcomed Rebekah and felt drawn to give her a little hug, but, unsure how she'd respond, she decided not to. Instead, she took the woman's coat and outer bonnet and hung them up for her.

She led her into the front room, where the heater stove made the place cozy for their hour-long lesson. "I thought it might be nice to read aloud together some of the rhyming verses from *Ideals Magazine*'s Christmas edition," Lena said, trying not to stare at Rebekah's forlorn expression. "Would ya like that?"

Nodding, Rebekah reached for her hankie. "Whatever ya think best."

With Mimi's permission, Lena had brought out the woman's cherished magazine and had chosen an easy Christmas poem. "Here's the first one," she said, handing it to Rebekah. "Read it to yourself silently, then out loud."

Rebekah did so, her voice sounding stronger now than when she'd first arrived.

"Okay, now let's read it together. I'll match your pace, and then each time we read it, I'll move up the pace just a bit, all right? Are ya ready?"

Rebekah said she was.

They used this approach on another short poem, but on the third one, there was a catch in Rebekah's throat, and she put the pretty magazine in her lap. "*Ach*, not feelin' so *gut* today," she said in a near whisper.

"You rest here," Lena said, getting up. "I'll bring ya somethin' to drink."

"*Nee* . . . no need for that." Rebekah forced a smile. "I'd much rather you just sit here with me."

Rebekah sighed, then covered her mouth with her hand for a moment.

"Are you all right?" Lena asked gently.

"What with Christmas so near . . ." She paused. "It's nice to be with Cora Ruth and her family, but I'm missin' my family back home . . . all the gatherings there."

"I understand." Lena nodded. *Believe me.*

Rebekah turned to look at her. "Oh, just listen to me goin' on so, and here you are so far removed from those you love."

Not wanting the focus to shift to herself, Lena shook her head. "I'm sure it must be hard for you, too, Rebekah."

"Honestly, I'm not sure I did the right thing, leavin' home when I did."

Of course, Lena hadn't the slightest idea why Rebekah had chosen to come to Leacock Township when she did.

"All of us second-guess sometimes," Lena said softly.

Rebekah paused and touched her *Kapp* strings. "My older sister Rachel sends letters and cards every week, missin' me, too."

Lena was glad Rebekah had such a special bond, but she also understood what it meant to have a dear sister living so far away. "Could Rachel ever come to visit you here?"

"*Ach*, she's up in years, so that's out of the question." Rebekah shook her head, seemingly resigned.

"Well, maybe you can visit her sometime," Lena offered, not really knowing what more to say.

Rebekah brightened, and for the rest of their time together, Lena noticed how much happier her student appeared to be.

After Rebekah left, Lena breathed a prayer for the poor woman and went to help Mimi make supper, first offering to go out and bring in more split logs for the cookstove.

"Would ya mind?" Mimi said as she put on her half work apron over her dress and long black apron. "Bundle up."

"*Jah*, I don't want to get a chill before Christmas." Lena went to the utility room for her outdoor things.

After donning them, Lena was just stepping outdoors when she saw Lydia Smucker coming up the back steps, her neck and part of her face wrapped in a black woolen scarf that matched her mittens. "*Kumme* in right quick—your cheeks look like ripe cherries," Lena said.

"*Denki!*" Lydia said once she was inside and had removed her scarf. Her eyes were tearing up from the cold. "My buggy wheel flew off on my way back from delivering Christmas cookies to my Dawdi Smucker, down the road a piece."

"Heavens! Are ya all right?"

"I'm fine," Lydia said, though her teeth chattered. "And the horse wasn't hurt, either, thank goodness."

"How far'd ya walk in this cold?"

"About a quarter of a mile, maybe a little more. But even though I put a blanket on the mare, I'm worried 'bout her bein' out for too long in this weather." Lydia's quick concern for others, whether person or animal, made Lena like her all the more.

"Harley and Eli will get the horse soon as they're home. Should be any time now."

Lydia thanked her and looked a bit less worried.

"For now, let's get *you* warmed up. Just make yourself comfortable in the kitchen while I get more wood for Mimi." Lena excused herself.

When she returned, Lena quickly placed two more pieces of wood in the bottom of the stove to keep the fire going. "There. Now the room will stay plenty warm."

Lydia hugged herself. "I'm glad I didn't have to walk much farther, to tell the truth."

Mimi agreed and offered Lydia a pretty smile. "I daresay the Lord must've put our farm right here for a reason, ain't?"

"That's one way to look at it." Lydia went to stand near the cookstove. "Mamma says the Good Lord knows just what we need . . . and when we need it."

Mimi nodded in agreement. "You can always count on that."

Lena invited Lydia to sit with her at the table, insisting she have some hot cocoa with them. "Don't ya worry none. Cousin Harley will repair your buggy wheel in no time," she told her.

Mimi stirred the milk and added the delicious homemade cocoa mix, which Mimi said she and Tessa had first concocted one rainy morning years ago. When the milk was hot enough and the cocoa blended in, Mimi poured the steaming drink into three mugs, topping them with whipped cream, and then set them on a round tray to carry to the table. "Here we are," she said with a smile at Lydia.

Lena glanced out the window and could see that it was snowing much harder. Thankfully, Harley and Eli were making the turn into the driveway just now, and she told Lydia so. "I'll go out an' let them know what's happened, okay?"

She hurried outdoors and waved Eli toward the house before the men could unhitch. "Might ya go an' see what can be done to fix the wheel?" she asked after briefly explaining Lydia's plight.

His face solemn, Eli quickly agreed. "Tell her not to fret. Dat keeps a toolbox in the buggy for such emergencies. We'll have her and her horse back on the road in no time."

Lena thanked Eli and headed back inside, hoping he was right. Twilight was nearly upon them, and with the snow still falling heavily, it was best Lydia got home safely as soon as possible.

14

With Eli's able assistance, Harley made quick work of putting the wheel securely on the carriage, screwing a large nut onto the axle to hold the still solid wheel back in place. Eli hardly said a word as they worked, though he had been full of talk during the ride back earlier.

Harley directed Eli to take Lydia's buggy back to the house while Harley drove his, replaying in his mind some of what Eli had said earlier. Mostly, his son had talked about the dairy farm . . . kept saying how much he enjoyed working around the cows and the barn, no matter the weather. *"Guess I was born to be a dairyman,"* Eli had declared, grinning as he added, *"And I can never be fired."*

Harley had to smile now. Was his youngest son hinting that he wanted to take over the farm in the near future, maybe ease himself into managing the operation? If so, did it mean Eli was thinking ahead to tying the knot with Lydia Smucker?

Harley tried to imagine what it would be like with Eli married and living in the family farmhouse. Having observed him with Lydia, surely that wasn't too far off—at least if Harley assisted him financially for the first few years. If Harley could afford to, he and Mimi would build on another smaller abode for Uncle Solomon so they could move into the *Dawdi Haus* and still have space for a sewing room for Mimi.

"Don't get ahead of yourself," Harley murmured, directing his horse into the lane and up toward the stable. "'Take no thought for your life, what ye shall eat, or what ye shall drink. . . .'"

Unhitching as fast as his gloved hands would allow, Harley called to Eli, who in the meantime had brought a bucket of feed to Lydia's horse. "Go inside and let Lydia know we're back, won't ya?"

"First let me take Barney to the stable for ya, Dat," insisted Eli as he came over. "You go in and get warmed up."

Too cold for an old man, Harley thought, reading between the lines. But he didn't hesitate to take Eli up on the offer, and made his way toward the house. Seeing the kitchen shades drawn, golden strips of light beneath them, he picked up his step, shivering and hungry. And eager to see Mimi again after the long day away.

⎯ᖗ ᖆ⎯

Once Lydia was on her way, Lena took supper over to Solomon next door, taking care not to slip on the ice and snow over that short distance. This time of year, she felt an almost aching hunger for longer days. The limited daylight was hard on folk, her mother used to say.

Noticing the stiff, frozen remnants of a few plants protruding out of the snowy whiteness near the house, Lena made her way up the porch steps of Solomon's little *Dawdi Haus.*

When he came to the door, an instant smile brightened his wrinkled face. "*Denki,* Lena Rose," he said, waving her inside. "I wondered how I'd get over to the main house tonight."

"There was no way Mimi or I expected that." She set down the container of hot soup and the wrapped plate of toasted cheese sandwiches on the small table for two, and Blackie came over to investigate from his resting spot near the coal stove in the sitting room, sniffing about. "Eli will prob'ly eat next door since he's still helping Harley with a few things, which means you'll have plenty here for seconds . . . even thirds."

Solomon smacked his lips, smiling as he sat, and she dished up his soup bowl with a generous portion.

"If ya want dessert, too, I can bring it over later," she offered, serving the rest of his meal on a plate.

A sad look crossed Solomon's face just then.

"Are you all right?" she asked after he'd bowed his head to pray before eating.

Solomon slurped up a spoonful of soup, then paused to say, "Ain't anything wrong with me. It's my ol' friend James Zook I'm concerned 'bout."

"Is he ailing?"

"Ain't ailing so much as sufferin' from a bad case of loneliness. I'd go over and spend more time with him if it wasn't so difficult to get myself out the door and in the buggy." He chuckled. "I guess he an' I both have some stories to tell, ain't?" Then, studying her, Solomon asked, "Say, would ya mind takin' me over there sometime—if ya can fit it in, that is?"

"Why sure. Actually, I have some mending to deliver to him. It's ready, so I could even take ya tomorrow, if you'd like."

Solomon, whose aged head and hands rarely stopped shaking, was stunned motionless. "A visit would be the nicest thing for ol' James." He sighed and glanced down at his soup. "And me."

"Consider it done, then," Lena said. "I'll take some goodies along, too."

"Well, now . . . I like that idea, and so will James, let me tell ya."

They visited a while longer before Lena said she should head back to set the supper table for Mimi. "Do you want me to send Eli over to eat with ya?"

Solomon shook his head. "Don't rush him. I've got Blackie here to keep me company. Ain't that right, boy?" he said, reaching down to pet his German shepherd. "I appreciate the hot meal, Lena Rose." He started to get up when she made a movement toward the door.

"*Nee,*" she said. "No need to see me out. And I'll be sure to return with something for your sweet tooth."

"Chust no ice cream." He grinned, waving her on.

"Definitely not anything shivery." She laughed as she headed out into the cold.

─◦҉ ҉◦─

While Lena ate Mimi's homemade chicken noodle soup and toasted cheese sandwiches, Mimi told Harley of Lydia's repeated thank-yous for coming to her aid.

"Bless her heart," Mimi added. "I'm thankful she was spared any injury."

"*Gut* thing the wheel came off when there was no other traffic nearby," Harley observed. "That stretch of road is pretty quiet toward evening anyway, and there wasn't a soul in sight tonight."

Eli nodded his head. "That's the truth."

They talked further about how cold it was; then Harley mentioned the kitchen remodel at the Grants' place. "Mighty fine workmanship," he said as he reached for his tumbler of water. "Manny and Arden certainly know what they're doing."

Mimi smiled. "I'm glad to hear you say that. Tessa's really hoping he can make a go of this."

Mimi rose to get her pecan pie and bring it over, and Lena remembered her promise to Solomon. "By the way, I offered to take dessert over to Solomon later," she said.

"Actually, I'll be goin' over there soon. How about I take it?" Eli suggested. "Doesn't make sense for you to go back out, Lena Rose. Not tonight."

"Maybe you'll have yourself a second piece of pie, too, eh, son?" Harley added with a wink.

Lena also told of her plan to take Solomon to visit James Zook. "That is, if ya don't mind if I use the carriage tomorrow."

"Go right ahead," Harley agreed. "I'll help ya get Uncle Solomon into the buggy," he offered as Mimi gave him the first slice of pie.

Lena nodded. "He is a smidgen bigger'n me, so that might be a *gut* idea."

Eli chuckled as he seemed to appraise her. "Well, now . . . only 'bout a foot or so."

Lena laughed and reached for her coffee mug.

"He doesn't have as much trouble getting out of the buggy," Eli mentioned. "But I'd still take it slow and easy once you're on your own."

"Oh, I will," Lena promised.

Mimi handed a large slice of pie to Eli. "Solomon's not quite as frail as he lets on."

"Now, Mimi . . ." Harley's eyes widened.

"Well, 'tis true."

"She's right, Dat," said Eli, wasting no time in picking up his fork and digging into the dessert.

Lena enjoyed the table banter even though it triggered memories of such amiable chatter with her own dear family. *The happiest days . . .*

After evening prayers, Lena headed to her room and stooped to raise the bed quilts. Pulling out her suitcase from under the bed, she paused for a moment before unlocking it and carefully

removed the packet of postcards her father had written to her
mother so many years ago.

"Am I ready?" she whispered, holding them reverently.

The first postcard featured a color photo of the old stone
Holmes County courthouse in Millersburg, Ohio, with its majestic
clock tower. The second one showed the quaint Heini's Cheese
Chalet, home of the world-famous wheel cheeses made in Berlin,
Ohio. On the back of the latter, Lena read these words:

*How I want to see you, Elizabeth! These summer days apart from
you creep along at a snail's pace. Your pretty face is constantly on
my mind, and I'm counting the hours till you're in my arms again.
May God keep you in His care till we're together again, in His time.*

Lena pressed her lips together, lest she cry. *Dearest Dat . . .*

She read the next postcard, where her father had written more
words of devotion to her mother. His love seemed so certain, so
true—the strength of it jumped off the card, in fact, reminding
her of all that her parents had shared. Lena had long known
they were devoted to each other but never considered how they
might have been as a young courting couple.

But reading these cards, it was easy to see why Mamma had
fallen for Dat so long ago. And in that moment, Lena felt a rush
of longing for a very special love of her own. *One like Dat and
Mamma's . . .*

⟞ ☙ ❧ ⟝

Not yet ready for bed, Lena found Mimi downstairs sitting at
the kitchen table, writing a letter. "Got a minute?"

Mimi smiled warmly as she put down her pen. "Of course, dear.
Sit with me." She offered Lena another piece of the pecan pie.

"It's delicious, but I'd better not. *Denki.*" Lena took a seat across
from her, still weighing exactly what she wanted to say. "When
my parents' possessions were being divided up, I chose my Dat's

postcards to Mamma as my keepsakes," she told Mimi. "And tonight I finally felt ready to take a look at them."

Mimi removed her bifocals.

"And you know what? My father was perty romantic."

Smiling, Mimi said softly, "A man who loves a woman doesn't mind sharing his heart. He'll do whatever it takes to be with her."

"I should have known, since Dat and Mamma always seemed so happy together."

Mimi nodded approvingly. "Sounds like their marriage was the best sort of example. They must've taught ya that a *gut*, lasting relationship is a two-way street, *jah*?"

Lena had contemplated this very thing while reading the postcards upstairs. "Oh, most definitely." She paused a moment. "And thank you for carin'," she said. "I've really missed talkin' to Mamma . . . and to Emma. You're kind to take time for me like this, Mimi."

Mimi squeezed her hand. "I've been wonderin' if you're struggling over something related to a young man, maybe."

Lena was a bit surprised. "Not struggling, really . . . just trying to make a courtship work from a distance. Guess it's safe to say it's helping me to understand myself better, and the postcards pushed me to think on what I should look for in a mate."

"What you share with me is always safe, Lena. All right? The Lord sees your heart and knows your future. He understands the sufferin' you've endured, losing your parents so young . . . an' bein' away from your siblings, too."

Lena opened her heart and let Mimi's wise words enter in. Truth be known, Cousin Mimi had no idea how significant this talk had been, or what it meant to Lena to know that she had an understanding ear so near at hand.

CHAPTER

15

It hadn't taken Harley long to realize there was something special about his cousin Jacob's daughter. Lena Rose's comment last evening at supper about taking Uncle Solomon to see James Zook was just one more indication of that. And even though he'd planned to go over today to help at the Grants' between milkings, Harley didn't mind letting Lena and Solomon have the carriage for their trip up Stumptown Road to James Zook's redbrick farmhouse.

While Lena held Solomon's cane, Harley helped the man into the family buggy. Harley also supplied Lena with several hot bricks to put at their feet, along with an exceptionally thick buggy blanket made by Mimi years ago. It was the warmest of those they owned.

Solomon and James will have themselves an enjoyable time, he thought, heading back to the barn, scuffing his work boots against the snow in the yard and remembering when the children were little, running around and playing after chores. One year, the three older boys—Aaron, Caleb, and Will—had decided to make a large snowman, which took a couple of hours.

Another year, Caleb and Will had made a fort for protection against the onslaught of Eli and Ada's snowballs. What a time that was! Harley recalled that Mimi had worried they were making the snowballs too hard with ice before hurling them at each other.

"All in fun," he'd assured her.

But in the end, Will had gotten his eyeglasses smashed and had to walk around half blind without them till they could get down to the Grants' and call for an appointment to replace the shattered lenses and bent frames.

It was one of a number of times over the years when Mimi's worries had been founded. *A wise one, she is,* Harley thought, smiling at himself for making such a good choice in his mate. *I married well.*

He hoped Mimi's former concerns about Rebekah weren't also on target, and that her spending time with Lena Rose wouldn't pose a problem. Truth was, Mimi would have been hesitant about having Rebekah around, back before her husband died, when the woman had first come to Leacock Township. It wasn't so unusual for a grandmother to help her daughter after the birth of a baby, but Rebekah's coming long before the twins were born had caused plenty of talk, and Harley had learned in confidence from Abram Mast that Rebekah and Cora Ruth weren't saying all there was to say. In fact, if what Abram had told Harley was true, Rebekah's husband, Michael, had needed more than a good talking to years before he passed so suddenly.

Nee, Lena Rose needn't know all the ins and outs of poor Rebekah Petersheim's life. . . .

Harley shook his head. "All of that's in the past," he murmured while stepping into Barney's stall, where the horse was nose-deep in his feed.

⸻ ୧ ୨ ⸻

Occasionally, Lena caught a glint off a not-too-distant silo as, now and then, the sunshine broke through the leaden clouds that morning as she and Solomon made their way to see James Zook. She had expected Solomon to be talkative today after her short visit with him last evening, but for the first fifteen minutes of their trip, he was silent except to remark about how pretty the landscape looked in the wintertime.

It wasn't that he didn't feel well, she was certain. Rather, he seemed calm and content to just ride along and watch the country-side go by—the landscape of his childhood, he said later, before pointing out one or two of his friends' farms. For a man who had never married—unusual for an Amishman—Solomon seemed quite happy.

Lena decided not to press for conversation and simply took in the view. She was becoming accustomed to not talking much during the day, other than when Rebekah Petersheim came for her Friday lesson, which Lena found to be a highlight of the week. The woman was just so eager. *"A willingness to learn makes all the difference,"* Mamma had often said of young students, which Lena recalled as they came up on Mascot Roller Mills on the left side of the road. The place had been owned by three generations of the Ressler family.

Solomon sat up straighter and broke the stillness. "Say now, has anyone told ya any stories 'bout that old gristmill?"

"Only what Harley mentioned the other day." Lena glanced at the stone mill.

"The owner's close to retiring, but he still grinds corn for some of the neighboring farmers," Solomon told her. "Harley says the floor shakes real *gut* when the dried corn goes through the mill."

He chuckled. "It's like goin' back in time to my grandfather's day." Solomon seemed to be enjoying himself.

He pointed out James Zook's house as it came into view. "Sure hope the old fella's up and around."

"*Jah*, and I hope he's happy to see us," Lena said, glad she'd baked chocolate squares to deliver along with the repaired trousers and a few other mended items.

When she had tied the horse to the hitching post and covered the horse with a blanket, Lena went around to help Solomon down from the carriage. She took it ever so slow, thinking she could catch him if he slipped and fell, unsteady as he was.

Together, they picked their way through the snow toward the side door, where Lena knocked and listened for signs of life.

"Might need to rap harder," Solomon suggested. "James is hard of hearin', and he prob'ly doesn't bother wearing his hearing aid at home."

Lena began to worry that they'd come all this way for nothing.

A few more minutes passed, and she looked at Solomon. "Shall I go round to the front, maybe?"

Just then, they heard someone coming.

"Thank goodness," Lena breathed as an older gentleman swung the door wide open, a bright smile appearing on his deeply lined face when he spotted Solomon there with her.

"Thought we'd drop in for a visit," she said. "I'm Lena Rose Schwartz . . . perhaps you've heard I'm staying with the Stoltzfuses for the time being. And of course ya know Solomon."

"Well, well . . . *wunnerbaar* to meet you, Lena Rose. You've lifted my spirits already," James said, his hair all *schtrubbich*, like he'd been lying down. His billowy white beard was not unlike the fake beards the bell-ringer Santas wore, and he ran one hand through it as if to tame it down. "Make yourself at home." He stepped aside to let them in.

"Lena baked some goodies for ya," Solomon announced as he removed his gloves and stuffed them into the sleeves of his woolen coat. He extended his hand to his friend.

They shook hands, and a grin appeared on James's face. "Can't complain 'bout that, now, can I?"

Lena smiled and set the plastic container of pre-cut chocolate squares on the small table. The kitchen counter was piled up with newspapers and other papers, as well as empty grocery bags, but a beautiful large sampler hung on the wall nearby. She wondered if it was his late wife's work. "Do ya have a sweet tooth?"

"Does Christmas come round once a year?" James chuckled. "We'll all have us some sweets, how's that?" he invited them, a mischievous look on his face.

"I just ate myself full at breakfast," Solomon said, "but I'll do my best."

"*Jah*, well. Ain't ever too early for dessert, right, Lena Rose?" James pulled out a chair at the table and sat down. "Won't yous join me? The neighbor just delivered fresh milk earlier this mornin', so we'll have some with Lena's treat."

She offered to get the milk from the icebox and brought the bottle to the table, then found the glasses. "Do you both want some?"

"How 'bout some coffee?" Solomon asked.

"Do ya take instant?" James asked, motioning to the counter, where he kept the coffee jar.

"Whatever ya have is all right," Solomon said. He draped his coat over the back of the chair. "Haven't seen ya at Preaching lately, James," Solomon said. "Under the weather?"

"It's hard anymore to get out an' hitch up in the ice and snow," James said. "Not like it was a few years ago when I was spryer." He glanced at Lena Rose. "Don't ever get old, young lady, ya hear? Ain't no future in it."

Lena laughed, and James grinned as he reached for the glass of milk Lena had placed before him. And he didn't wait long to take a chocolate square, eating it in just a couple of bites.

"Maybe one of the neighbors could come by and haul ya to next Preachin'. Abram Mast's hosting it," Solomon said.

"Well, the neighbors all have big families, though. 'Tis a hardship to have another body takin' up space in the buggy."

The way he was making excuses, reasonable though they were, Lena wondered if James would rather not go out on a wintery Lord's Day.

"I believe I could find someone to come an' get you, if you're willing," Solomon persisted.

"Honest to goodness, I might've overdone it here lately, tryin' to keep this old house clean on my own," James said, changing the subject. "Been pushin' myself to do what my bride used to." James pointed to the untidy piles on the counter over near the sink. "*Es Haus* was never so *schlappich*."

"Need yourself a housekeeper?" Solomon glanced not so subtly at Lena Rose.

"Do ya?" Lena asked, very interested. "'Cause if so, I could come every other week and clean."

"Oh, now, that'd be right fine, and I'd make it worth your while," James said.

"I could come over early next Saturday mornin' for a few hours," Lena offered.

"'Tis music to my ears." James's face broke into a smile.

Lena asked if he had a mop and bucket, dustrag, and other cleaning supplies. She didn't think it would be right to bring Mimi's.

"I believe we have everything needed to redd up this ol' house," James assured her, a tear in his eye. "*Denki*."

We . . .

The word stuck out, and Lena remembered that Mimi had said

James Zook still didn't seem to think of himself as a widower. He was very much in love with his deceased wife.

"Thank you," Lena said, knowing this opportunity was an answer to a prayer she'd never even prayed. *I could use the extra money . . . and it's good to keep busy on my day off.*

⁓ ⁓

It was a bit challenging to get Solomon back into the buggy, but Lena was cautious and made sure he was situated and safe before she went around and untied the horse. Once done, she got into the right side and slipped under the heavy woolen blanket.

Interestingly enough, Solomon had a big talk on for the return trip, and Lena listened as he raved about her chocolate squares. "It wonders me if James'll be tempted to devour them all at once, after we're out of sight."

"Well, he only ate *one* while we visited," she said, trying not to laugh.

"*Jah*, I should talk. I was the one who gobbled down three . . . and after I said I was too full from breakfast." Solomon guffawed and clapped his gloved hands together. "Such a mornin', ain't so?"

They talked more about having assured James he could get a ride to church with them as long as he bundled up. She made a mental note to follow up on that with Mimi or Harley. "And to think I have myself a second job, too," she said with a smile at Solomon as they rode through the snowy countryside.

"A providential visit all round," Solomon said, bobbing his head. "Say, this might seem nosy of me, but looking around James's kitchen, I didn't get the sense he does a lot of cookin'."

"Well, I noticed his icebox was fairly well stocked when I got the milk. He looks like he's doing okay, or it could be someone is bringing him meals."

"*Des gut,* then." Solomon sighed loudly. "Mighty grateful to ya, Lena Rose. Had myself a real nice time with my old friend."

"I think the visit did all of us some *gut,*" she admitted and realized she was genuinely looking forward to chatting with the old widower again.

16

"I really appreciate the ride," Lena told Mimi a week later on the way to clean James Zook's house. It was convenient that Mimi was headed to see her oldest son and family, who lived a mile or so past the widower.

"I'm glad to get out right away this morning. I'd like to be home later when Tessa stops by."

Lena had noticed that Tessa was coming to see Mimi each Saturday here lately, and Harley had been coming in from the barn to welcome her, too. *They seem to be bending over backward to make Tessa feel at home,* Lena thought as she waved good-bye to Mimi and made her way up the walkway to James's back door.

She knocked, and quickly James ushered her inside, his bushy white beard the first thing Lena saw as he welcomed her in. He looked tired, she thought, and once he showed her where the mop and cleaning things were kept, she urged him to sit and relax. "I'll make you a cup of tea first, if you'd like," she offered.

"*Ach* now, tea's for womenfolk," he shot back, waving his wrinkled hand and cracking a smile. "Well, I shouldn't say that, really. Some folk think it helps make things better. In fact, there's a woman in Hickory Hollow who makes peppermint tea for her friends who need a listening ear. Ever hear of such a thing?"

"Coffee and hot cocoa have the same effect, if ya ask me." Lena Rose glanced around the room and wondered if he'd eaten any breakfast. She was relieved to see a few dishes in the sink. "Can I get you anything else?"

James shrugged. "Just feelin' low today. Woke up like this."

"My Dawdi Schwartz is rarely ever energetic in the morning."

Leaning his head into his hand, James sighed, his lips chapped. "I sometimes take forty winks before getting up the willpower to do the dishes. Other times, I just take a nap and hope the urge to do anything passes right quick."

Lena felt better . . . surely he was pulling her leg now. Or was he? "You certain you're all right?" she asked. "Sometimes a small glass of orange juice can perk a body up."

He rose just then and sauntered over to the icebox and opened it. Out he took a pitcher of orange juice and set it down on the counter, then reached up to grab a small glass from the cupboard. He poured some of the juice; then with one of his mischievous smiles, he turned and handed it to Lena. "Here you are, young lady."

"*Nee*, I meant for *you!*" She offered the glass back, and he accepted it with a nod of his head, taking the glass with him to the table, where he sat down.

"I'll get started in the front room," she said, knowing she'd better get busy, since it would be too easy to just sit and talk with him.

"No need to clean upstairs, really," he said. "No one's ever up there."

"Then it might need a *gut* dusting," she suggested.

"*Jah, gut* riddance to the dust bunny population." James gave a short laugh.

Lena headed to the front room and began to clean as her mother had taught her, removing all the rag rugs and taking them out to shake. Next came the dusting and dry mopping, and last of all, she mopped the floor. She had also noticed the windows were in need of a good shining, but she let them be today, planning on giving the place a spring cleaning come the thaw.

Now and then as she worked through the rooms, she could hear James either talking to himself or humming. This made her smile—perhaps he wasn't as low as he'd indicated earlier.

By the time she was ready to wash the kitchen floor, James had wandered into the front room, where he sat by the coal stove, warming himself into a nice nap. She could see him from where she stood in the kitchen, his chin resting on his cushion of a beard against his chest. *He was tired,* she realized, thinking that a nap and the orange juice should help.

Lena finished up a little before eleven, right around the time Mimi was coming into the lane. "I'll be goin' now," she said, making her way into the front room.

"Not without pay, ya ain't." James yawned and pushed himself out of his chair. He went with her to the kitchen, where he opened the cookie jar, reached in, and handed her a wad of bills. "This is so you'll come back. I'm mighty grateful."

She accepted the money and wondered why he hadn't bothered to count it out. Then, as she went to put on her coat and outer bonnet, she asked when he'd like her to come again. "I'm goin' home for Christmas, so I won't be around to clean till New Year's Eve morning. Will that suit ya?"

"Ah, *wunnerbaar* . . . a spotless house to start the New Year." James grinned. "That's right fine," he said, standing there with his bony hands on his hips.

"Oh, and be sure to watch for the Stoltzfuses Christmas mornin'. They'll pick you up for Preaching."

137

He nodded repeatedly. "'Tis *gut* of you to remind me." The man followed her like a puppy dog to the back door and even out onto the screened-in porch. "Have yourself a nice day."

"You too!" Knowing how helpful this cleaning was to the old man, she felt happy. *He has to be around Dawdi Schwartz's age,* she thought as she walked to the waiting carriage and to Mimi, who smiled when she spotted her.

It wasn't until Lena returned home that she took the wad of bills out of her pocketbook and counted it. *Forty dollars!* She knew she had been overpaid. The next time she returned to clean, Lena would speak with James and let him know of his mistake.

One thing she knew for sure: She would not frivolously spend the money from this unexpected job. If possible, every penny must go toward a nest egg for her future.

❧

The following Wednesday at breakfast, Eli dismayed Lena with news of a massive blizzard taking place in Michigan and Indiana and the Ohio Valley region. Newscasters were calling it "the White Hurricane," it was so vicious. Already in some areas, fifteen inches had fallen.

"I'd better check on my trip home," Lena said, thinking she might have to return to the Grants' home to call to the bus station in downtown Lancaster. "Would this be considered an emergency?" she asked Cousin Harley, who sat in his customary spot at the head of the table. Though it made things hard sometimes, she wanted to respect the Leacock church ordinance even though she was a member in Centreville.

"I'm thinkin' so . . . ya best go ahead and make the call," Harley replied, his expression serious. "I'll be sure an' see what the mailman has to say 'bout this storm."

Eli continued talking about the blizzard, saying he'd heard

from several *Englischers* in town late yesterday that airplanes weren't even flying. "With the interstates closed, too, there's no travel in or out of the area."

Lena's heart sank. Oh, she hoped the reports were wrong and she could still get home for Christmas. *Hans and my family are counting on it!*

"Let's not jump to conclusions," Mimi said, looking at her from across the table.

Lena nodded, but there was a growing knot in her stomach. After all, she was packed and ready to go, more than excited to see everyone in Centreville again. It was all planned, too— she would be staying with the family that had taken in Emma, Verena, and Liz.

But if the bus doesn't leave for Michigan tomorrow . . . she thought, holding her breath. Really, that prospect was too depressing to contemplate.

—⁂—

By midafternoon, Lena had read the latest newspaper account of the Great Blizzard. She showed Mimi the front page and a photo of the storm. "Have ya ever had such a blizzard?"

"Well, back sixteen years ago in February, sixteen inches of snow fell here. Most everything came to a standstill," Mimi told her, folding the paper and placing it on the table. "I remember Harley sayin' he measured twelve-foot drifts along our road."

Lena tried to imagine such terrible drifts.

"And before that, when I was just a young married woman, a powerful snowstorm blew through here and blocked the roads, closing the schools. No one could get anywhere, not even Amish folk." Mimi went to the pantry and brought out a pint of dill pickles, which she put in the refrigerator. "What 'bout you, Lena Rose? Do ya typically get deep snow out in Michigan?"

"Oh, we always have lots of snow, but there was one really big blizzard when I was nine or ten that dumped at least twenty inches. After it stopped falling, my father went out and took his yardstick and pushed it all the way down into the fresh snow to measure it. Liz and Verena were real little then, and they were inside the kitchen with Emma and me, pressin' their noses against the windowpane, pleading with Mamma to let them go out and make a snowman." Lena loved this memory. "They were so happy when Dat came inside and insisted that all of us bundle up and go out to make snow creatures, I guess you could call them."

"Why's that?" Mimi wore a big smile.

"Well, because two of them didn't look anything like snowmen." Now Lena was laughing as she recalled aloud the one-eyed creation Wilbur had made—he'd run down to the cellar to get a single piece of coal for the eye, then added some straw to the top of its head. "Little Liz and Verena had plenty of help from Dat, so theirs looked like a snowman you'd expect to see, but the one Emma and I built was as silly-lookin' as Wilbur's, with two carrot noses and three lettuce-leaf ears."

Mimi chuckled as she wiped down the front of the cupboards. "Sounds like you have some real happy times to remember."

Lena nodded as she went around and dried the fronts of the cupboards with a dry rag, still remembering the snow creatures she, Emma, and Wilbur had made that winter. How Mamma's peals of laughter had rung through the cold air when she, too, came out wearing her warmest black coat and scarf.

"That was one of the few times I secretly wished for a camera," Lena confessed to Mimi.

"Well, ya really don't need a photo, now, do ya, clear as your memory of that moment is," Mimi pointed out.

Mimi's right, Lena thought, thankful when Eli offered to take her over to the Grants' to call the bus depot. Soon she learned that, due to deteriorating road conditions, bus transportation to Michigan was postponed until next week. *After Christmas,* thought Lena Rose, thoroughly disappointed. *I've been waiting all this time, and now this!*

The mood at supper was subdued as Lena shared the news about the buses. "I guess I'm not goin' anywhere," Lena declared. "Even mail delivery in the area has been canceled."

Mimi sighed and gave her a caring yet concerned look. "I'm so sorry, Lena. Wish there was something we could do."

Uncle Solomon spoke up. "I know you'll miss your own people, but we'll have us all a real nice time here."

Lena tried to smile, but her hopes were dashed. "That's real thoughtful of ya, Solomon."

"I'll make your favorite pie," Mimi promised.

"*Denki,* Mimi, but don't go to any extra trouble, really." Lena meant the words for all of them, knowing they were trying to make the best of it for her sake. She fought back the tears that threatened, wishing to escape to her room and bury her face in her pillow.

17

Friday brought yet another day of bitter cold, but Rebekah Petersheim braved the weather to arrive in her son-in-law's carriage in time for her lesson. Initially it had been postponed because of Lena's plan to be gone over the holiday, but the effects of the terrible blizzard lingered on in Michigan.

Lena went to the back door and down the shoveled steps to meet Rebekah, relieved to have something to occupy her troubled thoughts. Rebekah had brought along *Henner's Lydia*, the children's book that her granddaughter Emily had wanted her to read weeks ago.

Indoors, settling into the front room near the stove, Rebekah took one line at a time, doing as Lena had suggested the week before—Rebekah reading silently first, then reading aloud, albeit painfully slowly. Lena joined in as they repeated the same line again and again.

After a time, Lena proposed that Rebekah attempt to read with a bit more expression, if she felt comfortable trying. There were no puffy eyes this time and no tears in Rebekah's voice, but she did set the book aside to say that a dear friend in her hometown had sent a pretty Christmas card and letter. "It sure makes me homesick," Rebekah said, going on to mention how much she missed that community, as well as her family. "My husband's buried there, too." She said it so quietly, Lena nearly had to lean forward to catch the words.

"If he was still alive, he'd want me home," Rebekah whispered as her chest rose and fell. Then, shaking her head, she added in the same soft voice, "It was such a complicated marriage." She sighed and ran her hand over the cover of the book. "*Ach*, no need to tell you any of this."

Feeling at a loss over how to respond, Lena said nothing and reached to cover Rebekah's hand with her own.

She wished she were as bold and wise as Mimi and had something meaningful or even helpful to say to the woman. But no words or Scripture verses came to mind. All she could think to do was offer a silent prayer for her friend.

O Lord, comfort Rebekah, and grant her peace.

⁓ ᔐ ᔑ ⁓

Harley could see that the sky to the north was almost clear of clouds, and because of it, he felt a lift in his spirit as he helped Mimi and Lena into the family carriage.

"Our grandchildren will be thrilled you're goin' to see them in this year's school play," Mimi told him as he picked up the driving lines. "All of Aaron and Caleb's school-age children are in it, and Ada's Johnny and Ada Mae, too."

Lena sat quietly in the back, and Harley wondered if hearing Mimi talk so would make her all the more homesick. For that reason, he didn't comment, though he could see how very excited his wife was about going to the schoolhouse for the annual event. Mimi had faithfully attended each and every Christmas program since their first child was in school.

When they arrived, Harley waved at Aaron, his eldest, and his wife, Sadie Ann, as well as their four children, now climbing out of the buggy. "Hullo! Real nice day for the play, *jah?*" he called as he went around to help Mimi and Lena down.

"I was kinda hopin' we'd get more snow," Aaron said, shifting his black felt hat.

Harley chuckled at that. "*Ach*, there's been no shortage of that this year. Seems like I'm always out shovelin'."

"Dat says we're gonna have a white Christmas," said Aaron's youngest boy, Levi, as he came around the carriage and stood beside his father.

Harley gave a nod. "Say, I hear there are candy canes for everyone at the program." He winked at his grandson.

Levi's eyes grew wide, and he glanced up at his father for confirmation.

Laughing, Aaron patted his shoulder. "We'll have to see about that, son." He turned to Harley again and added, "We're lookin' forward to having Christmas dinner with yous."

"Your mother's tickled pink 'bout it," Harley said, nodding at Mimi.

"That's for certain," Mimi said with a smile and a hug for Levi. "I'm bakin' a real big ham," she said. "There'll be plenty for everyone."

"We'll see ya inside," Harley said with a glance at Lena, hoping that the sight of all these youngsters would boost her spirits.

During the play, when the scholars lined up at the front of the large classroom in front of the chalkboard and began to sing carols, Lena's memories flew back to her siblings' school programs.

The Amish teacher and her assistant motioned for everyone to join in singing, and Lena's mouth went so dry that she could only mouth the words. It was all she could do to keep her emotions intact, so acutely aware was she of not being able to see her brothers and sisters perform the Nativity back home.

Lena took a deep breath, wishing to sing along with the others. This special program was one of the highlights of the Christmas season, and she wanted to enjoy it and appreciate the heavenly Gift that had inspired it.

Spotting Harley and Mimi's grandchildren sprinkled throughout the scholars, Lena watched their joyful little faces, the way they opened their mouths wide to sing, eyes shining with happiness. Observing them and eventually joining in was the best remedy she could find for getting over the surges of sadness that had a way of sweeping over her when she least expected. Some days, she would start to think she was all right, and then this would happen. Today, however, it was worse than usual, because she knew that her younger siblings were likely singing some of the same songs and saying some of the same recitations this very day.

And I'm not there to witness it.

───── ໐ ໐ ─────

Lena was surprised when, late that afternoon, Mimi urged her to carol with the youth that evening. "I daresay you've already baked plenty of pies and cookies for our Christmas dinner," Mimi said as she wiped her brow with the back of her hand.

"Are ya sure?" Lena asked, quickly doing another count of the dozens of cookies. "There'll be lots of people at the table. We'll want to have enough."

Mimi nodded and reminded her that Ada and Tessa planned to bring along baked goods, too. "Honestly, I think we'll have ample choices for seconds of dessert, even thirds, maybe. So just go on and have yourself a nice time with *die Youngie*. Lydia and the others will be glad to see ya."

Lena saw through Mimi's eagerness to get her out caroling

and smiled her appreciation. *She thinks I'm stuck in the house too much. . . .*

—◌ ◌—

Lena breathed a sigh of relief when she learned from Mimi that Lydia's parents were hosting the snacks and desserts after the caroling. That and Eli's eagerness to take her were the only reasons she'd agreed to go.

"I know you must be disappointed 'bout bein' here instead of home with your family," Eli said at the reins of his open buggy. "I wish things had worked out differently."

"It's awful discouraging." She shook her head. "It's nice of you, though, to bring it up."

He shrugged. "I know my parents and Uncle Solomon will do their best to make you feel included. It won't be the same as bein' with your own brothers and sisters, but we do care for you."

Moved by his compassion, she nodded, unable to speak until a few minutes later, when they arrived and joined Lydia.

Soon the youth began to raise their voices in unison, the deep and resonant sounds of the young men rising behind her as they caroled. Lena began to feel better than she had earlier at the schoolhouse. At each farm, the youth began with "Hark, the Herald Angels Sing," one of Lena's favorites that never failed to boost her spirits. She stood with Lydia and Lydia's younger cousin, seventeen-year-old Vera Smucker, surprised to feel almost as if this group were an extension of her Michigan family.

Mimi must have suspected this outing would be a good thing; she'd practically waved Lena out the door with Eli. And being with these friends on such a brisk, invigorating evening was indeed a blessing. Lena let herself drink in the feeling of being surrounded by the other carolers, including dear Lydia, who stood by her side. *What would I do without her?*

They stopped at no fewer than eight farmhouses before return-ing to the home of Lydia's parents. As Lena Rose assisted Lydia's mother in bringing mugs of steaming cocoa to the table, Lena marveled at how close-knit this group really was. Several of the other young women were also helping Lydia's mother lay out the treats as young men brought in more firewood for the cookstove and the heater in the front room, all of them talking in *Deitsch* about activities this Christmas weekend.

At one point, Arden came over to talk with her. "I was sur-prised to see you at the program with Harley and Mimi."

She told him about her canceled trip, and his eyes showed concern.

"*Ach*, for your sake, I'm sorry to hear it," he was quick to say.

"It couldn't be helped, really."

They talked about the Nativity, and then Arden said, "I thought Harley was gonna pop some buttons when his third-grade grandson was the first to stand up to give his recitation."

"I thought the same thing," she said, laughing lightly and thinking how nice it was to see Arden again. She asked about his family's plans for Christmas.

"We'll leave for home right after Preachin' service for our first dinner gathering," he told her. "Then on Second Christmas, we're goin' to my oldest sister's house to visit with more rela-tives."

Lena, in turn, shared about the Stolzfuses' plan for tomorrow. "I'm not sure what's happening on Second Christmas, but it will prob'ly involve plenty-a food."

"Well, I hope it's a special time of remembrance for ya. This season, I always find myself thinking back on the old year," Arden said, "and I s'pose that's especially true for you just now."

She nodded, appreciating his sensitivity.

"We never can guess what's round the next corner. There's a

lot of comfort in knowin' that it's not up to us to figure out such things, I think."

He accompanied her to the large spread of desserts on the long kitchen table, and they stood with their paper plates filled with slices of pie and cookies and continued talking for a while longer, till Eli was ready to head home so he could be up before the morning's four o'clock milking.

Arden wished her a merry Christmas, and she said the same. "Since you'll be here for the holidays, do ya plan to come to the skating party on Second Christmas?" he asked.

"Hadn't really thought about it," she replied, surprised he'd mention it.

"Well, if you're up for it, you're certainly welcome."

Lena Rose couldn't commit one way or the other. Here lately, she could only manage one day at a time. And all the way back to Harley's, Lena pondered the precious hours she had lost with her siblings and Hans, her heart heavy yet again.

18

For Lena and Mimi, the particulars of Christmas Sunday began earlier than most Lord's Day mornings, what with the extra preparations required to host a portion of the family at noon. They all ate their breakfast earlier, too, so Lena and Mimi could wash the dishes and set the table before they headed out.

Yesterday evening, Harley and Eli had opened the kitchen table and put in all four leaves to accommodate the dinner guests. And they'd set up a large folding table for the school-age grandchildren, as well.

Lena was looking forward to seeing so many of the little ones again. She hoped she might break through the wall that seemed to surround Tessa. *But how?* Lena wondered, determined to assure her that she had no intention of taking her place.

Then later, at Preaching, Lena focused on the words of the traditional hymns, trying to keep her mind on worship. She offered her gratitude to the heavenly Father for bringing her together with this group of People, and for dear Mimi and Harley, too. *Bless them abundantly for their kindness to me, O Lord. And be near to my brothers and sisters this Christmas Day.*

During the silent kneeling prayer, Lena thought of her family back home, all kneeling in reverence at their own Preaching service. Were they also thanking God for the loving families that had taken them in and given them homes? Were they praying for Lena, too, missing her—and as disappointed as she was?

When church was over, a good half or more of the families slipped away for home, not staying for the usual common meal. As Lena walked with Mimi to meet Harley at their carriage, she noticed Arden Mast discreetly wave at her, just ahead in the line of buggies ready to head out to the road. Seeing his contagious grin made her smile, too, and she nodded as she quickly stepped into the Stoltzfus carriage.

Harley was pleased to see his family including Lena Rose in conversation before the meal. He admired the festive paper snowflakes little Levi and his older sisters had made to stick on the windowpanes. *"To make Mammi Stoltzfus's kitchen extra perty,"* Levi had announced, eyes sparkling.

Mimi had placed three-dimensional Moravian stars here and there about the main level of the house, as well, but it was Lena who'd suggested putting two tall green candles with miniature holly rings at either end of the long table. That very table was now laden with an enormous baked ham. Mimi and the girls had also made all of Harley's favorite side dishes—mashed potatoes with ham gravy, buttered corn, and baby limas swimming in butter. Harley's stomach rumbled in anticipation as he signaled for the prayer of gratitude by folding his hands and bowing his head.

Once the meal was under way, he was glad to notice that even Manny was talking with the others. But when Lena Rose offered to hold baby Joey, Tessa merely shook her head. Harley couldn't understand why his daughter was refusing Lena's help with the fussy baby. *It's Christmas,* he thought. *Why would Tessa act so? Is she out of sorts?*

After the meal, the young women worked together to redd up the kitchen, letting Mimi rest a bit. When every last plate, utensil, and pan had been put away, the family gathered in the front room, where it was nice and warm because Harley had stoked the fire in anticipation of this special time of fellowship.

When everyone was quiet, he read Luke chapter two from the *Biewel*. Lena sat on the floor near six-year-old Joanna and the other children, Joanna whispering to her every so often. *Looks like Lena's having a pleasant time,* thought Harley, glad for her sake.

Then he asked Uncle Solomon to share a Christmas memory from his boyhood.

As expected, Solomon had a story on the tip of his tongue. "There once was a young Amish lad named Solomon, who wanted a pony for Christmas more than anything else."

Several of the children turned to look questioningly at their parents, and Lena smiled at Joanna, who giggled.

"But little Solomon forgot to say exactly what *kind* of pony. So, when his Dat and Mamma presented their gift to him after Christmas dinner, he took one look at his new pony and thought for sure it must've shrunk." Solomon paused to look around at all the children. "'Cause there it was, in a small wrapped box . . . just the size of a half dollar."

Ada's little girls, Ada Mae and Joanna, gasped, their hands flying to their mouths.

"That there pony had not only shrunk," Solomon said dramatically, "it had turned to wood!"

The smallest of the children looked astonished.

"Did that really happen?" Levi asked, leaning forward on his hands.

"I wouldn't tell yous a made-up story, now, would I?" Solomon said. But Harley detected a familiar glint in the man's eyes.

"You were the boy in the story, ain't so?" asked Ada's son, Johnny, after a glance at Levi.

Solomon slapped his hand on his leg and chuckled. "In fact, I can prove it right here, right now." And he pulled a miniature wooden pony out of his pocket. "See here?" He held it up.

Harley smiled at the *aahs* that rippled round the room.

Of course, then all the children wanted to get up and have a look-see. And they did, gathering close around Solomon.

Aaron, as well as Ada's husband, John, were the next to share a childhood Christmas memory. They told of going ice fishing, sledding, and helping to push motorists out of snowdrifts.

After Aaron and John were finished with their tellings and everyone began to engage in conversation, Harley tiptoed out of the room and brought back a large basket of goodies and small gifts that he and Mimi had secretly assembled.

Each of the children sat cross-legged on the floor, eyes bright as Harley distributed the homemade candies and sugared almonds wrapped in green cellophane. There were shiny red apples, toy tops, a nice tablet and writing pen for the older school-age children, and small, faceless rag dolls for the younger girls, and sets of jacks for the little boys.

Right away, Levi held his bag of jacks high, then jumped up to thank Harley by offering to shake his hand.

"*Ach* now . . . how 'bout a bear hug?" Harley said and bent down, arms wide.

This brought more of the younger children to their feet, and soon it was one hug after another for both him and Mimi. The older children came to thank them, as well, looking him right in the eye as they wished him a merry Christmas in *Deitsch*. "*Hallicher Grischtdaag,*" Harley said to each of them in return, his heart filled with the delight that only family could bring.

In the midst of this joyous setting, Lena recalled a past Christmas when she and Emma had worked together to make a multi-colored, quilted throw pillow for Mamma—their first attempt at such a complicated project. They had managed to keep it secret by sneaking over next door to work on it in the *Dawdi Haus* where Dat's elderly Aunt Ida lived at the time.

Oh, the look of surprise on Mamma's dear face when she'd opened their present, tears coming into her eyes. "*Such sweet little girls I have!*" she exclaimed as she knelt on the front room floor and swept them into her arms.

Emma has that throw pillow as one of her keepsakes, thought Lena, glad for her sister and so thankful for this special memory on this faraway Christmas Day.

19

Lena began Second Christmas by making a birthday card for Verena, tucking a note inside. What with the U.S. mail still playing catch up after the Great Lakes blizzard, and her sister's birthday coming up January 8, Lena wanted to be sure to get the card sent off soon.

Harley and Mimi had invited Lena to join them and Solomon for the noon meal at son Caleb's farm—a merry Second Christmas celebration indeed. Eli met them at Caleb's in his open buggy but excused himself following dessert to visit Lydia.

"I'll come back to get you for the skating party tonight if ya want to go," he offered to Lena before leaving. "If ya ask me, it would beat a night staying home."

Lena knew he was right, and she decided to go ahead and attend.

True to his word, Eli returned for her, as well as to grab his skates and a heavier pair of gloves. While they rode together toward the Grants', Eli brought up how peculiar it was for the gathering to be held at the farm of a Mennonite family. "*Englischers* hosting Amish skaters, of all things!"

Lena had wondered about this, too. "S'pose that doesn't happen often round here."

"Far as I know, it's *never* happened." Eli shook his head in apparent wonder.

Lena let the subject drop, thinking ahead to seeing Lydia again as Eli pulled into the long driveway leading up to the Grants' house.

Later, walking out toward the pond with the other Amish youth, Lena carried the white skates she'd borrowed from Ada. It was impossible not to stare at the full moon's reflection in the large pond behind the house.

When her skates were laced up, Lena stepped onto the ice. Within seconds, Lydia was right there beside her, and they linked arms and sped across the glassy surface, finding their way in and around other skaters.

"Wasn't sure you'd show up," Lydia said, out of breath.

"I wasn't sure, either." Lena gave her a mischievous look. "But don't worry, I won't keep ya from skating with Eli."

Lydia laughed softly, the sound floating up into the cold air. "Oh, we won't pair up just yet."

It was a good half hour or more before Eli skated over to Lydia and whisked her away. Lena decided it was fine to keep skating without a partner. *Best way to keep warm.* The skaters' merriment filled the night, and her thoughts were with dearest Emma as she wondered if her sister was out skating this very evening—perhaps with a young man.

I'm missing out on everything. She recalled how hesitant Emma had been the first time she'd gone to a Sunday Singing after her sixteenth birthday. Emma had confided in her that she almost wished she could wait another year, but Lena had been her guide, looking out for her and making sure Emma sat with her at the long table next to all the other girls. Even so, it had taken nearly ten months for Emma to decide to go out with a boy.

"Mind if I skate with you, Lena Rose?" Arden asked, bringing her out of her musing as he caught up to her.

"Hullo," she said, feeling a bit reluctant at first. Then, realizing it was more awkward to just stand there, she pushed off over the ice, and Arden matched her pace.

Soon, she wasn't sure who was keeping up with whom as they zipped around the pond. "How was your Christmas?" she asked.

Arden described the feast his mother had prepared. "How 'bout yours? I'm sure it was hard bein' away."

She gave him a quick smile, not wanting to reveal how very homesick she felt. She told him instead about Harley and Mimi's sweet grandchildren and the fun they'd had with their great-uncle Solomon. "The children were spellbound by his story."

"Sounds like a *gut* tellin'," said Arden. "Doesn't surprise me, knowin' Solomon."

They talked about each person present at each of their homes yesterday, and Arden brought up the various delicious desserts his mother and sisters had made.

The way to a man's heart, Lena thought, suppressing a smile.

A few of Arden's girl cousins skated past them two by two, calling to him. And when even more skaters overtook them, Lena realized that she and Arden must have slowed their pace. *It's all the talking we're doing.*

Eventually, they picked up speed, talking less now. As they turned into the curve a bit too swiftly, Lena tripped over her own foot and lost her balance. Just that fast, Arden reached for her hand and managed to keep her from falling to the ice.

"Goodness, not sure when I've done *that* before," she sputtered, forcing a laugh and feeling foolish as she righted herself.

Arden seemed reluctant to let go of her hand. "We'd better watch these curves more carefully," he said, and they fell into a slower rhythm than before, their blades making a whisper of sound on the pond's glistening surface. The cold and wintry night was still young, and even more skaters arrived as the enormous moon rose ever higher.

"I had a long talk with my father early this morning," Arden told her and then was silent for a long time, which seemed strange. Lena almost wondered if he was waiting for her to say something. Then he added, "It was the most difficult thing I've done in years."

"What sort of talk?" She really had no idea what else to say, considering she suspected this had something to do with what Tessa had told her and Mimi.

"You surely know by now that my father's a dairy farmer." At her nod, Arden continued. "He's always expected that I'd take over the operation . . . and till just recently, I thought I would, too." He sighed and gave her a sidelong glance. "But it's not the place for me. I have other ideas."

"Sounds like a weighty decision," she said.

"It was all I could do not to give in to what Dat wants."

Lena was curious why he was entrusting her with these rather personal details.

"You see, I'm starting a cabinetmakin' business with Manny Beiler." Arden went on to say that he and Manny had been working toward this decision for some months now, trying to keep it mum till the right time. "I needed to talk with my Dat about it, though," he added, sounding almost sad. "Like I said, real hard to do, but necessary, so Dat can line up one of my brothers or someone else to go on with the farm when he retires."

Lena held her breath, wondering how the conversation with his father had turned out.

"I wish I'd told Dat sooner . . . but I never had an opportunity like this before, and I don't think I'd be pushin' ahead without a partner. I've always liked makin' furniture—kinda got the knack from Dat, who's *wunnerbaar* with wood. I like making two pieces of wood look almost like they've grown together that way."

She listened, caught by the rise and fall of his emotions in the space of only a few minutes. "I s'pose your father understands your keen interest in this work, then."

"Well, he wants to discuss it more, no doubt to see if he can talk me out of it."

"And can he?" Lena asked.

"*Nee*, I'm not a second-guesser." Arden sped up, moving ahead of the other skaters now. "Do ya think I'm doin' the right thing, Lena Rose? I haven't told anyone else this yet."

She had to stop and think about that. No other man had ever asked her opinion on an important issue. Most men just expected her to agree with them. "Do what you believe you're s'posed to do. What God has put in your heart."

"*Jah*, trustin' in His guidance is best," he replied.

The cold had seeped deep into Lena's bones, and Arden suggested they go warm up near the big bonfire. Across from them, Lena could see Eli with Lydia, warming themselves, too.

"Cabinetmaking and remodeling are ideal for me—I can't imagine myself as a farmer for the rest of my life," Arden went on. "But I'm real sorry to disappoint my father."

"Do your older brothers—or brothers-in-law—have farms of their own?"

"That's the tetchy part. My brothers are all set, so we'll see what happens."

She understood now why Arden felt so stuck.

"I don't mean to burden ya with this, Lena Rose. Sorry."

"It's not a burden," she said quickly. "Not at all."

Once they'd gotten almost too warm, Arden asked if she wanted to skate again, and she agreed, realizing how good it felt to be asked. This friendship with Arden was unlike any she'd had with fellows back home, including Hans, she thought as they walked toward the frozen pond once again. She appreciated Arden's treating her as though her thoughts really mattered.

After the skating party, the youth were served popcorn, cupcakes, and hot cocoa at Calvin and Deb Grant's farmhouse overlooking the large pond. There was much *Deitsch* chatter inside the comfortable home with its high-beamed family room and a wall of windows overlooking the snowy acres of land.

A tall Christmas tree stood over in one corner, shining with ornaments and white lights, and a large wreath with a silvery bow hung over the mantel. On either side of the wreath gleamed white and silver candles, and an antique-looking Nativity scene graced the coffee table.

Even though she had come here twice to use the phone, Lena felt nearly out of place in this house. She remembered how Harley had talked about the kitchen remodel that Arden and Manny had completed earlier this month. Arden must have been trying his hand at remodeling and cabinetmaking well before telling his father.

Because it was growing late, Eli came over and asked Lena if she was ready to head home.

"Whenever you're ready," she replied. "And if you'd like some time alone with Lydia, you can drop me at home first."

"She says she's tired."

"Then I'm ready now." Lena turned to say good-bye to Arden, adding, "I hope ya get things sorted out with your Dat."

"*Denki*," he said, giving her a wink. "I appreciate that."

Ach, *he likes me too much,* she thought as she hurried out to Eli's open buggy and climbed in next to Lydia. *I need to be more careful around him.*

20

Lena worked with Mimi the following Friday until that afternoon, when she read with Rebekah Petersheim, noticing even more progress. She could tell that Rebekah was becoming more confident in reading aloud each week and wished someone had taken the time to help her long before now. The woman had known and understood far more than she'd given herself credit for, and she'd been working hard to practice in between lessons.

As Rebekah was preparing to leave, she hesitated at the door and, turning back, said, "*Ach*, Lena . . . last week I told ya some things, and I might've given ya the wrong impression."

Lena didn't want the woman to feel like she had to share more than she was willing. "It's all right, really."

Yet Rebekah seemed determined to forge ahead. "There are some rumors swirling. . . ."

At Lena's nod, Rebekah continued. "I shouldn't care what people think of me, 'specially if they don't know the truth. But I *do* care what you think, Lena Rose."

Lena smiled. "Remember, no one knows the troubled path other folk must walk."

Rebekah blew out a breath. "Ain't that the truth."

"And I truly care about what happened to you."

Rebekah's eyes glinted with tears. "Then you're one of the few, if I dare say it." She seemed to steel herself, as though gathering pluck to say more. "Here's what most folk ain't willing to hear. You see, at the time I came to be with Cora Ruth and her family—nearly a year ago now—my husband had just been put under a severe *Bann* for his drinking habit. The ministers wanted him to quit. Well, he didn't quit—he drank all the more. And eventually, the bishop put his foot down, and the brethren put a probationary shunning on Michael."

Lena sighed. "I had no idea."

"Things were awful tense between us, since I was expected to shun him, too. You can only imagine." Rebekah shook her head. "S'pose I felt somewhat guilty, too, because I was nearly the last one to realize he'd been tinkering with our grape juice, makin' his own wine!" She wrinkled her brow into a hard frown. "Finally, one of the preachers thought it would be best if I left home for a time, in hopes of getting Michael to understand the foolishness of his ways. I had my doubts, though, whether that might just push him further over the edge, but I obeyed and came here to be with Cora Ruth and her family.

"Truth be told, I shouldn't have stayed as long as I did, considering Michael's awful state, but once the twins were born, Cora Ruth needed me. I kept thinkin' I should get myself home, but before I could, the worst possible thing happened. My husband died suddenly." Rebekah wiped her eyes.

Lena sighed, bearing the pain of it. "I'm so sorry, Rebekah. I didn't know you were carrying such a burden." Lena reached to embrace her and wished she could do something to ease the poor woman's pain and the *guilt* Rebekah was enduring, as if she were responsible for her husband's untimely passing.

"My deacon does say there's a bright side to all this, though," Rebekah added.

Just at that moment, Ada and her two daughters, Ada Mae and Joanna, opened the back door and walked in. "Oh, so sorry . . . didn't know you were getting ready to leave," Ada said, clearly embarrassed to have broken in on their conversation like this.

"'Tis all right," Rebekah said. Then she glanced at Lena. "We'll talk later." And she headed outdoors.

Lena felt sorry for the interruption and wondered how Rebekah managed to be so resilient, given her circumstances. To think she was willing to better herself so that one day she could read to her grandchildren. *She's surprisingly determined, even optimistic, despite all she's suffered.*

_____

The next morning, Lena made time before breakfast for some letters to her siblings. Now that she didn't know when she'd be home for a visit, she was drawn to writing like never before. The letters would have to be enough till she found a time and a place to return—preferably for good.

When Lena was ready to go to James Zook's to clean, she had in mind to discuss his too-generous pay of two weeks ago. But when she brought it up first thing, he only chuckled and drummed his thick fingers on the table. "I'm fine with what I paid ya—it's a closed case. Besides, I'd like for you to cook sometimes, too. All right?"

She agreed despite her objections, knowing that the more she saved, the more money she would have toward rent or whatnot when she returned home.

Lena considered the folk she had gotten to know during her months here—Mimi, Rebekah, and James Zook. Somehow, they had come to rely on her, and that knowledge softened her homesickness. The way Harley talked, a person might think she was indispensable, although Lena expected that at least Rebekah Petersheim would be ready to be on her own in a few short weeks. Her connection to the Stoltzfuses and the others she'd met here sometimes made her feel as though she were playing an inner tug-of-war. Was it risky to put down roots of any kind when she hoped to be on her way soon? Yet the longing for home seemed all the worse when she just kept to herself. And here lately it had been all the stronger because she had yet to receive a letter from Hans, even a belated Christmas card.

After she'd cleaned and scrubbed the kitchen and even cooked up a nice hot dish of noodles and roasted chicken, Lena took a few minutes to look at the Christmas cards James had strung up across the entrance to his front room, smiling to see the many he'd received from grandchildren and other family.

Before she left, Lena asked if he needed any letters taken out to the mailbox, and right away he asked if she'd help him write a few thank-you notes. "My handwriting ain't so legible no more," he said. Briefly, he went to the next room and returned with a box of notes and a worn brown address book. "*Denki*, Lena Rose."

"I'm delighted to help." And she sat with him at the table as he dictated the short notes to several relatives in other communities.

His eyes welled up. "This may seem like a small thing to you, but it's a big help to an old man like me."

She patted his arm and asked if he had plans for New Year's Day tomorrow.

Nodding, he pulled out his red kerchief and wiped his eyes. "Melvin and Cora Ruth Ebersol invited me over for the noon meal. I guess they're havin' a big group in—some family, some spares like me." He stuffed the kerchief back into his trousers pocket.

"Well, I know you'll have a *wunnerbaar-gut* time," Lena said as she rose and prepared to leave. "And you'll enjoy those cute Ebersol children, too!"

"*Hallich Neiyaahr!*" James said as she put on her coat and bonnet.

"Happy New Year to you," she replied, a tear in her eye as she headed outdoors. Her Dawdi Schwartz had come to mind just then, and she wondered how he and Mammi and Chris were really doing together in their little *Dawdi Haus.*

And Hans, too. What's he been up to that has kept him too busy to write?

Surely the aftereffects of the storm hadn't occupied him *all* this time.

But Lena decided not to let herself brood over her disappointment. Instead, she would do her best to enjoy her new friends and the compassionate family where God had placed her for the time being. *I must try to bring joy to others and not dwell so much on myself.* . . .

─◌ ◌─

On the first Tuesday of the new year, Lena heard loud knocking at the front door. She hurried through the house to see who was there and found Alan Reese, their mailman, standing on the porch with a box. "Hullo," she greeted him as she opened the door.

"I've got a parcel for a Miss Lena Rose Schwartz," the stout man said with a smile.

"That's me."

"Just sign on the dotted line, please." He held out a clipboard with a piece of paper on it, a pen attached.

Lena quickly signed, and the postman handed her the box. "It's not heavy, just a bit awkward."

"*Denki.*" Closing the door behind her, she carried the box into the kitchen and peered at the return address. "From Uncle Noah?" Since she and Hans had missed spending Christmas together, she had actually wondered if it might be from him. Could it be from her brothers and sisters instead?

Mimi came over just then, having been in the nearby pantry, and watched Lena cut the packing tape to open the top. "Has Christmas caught up with ya, just maybe?"

Lena stared into the box. "Oh, Mimi . . . look at all the wrapped presents!" Tears sprang to Lena's eyes. "*Ach*, now I wish I'd sent something special to each of my siblings, not just some money in their cards," she told Mimi. "Well, except for Chris's little puzzle."

"Oh now." Mimi shook her head. "I'm sure your siblings understand. After all, a good portion of your earnings goes their way every month."

Even so, Lena wished she had done more as she lifted out the small gifts one by one and placed them on the counter, lining them up according to the gift giver's age—Emma all the way down to little Chris.

Mimi gave her a quick hug. "Take heart and remember that surely next Christmas you'll be in Centreville to celebrate with all of them." She paused. "And with your beau, too."

Lena thanked her for understanding.

"I daresay the days between now and then will go by quickly, busy as you are," Mimi said as she touched one of the pretty bows. "*Ach*, you're only here as long as the Lord has planned. Ain't that right?"

Lena nodded, but she hoped and prayed that God in heaven knew that sooner was better than later, at least for her. Surely the Lord heard all the earnest prayers she was sending heavenward each day!

—ᴄ ᴐ—

Lena saved the gifts to open privately in her room that evening, where she could take her time and enjoy all the handmade items—potholders for her hope chest from Liz and Verena, a crocheted doily from Emma, and several whittled animals from the boys. Chris, however, had drawn a self-portrait, and Tubby Tabby was in the picture, too, right in his arms!

Looking at her wall calendar, Lena sighed as she realized that, come Sunday, Verena would be a teenager! She would likely celebrate with Liz and Emma over one of Emma's delectable birthday cakes, and surely they would get together with the rest of their siblings. Lena hoped her homemade card would arrive in time. *Oh, to be a bird and wing my way home!*

_ɔ ᴐ_

A day later, Lena received a long, newsy letter from Emma thanking her for the belated Christmas card and the dollar bills tucked inside. *I'll save the money for a rainy day like Mamma taught us, or maybe buy a new book.*

Standing there near the mailbox, Lena continued to read, unable to pull herself away from the letter even though she shivered in the cold.

There was no mention of Hans, but Emma had plenty to write about concerning the awful blizzard. *The roads were closed for nearly a week. It's a good thing you weren't already on your way, or your bus would have had to turn around and head back to Lancaster County,* Emma had written, going on to describe how they'd remained inside for days because of the subzero temperatures and fierce wind. *And the snow—it seemed like it would never quit! Thankfully, we kept warm by the wood stove and took turns reading out loud to each other. And when we tired of that, we played checkers. I daresay it'll be a good month before any of us wants to see that game again!*

Lena shook her head at the thought of such a serious storm, one worse than any blizzard she'd experienced. Tucking the letter away to finish reading in the warm kitchen, she made her way up the driveway and into the house, wishing Hans had written to share what he and his family had done during the Great Blizzard. *What's taking so long?*

Pulling out a chair at the table, Lena began reading again and learned of a youth gathering Emma was looking forward to toward the end of January—a dessert social at the home of Emma's new beau's parents. *I've just started seeing someone special, Lena. Someone you know, of course—Ammon Bontrager, Hans's younger brother. Now, isn't that something? I meant to tell you about him at Christmas, but this letter will have to do.*

Lena continued reading, soaking up the updates on all of the children. Then Emma confessed how hard she found it to walk past their old house, which had been purchased by a young Amish couple with a number of children. *I just don't have it in me to go up and knock at the door to meet them. Everything that's happened to our family is still like a very bad dream.*

Lena swallowed hard. Emma was right: Losing Dat and Mamma was never going to be something any of them would just get over. Yet with God's help, somehow they would eventually move past the deepest, most searing sorrow. Lena knew this in her head, but her heart was with Emma's.

Later, when Lena returned to her sewing, she felt compelled to share parts of the letter with Mimi, remarking that she was sorry to be cut off from the youth activities in Centreville, especially now that she knew Emma had her first-ever beau.

Life goes on there without me, she thought dolefully.

The mail was late in coming that Friday afternoon, and Lena hurried out to get it the minute she heard the mail truck coming down Eby Road. At long last, an envelope that looked like a card from Hans had arrived!

When she opened it in the chilly outer room, she pulled out a rather ordinary-looking Christmas card. It was pretty enough with its scene of a snow-covered hedgerow and a lamppost neatly tied with a red ribbon and holly, the words *Merry Christmas to you* centered on the front. But Lena Rose didn't know what to think of the inside—Hans had merely signed his name at the bottom, although there was a separate note on a plain piece of paper, apologizing for being late with his greeting. *The blizzard canceled our mail delivery,* he'd written. *I hope you had a nice Christmas even though we didn't get to see each other.* Beyond that, there was nothing else—no words of affection or discussion of future plans, or even questions about when she might be coming home. This was nothing like his other correspondence, which she'd cherished over the past months. If anything, she almost wished Hans hadn't bothered to make the effort, impersonal as the card was.

Lena swallowed her disappointment. Now that work on the Bontrager family farm was at a seasonal lull, Lena had really hoped that Hans would suggest visiting *her* sometime in the new year.

She wondered now if she *should* have sent the card she'd hand made for Hans—she had held on to it, not wanting to appear forward while awaiting his reply to her last letter. *Was it a mistake to wait?*

Removing her snow boots, she sighed and wondered if she ought to reveal her feelings about this to Mimi.

She carried the rest of the mail into the kitchen and placed it on the counter. From where she stood in the kitchen, Lena could hear the treadle running steadily in the sewing room. Then, hurrying upstairs with Hans's card, she stared at it again, and instead of displaying it on the dresser, she pushed it into the top drawer.

"What's really goin' on?" she whispered, worry replacing discontent.

—☙ ❧—

By midmorning the next Wednesday, everyone was abuzz with the news that Harley's son-in-law, Manny Beiler, was moving to Leacock Township to partner with Arden Mast in a cabinet-making and remodeling business in a shop to be located adjacent to Manny's new home. Harley himself had heard the news from Abram Mast when both of them showed up at the same horse auction in Gordonville. And Abram's gloomy expression made it clear he was none too pleased.

Harley was a bit peeved, as well. Why was he hearing all this from his neighbor instead of directly from Manny, or even Tessa? Abram also relayed that Manny and Tessa had put down a rental deposit on a house on West Eby Road, of all places. *Not far from us,* Harley thought, downright surprised.

Eager to tell Mimi, Harley first had to wait around awhile at the auction to bid on a road horse to replace his ailing mare, Jennie, who was no longer able to pull even a lightweight wagon.

Will Manny's move change things for our family? He knew for certain Mimi would be happy to have Tessa nearby once again.

Harley eyed the hoped-for mare, having carefully checked her over two hours ago. She was strong and possessed a gentle temperament. He pulled out his pocket watch. If all went well, it wouldn't be much longer before he could make a bid on the fine horse.

———⌒ ⌒———

"*Jah*, Mimi, you heard right," Harley said from the doorway to the sewing room. Lena Rose had made herself scarce, quickly excusing herself when Harley arrived. "Our younger daughter is returning to her church district."

At the treadle machine, Mimi turned around and smiled her sweetest. "'Tis *gut*, ain't so?"

Harley shrugged. "Not for Abram Mast, *nee*." Removing his hat, he ran his hand straight back through his bangs. "Arden's tellin' him that the dairy life ain't one he wants, and the man's havin' to scramble for the future of his farm." He sighed. "Can ya believe it?"

She tilted her head, her face turning pinkish. "Well, it'll be *wunnerbaar*, havin' Tessa so close by an' all."

"Tessa, *jah*. Just not sure how things will be with Manny round here—the Good Lord must know I need help in that area."

"Now, Harley. No one's more long-sufferin' than you."

He waved his hand. "If only that were true. Well, I must get the new mare settled before the noon meal."

"What 'bout our Jennie-girl? Are ya thinkin' of putting her out to pasture? She's been a part of our family for so long."

Harley nodded. "It's the best thing we can do for her now." While he knew it might be more practical to sell her to one of the Amish farmers who purchased ailing and older horses, somehow it didn't seem right.

Mimi said no more about that, and Harley put his hat back on and headed for the door.

⁓ ⁓

More than two weeks slogged by with no further word from Hans. *Should I be worried?* Lena wondered. *Why isn't he writing?* Surely he'd received the short letter she'd written him after receiving his card—a note which she'd purposely kept light, hoping to encourage a brighter response.

Ach, it's out of my hands. I shouldn't stew over nothing, she thought, trying to dismiss her worry.

Dispirited, Lena offered to go over and spend time with Solomon, wanting to keep him company this Sunday evening. *It won't matter if I miss Singing. . . .*

Mimi protested a bit at the arrangement, but she was down with a bad cold and didn't wish to expose Uncle Solomon to it, anyway. So Lena thought it probably was for the best, especially when she thought back on her exceptionally friendly conversation with Arden Mast at last month's skating party. Happily, she carried a simple supper of ham and cheese sandwiches, chow chow, and potato chips to the *Dawdi Haus* and ate with Solomon, who was eager to share more of his childhood stories. Like the time Solomon had discovered, to his chagrin, a pig's tail in the fresh stuffed sausage made after one fall butchering. Or how Solomon, as a boy, had looked forward to trips to the old general store with his Dat. Even during the Great Depression, the owner had had a tradition of allowing him to choose a single piece of free candy—ribbon candy, taffy, or a peppermint stick. "Lookin' back on it, havin' to make little choices like that helped prepare me for some big decisions later in life," Solomon told her as they ate at the small table.

"Was there any chocolate amongst the choices?" Lena asked, momentarily getting up for the dishes of chocolate pudding she had prepared.

"Nope, never was," Solomon said with a tug on his long beard. "Might've been too expensive to give away." He chuckled. "'Course, that would've made choosin' *real* easy!"

Lena laughed right along with him.

"Things were awful tight when I was growing up. Dat had to put cardboard in the soles of us kids' shoes to cover up the holes."

"Was there enough food to go around?" she asked. She'd loved to hear her Dawdi Schwartz talk about this time in history.

"Sometimes my Mamm made soup from little more than turkey bones and vegetables from our garden, but we never went to bed hungry. Things had to be kept simple—Mamm couldn't afford sugar to make desserts." He shook his head. "Can you imagine a meal without dessert?" he said, pushing a spoon into his chocolate pudding. "Mostly, it was a time of faith. We had to put our trust in *Gott*, and He took care of us."

Lena considered this as she savored her own pudding, thankful for this time with him.

When she'd washed the dishes, she and Solomon went to sit in the other room near the stove, where Solomon relaxed with a number of periodicals, most particularly *The Budget*. His faithful dog, Blackie, lay near his feet, rarely moving as Solomon dozed off now and then and caught himself with a shake of his head.

"Whenever you're ready to retire for the night, that's all right," Lena assured him, looking up from the letter she was writing to brother Benjamin. "No need stayin' awake for me."

But Solomon just picked up his paper again and read till he nodded off once more.

Finally, when the day clock struck nine times, Solomon folded his paper and said, "Well, *gut Nacht*, Lena Rose. *Kumm ball widder.*"

"Sure," she said, "I'll come again soon." And when Solomon had gone to his room, she headed back to the main house to make a card for Timothy, who would be celebrating his ninth birthday the end of next month.

Lena remembered clearly the day Timothy was born. The midwife had been late arriving because of deep snow on the unplowed side roads, so ten-year-old Lena had helped deliver her baby brother with only her Mamma's murmured instructions to guide her. Dat had been so pleased with Lena when he returned with the midwife late that afternoon—he'd gotten stuck in the snow near Murk's Village Store in downtown Centreville.

Lena had never been so glad to see her father, even though newly born Timothy was pink and obviously healthy, wailing as he was at the top of his tiny lungs. "*Sometimes, babies just don't wait for midwives or snowplows,*" Mamma had said afterward, and Lena had never forgotten.

Sitting now in her room at the small writing table, she heard Eli's open carriage rumble into the driveway around ten o'clock. She put down her pen and noticed a dent on the fleshy part of her third finger. Evidently she'd been writing for nearly an hour already.

Fleetingly, she wondered if Eli might have talked with Arden at the Singing. And if so, what might he have said?

But she rejected the urge to let her mind wander in that direction. After all, it really didn't matter if Arden was disappointed she hadn't gone.

CHAPTER

22

The next morning, after the four o'clock milking and a nice hot breakfast, Mimi suggested Harley take a lemon pound cake over to Abram Mast's for his birthday. Abram, moving more slowly than usual, motioned Harley out to his office in the barn, where they sat on old wooden stools, Abram leaning against the makeshift desk, shadows under his eyes.

"Just between us, Harley, I'm thinkin' of renting out my dairy and the cropland," Abram said, his brow furrowed deep between his shaggy dark eyebrows.

Harley was surprised. "Didn't expect to hear this from you."

"Honest to Pete, I can't get any of my family interested in takin' it off my hands." Abram shook his head, his eyes glistening just then. "Don't know whether to be mad or sad or . . ." His voice trailed off. "And I'm ready to call it quits."

Harley felt for his lifelong friend. "Understandable."

"Arden is bent on leavin' the farm and givin' working with Manny a try—says they've already accepted a couple of jobs and should do real well. So that's that." Abram grimaced and rubbed his stubby nose. "'Course, once I sign a lease agreement, it won't be easy to get out of, so I told Arden he'd better be mighty certain 'bout the path he's takin'.'"

"True, and somethin' for him to ponder but *gut*."

Abram nodded. "As for me, I need to keep busy. Don't wanna just sit around and rot. Maybe I'll make some furniture, like I used to, and sell it at market. Come to think of it, that could be what whet Arden's appetite as a youngster."

"Well now." Harley smiled. "But if ya rent out the dairy and your cropland, you'll still be tempted to roam about the farm, won't ya? Keep your hands in it?"

"Maybe so. But I'm not gonna twiddle my thumbs in the house and waste away." Abram chuckled. "Would *you*?"

"Prob'ly not." But truly, there were times Harley wondered what it would be like to be free from milking twice a day so he could take Mimi on a vacation, especially in the dead of winter—somewhere warm like Pinecraft, Florida, where some Amish folk went for months on end. *Amish snowbirds.*

Abram removed his knit black hat and placed it on his knee. "Surely you're thinkin' along the same lines as this ol' man."

"Some days more than others, *jah*."

Abram raised his eyes to look at Harley. "Eli ain't talkin' like this, is he, 'bout getting out of the dairy business?"

"*Nee*, says it's the life for him."

Abram nodded slowly. "I daresay you're mighty lucky."

"Well, I am thankful, that's for certain," Harley said as one of the nearby mules brayed loudly.

He laughed, and when Abram invited him to stay for coffee and some of the birthday pound cake, Harley said, "I thought you'd never ask!"

—⁓ ⁓—

When the mail came Wednesday afternoon, Lena had little hope of finding anything from Hans, given that the only correspondence she'd had since Christmas was his belated card and rather terse note. But she was excited when she spotted an envelope addressed to her from Emma. She pushed it into her coat pocket and rushed up the driveway, ready to get back inside, so biting was the cold.

In the house, she sought the privacy of the front room, where she sat right down on the daybed to read what her dear sister had written.

Dear Lena Rose,

How are you? I hope you're keeping warmer there than we are here. It's been a hard winter to be sure, but the hardest part is how it's kept us apart. I miss you so much!

I wish I had some good news to share, but the truth is that things aren't going so well here, and Wilbur's urged me to write, since you deserve to know.

You see, Hans started attending Singings again this month, and he's been showing attention to one particular girl. Well, that in itself isn't good, but last time he gave her a ride home. It looks very much as if Hans is moving on without you, and wrong as it is to say, Wilbur and I both want to strangle him! How could he?

I'm awful sorry to have to break this to you, Lena Rose, although Wilbur and I really hope that Hans has written to tell you this himself. Surely he'll assume that one of us would say something.

Lena pushed the letter aside and stared at the ceiling. She was surprised at how numb she felt—neither angry nor sad. She still had not gotten over the fact that Hans hadn't offered to come to visit *her*, once the highways were plowed. *The road goes both ways,* she thought, suddenly recalling Emma's concern about how Hans had set up their dates, simply telling Lena where to be and when. Even back in late August, Emma had somehow discerned that Hans was taking Lena for granted. Yet it was something that Lena Rose herself had never considered . . . till now. *Were the miles between us more than he could handle?*

Reaching for a quilted pillow, Lena pressed it against her. She replayed the discussion they'd had on the day he'd stopped by while she was packing. At the time, Hans had seemed sympathetic, agreeing that her coming here for a few months till something else opened up in Centreville was her only option. If she wasn't mistaken, he had been relieved by the news that she wouldn't be gone for too awful long.

Everything must've changed when I didn't get home for Christmas, she decided, yet deep in her heart, she knew better. That couldn't have been the sole reason, and Emma's letter seemed to prove that.

—❧ ❧—

While sewing that afternoon, Lena continued to think about Emma's disquieting news. Now and then she found herself glancing across the long sewing table at Mimi, wondering if she might talk it over with this wise and caring woman.

At last, when Lena felt she might burst if she didn't say something, Mimi put down her needle, leaned her elbows on the table, and looked right at her. "Somethin's botherin' ya, Lena. I can feel it clear over here."

Giving a nod, Lena admitted, "Ya know me so well." She finished a stitch, then sat back in her chair. "I've been tryin' to be patient, waitin' for a letter from my beau back home, since I know it's what he'd expect. Honestly, I was thinkin' he might propose while I was home for Christmas, but then I didn't get back, and I've only had one note from him in more than a month." Seeing how solemn Mimi's face looked, Lena went on. "Truth be told, I've been holdin' my breath for him to take the next step."

"Well, of course," Mimi replied, nodding her head. "Any girl in love wants to be pursued by her beau."

"But now it seems he's pursuing someone else." Lena told about Emma's letter.

Mimi tilted her head and frowned. "*Ach*, it'll be his loss if he chooses another young woman. You care very much for him, don't ya?"

Just the way Mimi said it made Lena feel all the more tender-hearted. "He's the first fella I've seriously dated."

"Well, dating is one thing, but cherishing someone is quite another," Mimi said quietly. "Mind if I tell you a little 'bout Harley's and my courtship?"

Lena listened as Mimi shared. "I was very shy at the time I started goin' to Singings, but knowing I'd never dated didn't scare away Harley. He wanted to make sure I felt comfortable with him, so he decided to approach Dat about his interest in me." Mimi smiled and shook her head at the thought. "Harley never balked, not once, when my father laid out to him how old I had to be for serious courtin'—older than sixteen, mind you. Harley had to wait a whole year before he could take me out in his courting buggy."

Lena was impressed by Harley's willingness to abide by Mimi's father's wishes—she doubted most young men would be willing to wait like that. "Patience was a trait I couldn't help but notice in my Dat, too," Lena said wistfully.

"An important characteristic, I daresay." Mimi smiled now. "'Specially in a spouse."

Lena pondered that. "I'm not sure patience is the main concern with my beau, though. I mean, if Hans felt impatient to marry me, I'd have had a proposal in a letter by now, seems to me."

"If he were ready to make a lifelong commitment, maybe so. But from what you've just shared, that hardly seems likely."

Lena bowed her head. She ran her hand over the shirt she'd been mending and sighed. "I thought *I* was ready to move forward with marriage, but 'specially since Christmas, I've begun to wonder. . . . Could be I've been foolin' myself about Hans." She lifted her head and fixed her gaze on Mimi. "I mean, is any courtship s'posed to be this hard?"

Mimi folded her arms and leaned back from the table. "That depends on the couple. And if Hans is seeking out another girl at Singing, that's not a *gut* sign, *jah*?"

Lena knew Mimi was right but said nothing. It was too hard to get any words past the tightness in her throat.

"I know you've expressed that you're tryin' to be, and *do*, what your beau wants." Mimi stopped to take a sip of water from the tumbler she had nearby. "But ya know that can only go so far. A beau needs to love you for who you are, not who you're tryin' to be. There's a danger there of tryin' to make things happen in your own power—not putting your trust in our heavenly Father."

The fact that Mimi felt comfortable speaking so plainly like this made Lena feel secure in their closeness. "I admit that I have difficulty trusting. I tend to want to make things work out my way."

Mimi smiled. "Realizing that can be the first step toward a better relationship . . . and I don't mean just with a young man."

Lena knew she needed to put more trust in God. Why was it so hard for her to do what seemed to come naturally to some? *Like Mimi*, she thought, thankful for her caring. The kindhearted woman had taken the time to talk with her the way her mother might have. "*Denki* for listening while I spilled my heart."

"Anytime ya need a listening ear, Lena."

Tears sprang to her eyes, and she nodded her thanks.

Truth be known, even though it might have seemed to others that she was beginning to recover from her parents' untimely death, Lena was, in fact, still trying to make sense of all the jumbled pieces of her life, like the jigsaw puzzles she loved to put together. Till Emma's letter arrived, Hans Bontrager had certainly been one of those important pieces, if not one of the most important.

23

A nother letter came for Lena that Thursday afternoon, this one from Mammi Schwartz. It told the news that Tubby Tabby had somehow escaped the house and run off.

> *Oh, Lena! Chris just fell apart when Tabby disappeared yesterday—he wouldn't stop crying. At the time, it seemed over-the-top, but that cat is so dear to him. I wonder now, however, if his sadness over Tabby isn't made worse by the loss of your parents and by being away from you and the rest of your brothers and sisters. The poor child has had to put up with so much in such a short time!*
>
> *Unfortunately, that wasn't the worst of it. . . .*

Reading on, Lena discovered that Chris had donned his winter things and headed out to find the missing cat without Mammi's and Dawdi's knowing. *For a couple dreadful hours, we had no idea where he was,* Mammi wrote, *but Wilbur and your uncle Noah went out there looking with many of the menfolk, and thankfully Wilbur found him—and Tabby—before too long.*

Lena felt nearly ill at the thought of her little brother alone in the cold, searching for his beloved pet. Why had Chris taken such a terrible risk? *Thank goodness he isn't still out there!*

Even so, the unsettling news made her realize how helpless she was to protect her siblings, and she wished all the more that she could be there in Centreville. *Mammi's right—Chris has gone through too much these past months!* she thought.

$\sim$

At supper, Lena told the others about Chris's disappearance and rescue. "Mammi said he went looking for his missing cat." She stopped for a moment and rubbed her temples; the headache she'd had since reading Mammi's letter continued to nag her. "*Ach,* I can't understand how this happened," she told them.

Harley's face was as solemn as Eli's, and Solomon shook his head across the table from her and Mimi.

Harley spoke up. "Well, I'm glad to hear Chris is fine."

"He may be fine now," Lena said, "but the fact he was able to slip away still troubles me. He needs someone to keep a careful eye on him, yet here I am." She shook her head. "I hate feeling so useless . . . so *stuck.*"

Solomon slowly put down his fork. "'Tis understandable, but it's quite all right not to be in charge of things, Lena Rose. No one but *Gott* can do that, and He knows our comin's and goin's from one day to the next, *jah?*" Solomon looked at her, so serious. "He knows just where Chris is from minute to minute. Why not do like the Good Book says and give your worries to *Gott*? It might not feel natural to do it, 'specially at first, but you can trust Him."

Eli nodded thoughtfully, and Lena turned to glance at Mimi, then at Solomon again. In that moment, Lena felt surrounded by love.

"*Denki,*" Lena said.

Harley cleared his throat and looked over at her. "If ya don't mind, I'd like to take a moment to thank the Lord for gettin' Chris home so quickly," he said, surprising Lena Rose. Then Harley bowed his head, and they all prayed together in silence.

_____

Lena did not dare reread Mammi's letter before going to bed. As it was, certain phrases had been going through her mind for hours. Instead, she tried to do what Solomon had said—to simply trust.

"I can't be there with Chris to keep him safe," she whispered into the darkness. She thought then of Emma's letter yesterday. "And I can't keep Hans faithful to me, either." She knew that was not her place or in her ability to control. What Hans did was up to him, and if it meant they had grown apart, then there wasn't anything she could do about it.

The more she pondered this, the more she realized that she, too, had been feeling uncertain about the ongoing plan to court through letters. But how could there be a courtship if both weren't doing their part to write?

Lying there, her weary head on the pillow, Lena prayed for the kind of wisdom Harley's uncle seemed to possess . . . and for Chris, safe tonight in his own warm bed. *O Lord, I must entrust my brothers and sisters—and my anxiety about Hans—to Thee. Help me learn how to do that,* she prayed. *Worrying like this is more than I can bear.*

_____

While Lena worked with Mimi in the sewing room the next day, she lifted her loved ones' names to heaven. *I will trust and not be afraid,* she thought each time she was tempted to fear. It helped knowing that Mimi, too, was faithfully praying for her family.

Lydia Smucker was a welcome sight to behold when she stopped by after the noon meal, bringing a freshly made shoofly pie. "Just had a feelin' ya might need a little pick-me-up," Lydia said as Lena invited her in.

"Ya did?"

"I missed ya at the last Singing," Lydia said. "Hope you're doin' all right."

Lena told her that she'd kept Solomon company. She motioned her friend into the front room, where she told about her youngest brother—and Hans. "I'm doin' my best to give over my worries to the Lord . . . but my mind just wants to keep workin' on them, no matter how much I try." Lena inhaled sharply. "All of this at once seems like a test, to tell the truth."

Lydia reached to give her a hug. "You poor thing! No wonder you looked surprised when I brought the pie."

"You're a godsend—that's for sure."

"Maybe I should have brought you something to read, as well. A good story or poem always soothes me," Lydia suggested. "The only thing better than reading them is writing them, I think."

"You're a writer?" Lena had known a woman back home who was a scribe for *The Budget*, but the reporting of everyday news was quite a different thing.

"Mostly poetry," said Lydia.

"Have ya ever had anything published?" Lena asked.

Lydia nodded. "Last year in *Family Life* magazine."

Despite her lingering concerns, Lena enjoyed hearing this. "I'd really like to read it sometime."

※

Lena had a hard time keeping her mind on Rebekah's lesson that afternoon. But in the middle of it, while they took a short break and Lena poured coffee for them, Rebekah began to talk about her husband once again. This time, she mentioned that Michael had, one desperate day, gone to the deacon's home to get help for his drinking. Later, while going through the painful process of drying out, he'd made peace with God.

"It turned out he was on his deathbed. I was so shocked when word came that he'd passed away," Rebekah admitted. "But oh, the relief in knowin' he was not alone—the deacon stayed right with him, and Michael knew the Lord had forgiven his sins. The deacon told me this in a letter."

Lena breathed deeply, thankful for this update. No wonder Rebekah had reason for peace. "God was with your husband to the very end, drawing him . . . bringin' him back to the fold, *jah*?"

Rebekah nodded, smiling now. "Hard as it was to hear he was gone, there's no doubt in my mind he was ready to go when it was time. So sudden it was."

"I'm real glad ya told me," Lena said, having wondered about it and prayed whenever she had thought of Rebekah that past week.

⁓ ⁓

After the lesson was over, Lena heard the postal truck. Lena offered to go and get the mail, ready for some fresh air and not caring how cold it was outside. She hoped with every heartbeat for a note from home.

Quickly combing through the letters, she was pleased to spot one from Wilbur. She carried the mail inside to Mimi in the sewing room, then excused herself to read Wilbur's letter in the kitchen, wondering what he'd written.

Dear Lena Rose,

Mammi told me she wrote to you about Chris. I was so glad when I found him carrying Tabby only a couple hours after he disappeared. He was walking toward Dawdi's and Mammi's, looking tired and cold. Turns out Tubby Tabby was trapped in an outhouse nearly a mile up the road, meowing noisily, all battle-scarred and ruffled up.

"What on earth?" Lena shook her head. Since when had that old cat become such a rascal?

Tabby looks like she's been in a fight for her life, but Chris couldn't be happier to have her back, though he gave everyone a scare. Dawdi warned him never, ever to leave the house without telling them.

Lena read through the rest of the letter, which was filled with updates on their siblings, as well as the news that Wilbur had found himself a job at the RV factory. *Dat and I had talked about my working there, too, someday, so I'm thinking he'd be happy that I've managed to get my foot in the door.*

"Ach, Dat and Mamma would be so pleased," Lena murmured. Indeed, despite the disquiet of the past few days, there was much to be thankful for at this moment.

~ ❧ ❧ ~

A sense of gratefulness lingered into the next day and Lena's morning cleaning for James Zook. As before, she did some cooking for him, as well, making a pot of beef stew and even baking biscuits, though the light in his eyes indicated they wouldn't last more than a few days.

The Saturday mail had already arrived when Lena returned home. And to her immense surprise, it included a letter from Hans. "You'll likely want to read this right away," Mimi said, presenting it to her with a sympathetic look.

Lena went to sit near the window in her room, needing the warmth of the sun on her back. Now that it was actually here, she felt hesitant to open Hans's long-awaited letter, but her heart was not in her throat as she had suspected it might be.

The first page was filled with mundane weather-related comments, and she began to doubt he was going to address the issue she expected was at hand.

Then her eyes fell on these words:

> *It's possible you've already heard about the Singings I attended recently. I should've written to you first, before spending time with any other young woman. And I apologize for that, Lena. You deserve better.*

Lena stopped reading and looked out at the now familiar scenery—even prior to this letter, she'd considered writing a note to Hans to tell him she was having second thoughts about their letter-writing courtship. The delays between letters and the belated Christmas card with its impersonal note had caused her to question the strength of the bond between them. Emma's letter had only confirmed the wisdom of rethinking their courtship.

But thus far, Lena had held off on writing, at least since sending her short response to his card. She'd wanted to convince herself that she was giving Hans more time, but she felt guilty at the sudden realization that it was more likely due to a fear she might now never get home if she mailed off such a letter. Truly, she needed to separate her feelings for Hans from her intense desire to return to Centreville.

Returning to the letter, Lena read on:

> *I've spent some time thinking about our relationship, Lena Rose. Much as I like you, it's awful hard to court when you're*

*so far away—it just isn't the same at all. I'm not cut out for it.
In my mind, we've drifted apart. Don't you agree?*

She spoke a resounding *jah* out loud. And knowing she was
in complete agreement with Hans, she now felt at peace about
writing him to share how she felt, with no hard feelings or lingering questions.

Her father's loving postcards came to mind. *Hans didn't show
me the same regard that Dat had for Mamma, or even Harley for
Mimi.* If she was honest with herself, Lena hadn't felt the same
love for Hans, either.

And I must marry for love alone. . . .

She set Hans's letter on the dresser and returned to the kitchen.

"I hope it's not bad news," Mimi said as Lena joined her at
the counter.

"Actually, it's not." And Lena told Mimi that her courtship
with Hans had mutually ended. "I'm just fine with it, which might
seem peculiar after all the fretting I've done."

Mimi listened without judgment, her expression relieved.

"God must have another plan," Lena said.

"That's the best way to look on it, ain't so?"

Lena agreed.

24

E ven before Lena was downstairs making breakfast for Harley and Eli early that first Thursday in February, Mimi was off with three of her sisters and Ada to help Tessa finish packing. Afterward, they would all unpack at the new place and at least get Tessa's kitchen set up while Manny and a few of the men put together the beds and the crib. According to Harley, the rented house was about a mile up the road. "An easy walk in nice weather," he told Lena and Eli at breakfast.

Lena had been content to stay behind and work on the mending and tailoring, adding some of Mimi's work to her own. But she doubted it would take very long for Mimi and the other womenfolk to accomplish the task of boxing things up. It sounded as though Manny's mother would look after little Joey during the move.

Seeing little Joey nestled in Tessa's arms during their last visit had stirred up a longing in Lena for her own babies someday. She wondered if she might have more opportunities to see that darling baby boy now that Tessa would be living just up the road. Lena smiled as she threaded a needle and made a knot at the end of the long black thread. *Mimi can scarcely contain her delight!*

But now that Lena was without a beau it was futile to be thinking about future babies. Of course, if Emma were sitting right here talking with her, like they always had when sewing new dresses or aprons, she would have encouraged Lena that the situation was sure to change. Why, knowing Emma, she would be happy to put a bug in a young man's ear if she knew he'd caught Lena's attention.

Unfortunately, as Lena recalled, there were no other young men her age in Centreville without sweethearts. And if there were, it never seemed to take them long to pair up by this time each year. *That's how it is*, she thought, not second-guessing her split with Hans. *And if I'm not there, I can't meet a potential beau.*

Finished with the hem of the jacket and now in need of some different colored thread, Lena rose and walked over to Mimi's work area. For the first time, she noticed what looked like a list of names written in Mimi's hand—a prayer list. And as Lena stepped closer, she saw the words *Lena Rose's future* at the top.

"Bless you, Mimi, for caring so deeply," she whispered.

$$\sim\!\!\!\sim\; \sim\!\!\!\sim$$

Rebekah arrived for her lesson that Friday afternoon looking cheerful and eager. She let Lena know that this would be her last lesson, since she was feeling much more confident, but she'd keep reading aloud at Cora Ruth's for practice.

Lena was secretly grateful that Rebekah had chosen to start with Isaiah forty-one, verse ten. "'Fear thou not; for I am with thee: be not dismayed; for I am thy God: I will strengthen thee. . . .'" Compared to two months ago, Rebekah read quite smoothly, stumbling only a few times, though she didn't let that bother her.

"Be not dismayed. . . ." Lena thought of young Chris's disappearance and of Hans's interest in another girl. She had certainly

experienced times of dismay herself, but God was showing her that He was with her. "You're readin' so much better—the words are flowin' so well now. Can ya tell the difference?"

Rebekah nodded, her chin quivering. "I've been thinkin' of what I might do to thank you, Lena Rose," she said.

"Ain't necessary. I'm just tickled you're feelin' confident."

Rebekah closed her Bible. "Well, I'd really like to have ya join us for supper a week from tomorrow. I've already checked with Cora Ruth, and besides, Emily and the boys are a-hankerin' to see you again."

Remembering how sweet her grandchildren were, Lena smiled and accepted the invitation. "You're really too kind."

"What's your favorite meal?" Rebekah asked, adjusting her black apron.

"Oh, don't go to any trouble."

"Well, I'm not gonna promise *that!*" Rebekah grinned.

Lena Rose accompanied her out to the waiting buggy. She would miss these weekly lessons, but she was glad for this chance to have done something useful, maybe even important, to the woman's happiness and well-being.

___ ⟋ᘓ ᘓ⟍___

Eli offered Lena a ride to town the next morning when she said she needed to run a few errands. And as they rode together, Lena was surprised when he mentioned that Arden Mast wasn't dating anyone. "In case you were curious," he told her.

"I had wondered why he wasn't engaged," she admitted, feeling peculiar talking with her cousin about Arden like this. While her breakup with Hans hadn't been the subject of suppertime conversations, it was common knowledge around the Stoltzfus household.

"Well, he was pretty serious about a girl a year or so ago, but her family moved away to Conewango Valley, New York. He couldn't follow after her because he'd always figured he'd take over his father's farm. Really, there was no way he could leave Leacock Township."

"So he loved home more than his girlfriend?"

Eli laughed. "You hit the nail right on the head. He let her go with her family to the new community. Guess he thought she'd stay if they really had a future together."

This revelation was an eye-opener, to be sure.

And while Lena hadn't asked to know any of this, she was secretly glad Eli had told her.

—⟨∽ ∾⟩—

While Lena and Mimi cleaned up the dishes that evening, Lena mentioned that, a week from tonight, she'd be away for supper at Melvin and Cora Ruth Ebersol's house. "I hope ya won't mind. Rebekah invited me yesterday at her final lesson."

"Go an' have a real nice time," Mimi said, glancing at her as she draped the tea towel over the drainer. "You've been an encouragement to her all these weeks, and it seems to have done both of you some good. At first, Harley and I weren't sure it was altogether wise, to be honest."

Lena was surprised. "For her to come here for lessons?"

Mimi nodded and looked regretful. "We were so very wrong." She sighed and turned to lean against the sink.

"Rebekah has shared some things about her past with me," Lena said, careful not to say too much. "Her life hasn't been easy, that's for sure. But she feels it was a blessing that, before he died so suddenly, her husband managed to get himself over to the deacon's to ask for help."

Mimi nodded her head, so Lena presumed she knew something about the years of drinking. "I heard about that. It was compassionate of the deacon to take it upon himself to stay with Michael while he went cold turkey," Mimi said.

Lena agreed. "Rebekah was ever so grateful—said he was awful bad off." Lena remembered what the woman had told her a week ago—that up until his death, she was praying daily for him to get sober and to stay that way, as well as for the bishop to lift the *Bann* once Michael was sober. Despite the troubles they'd had, Rebekah missed her shunned husband terribly. "It was Rebekah's hope she could return home. . . . To think the poor man died before they could be reunited," Lena said softly. "Talk about heartbreak."

Mimi lowered her head for a moment, and when she looked at Lena, her eyes were bright with tears. "Your heart was in the right place all along, Lena Rose."

"I think she and I were drawn to each other. We both feel displaced, I guess. . . ." She sighed. "Truth is, neither of us can go back to the life we once had. But that doesn't make me miss my family any less."

Mimi carried her coffee cup to the table and set it down. "We just never know what might be happenin' to cause a person heartache," she observed.

Lena agreed. "Mamma used to say that if we have the chance to be God's hands and feet here on earth, He can use us to lift someone's spirit . . . and make a difference in a life. We just need to be willin'."

Mimi nodded, motioning for Lena to bring her coffee cup and sit with her.

—◌ ◌—

The Saturday evening at Melvin Ebersol's turned out to be full of surprises. For one thing, Rebekah served a delicious ham loaf, and there was a white angel food cake with homemade chocolate ice cream and specialty candies—like a birthday celebration. So much so, in fact, that some of the children were a bit confused by it. "We're honorin' my *wunnerbaar-gut* friend tonight," Rebekah simply told them.

After the meal was finished and the second blessing was offered, Rebekah asked Emily to come and sit on her lap near the warm cookstove. And to little Emily's wonderment, Rebekah opened *Henner's Lydia* and began to read, just as she'd practiced with Lena Rose, sounding as comfortable as if she had been doing so all of her life.

When the story came to an end, Emily turned and wrapped her arms around Rebekah's neck. "*Denki*, Mammi . . . will ya read it to me again tomorrow?"

"I surely will," Rebekah said, looking over at Lena, tearing up.

A few moments later, there was a knock at the back door, and Melvin went to see who was there.

Lena could hear a snowplow rumbling past the house, then what sounded like Arden's voice. When he walked into the kitchen with Manny Beiler, she could hardly believe it.

"You've come to measure for the new kitchen cabinets, ain't so?" Cora Ruth asked right quick, and Lena thought she really ought to get going. "Stay an' have some cake after you're done," Cora Ruth added. "There's plenty left."

"Whose birthday?" Arden asked, his glance catching Lena's.

"No birthday. It's just the start of somethin' new," Cora Ruth said, looking now at her mother.

Blushing, Rebekah smiled. "Thanks to Lena Rose."

Looking from one woman to the other, Arden appeared down-right baffled while Manny stood over near the counter, pulling out his measuring tape.

Lena had no intention of explaining the reason for the cel-ebration to Arden, considering that Rebekah hadn't told her grandchildren, and was relieved when Manny called for Arden to help him measure the space for the new cabinets.

With some assistance from freckle-faced Abe, who leaned his little blond head against Lena's arm, Rebekah and Emily urged Lena Rose to stay for seconds of dessert once the fellows finished.

As it turned out, Arden took a seat directly across from her, so it was impossible not to interact with him or to see the wink he gave her. Surely he only meant to be friendly, although each time he fixed his stunning blue-green eyes on her, she felt a fluttery sensation.

Later, when Lena thanked Rebekah for the delicious supper and the very special evening, little Abe came over and shook her hand; then his younger brother, Bennie, mimicked him, grinning up at her. Even Emily stood on tippytoes to give Lena a peck on the cheek and ask if she'd come visit again. For a moment, it was a flashback to Lena's school days, when Liz and Verena were small and showed their gratitude with kisses.

Making her way through the snow out to the horse and buggy, Lena was surprised when Arden hurried out the door behind her. "By the way, I missed seein' ya at the last Singing. Eli said you were busy with Mimi." Arden fell into step with her.

"Mimi seemed glad for some time to put a puzzle together . . . to break up the monotony," she said.

"Well, I hope *you're* not bored here."

She looked at him. "Well, *nee* . . . but my heart's in Centreville."

Arden suddenly went quiet, and she remembered what Eli had told her about his ties to this area. "I'm sure you understand, *jah*?"

"Definitely," Arden replied. "I can't imagine leaving here. I'm putting down strong roots for certain . . . my partnership, ya know, with Manny Beiler."

She wondered if he might be disappointed that she didn't

appreciate Leacock Township the way he did. *I do,* she thought. *It's just not home.*

Arden gave her a smile in the dim light of the moon's waxing crescent. "I'd like to see you again, Lena Rose. I'd still like to take you out for coffee sometime."

"As friends?" she asked.

"Whatever you'd like to call it," he said as he helped her inside Harley's enclosed buggy before untying the horse from the hitching post. "Sure wish I could drive ya home tonight, what with this weather an' all." He paused near the driver's side, then brought around the driving lines and handed them up to her.

The wind gusted, and Lena thought how good it would be to get back to Harley and Mimi's and sit by the fire in either the kitchen or the front room. There were no hot bricks to warm her on the floor of the carriage, but she was thankful for the buggy blanket she pulled up around herself.

"You be careful, won't ya?" Arden said.

"I promise."

He broke into a grin. "Don't forget to think 'bout going for coffee with me, okay? Whenever you're ready."

With any other fellow, Lena might have felt pressured, but Arden had an endearing way about him that made her feel comfortable, and she liked talking to him. "I'll see," she said. "*Gut Nacht,* Arden," and she signaled the horse to move forward.

CHAPTER
25

Lena received two long letters that Wednesday afternoon—one from Wilbur, and the other from Emma, both asking how she was doing. Oh, with all of her heart, Lena hoped there might be news about a job or a place to stay in Centreville. But scanning the letter, she saw that nothing had turned up even though Emma said Uncle Noah and the deacon had been talking to quite a few folk, including some relatives who lived in Sturgis, fourteen miles southeast of Centreville.

Instead, Emma turned her focus to Lena's recent breakup:

Considering what's happened with Hans, I'm really hoping for a new beau for you out here. Is it too early to say this? If so, please forgive me, dearest sister. With all of my heart, I want you to be happy.

Now, I hope ya won't think I've lost my mind, but there is a nice young widower with three children who's looking for a wife. He's a man Dat knew and always seemed to have good fellowship with. Let me know if you would be okay with him contacting you. If not, please ignore this and try not to be upset with me. I just want you home again!

"A widower? Emma's thinkin' much too hard on this—tryin' to be a matchmaker now, too," Lena murmured. "I wouldn't have time for my family if I married someone with children of his own. And I can't marry someone just to find a way home."

What am I willing to do to get home?

Sighing, she opened Wilbur's letter next. After the jolt of Emma's desperate suggestion, Lena welcomed her brother's laid-back words. He thanked her for being so faithful about keeping in touch, then wrote how relieved he was that she seemed to be taking the breakup with Hans in stride.

All the better if he's serious about someone else by the time I move home, she thought.

Brushing that thought aside, she read the rest of Wilbur's letter, thankful to know that their five younger brothers were doing well in school, minding their manners, and praying every day for Lena Rose.

And finally, he wrote, *I've saved the most important news for last: Tubby Tabby's recovered from her escape and shows no signs of wanting to stray away a second time. Frankly, I think she'd have a hard time getting away—Mammi and Chris have kept a close eye on her, for certain. And the rest of us have kept a close eye on Chris!*

Lena smiled. *Oh, to be there,* she thought, folding the letter lovingly.

—◌ ◌—

Later, when Lydia dropped by, the two of them hurried upstairs and sat for awhile in Lena's room.

"I missed ya again at the last Singing," Lydia said, going to sit on the chair near the window.

Lena leaned back against her bed pillows, thankful for Lydia's friendship. "I just decided to spend the evening with Mimi, is all."

Lydia frowned. "What 'bout the next Singing?"

Lena stared down at the bed quilt, smoothing it with her hand.

"C'mon, you *know* ya want to go."

"It sounds a little like you've decided for me." Lena reached back and rubbed her neck.

"Besides, everyone was askin' where you were."

Lena wondered if by everyone she meant Arden, yet she didn't dare ask, not wanting Lydia to misconstrue the reason for her interest. *At least she hasn't mentioned how attentive he was at Second Christmas.*

They visited a bit more, and Lydia mentioned a wagon ride coming up on the nineteenth, after Sunday's Singing. "There was talk of taking out a few sleighs, but with the roads mostly clear of snow now, it's not practical, and besides, there's really much more room in a wagon than a sleigh. 'Course that might change if it snows 'tween now and then."

Lena wondered if Eli would be going. If he was, Lydia would naturally want to spend time with him, and Lena would likely be thrown together with Arden again. "I'll think about the hayride, but I'm not sure I should make a habit of going to Singings," she told Lydia.

"What could keep you away?" her friend asked. "You're part of our group here now."

Lena shook her head.

"Still sad over Hans?" Lydia asked her right out.

"*Nee*, I'm fine with things ending with Hans." Lena rose and walked to the window. "It's just sometimes I wonder if it makes sense to go, since I should be moving home anytime. To be honest, I thought I'd be back home by now. Can ya imagine how *you'd* feel if you were over five hundred miles away from your family?"

Lydia went to stand next to her. "Plain miserable. But I'd like to think that I'd do exactly what you've been doing . . . makin' the best of where the Lord put me. We need to be content with that, ain't?"

Lena nodded, knowing all too well how easy it was to talk about being at peace with where God had placed you . . . but much harder to live it out.

—✂ ✂—

Melvin Ebersol met Harley in the barnyard the next day with a strange request. "My mother-in-law's closest sister is terribly ill," Melvin said, pulling his woolen scarf tightly around his neck. "And Cora Ruth thought it might help comfort Rebekah some if Lena Rose could drop by for a while. She's takin' the news awful hard."

It wasn't Harley's place to speak for Lena Rose. "I'll see if she can get away from her sewin' later. If so, I'll bring her over . . . prob'ly after the noon meal."

"Lena has such a gentle way with folk, I'm sure ya know."

Harley clapped a hand on Melvin's big shoulder. "I'm sorry to hear 'bout this on top of all Rebekah's been through. We'll remember her sister in prayer."

Melvin nodded.

"Let us know if there's anything else we can do." Harley headed out of the barnyard with Melvin, through the wooden gate to the driveway. As they went, he glanced up and saw the smoke curling out from the chimney and counted his blessings— dearest Mimi and all the family were healthy and doing well this day.

We never know when our time is up, he thought, recalling how he'd felt when the word had come that Lena Rose's parents had died. His own father had impressed on him the importance of making every day count, and he hoped for Rebekah's sake her sister would pull through this illness all right.

—ᗡ ᗡ—

Lena Rose went as soon as she could and tried her best to console Rebekah. After a time, Cora Ruth urged her mother to go and lie down. Accompanying Rebekah to the bedroom just off the front room, Lena felt concerned enough to stay after getting the woman settled in for an afternoon rest. Lena covered her with the extra quilt at the foot of the bed as Rebekah lay there, trying not to weep. "I should be with her," Rebekah whispered, choking back a sob.

"It's all right to cry," Lena said quietly as she moved the cane chair close to the bed. "Holdin' it in is hard on ya."

"Tomorrow, I must make the trip home. I need to see her . . . can't bear the thought she might die before I can talk to her again," Rebekah said falteringly. "Cora Ruth can't go along 'cause the children need her, so I'll be goin' alone." The woman's hands trembled, and she folded them beneath her chin.

"Please try not to worry, Rebekah. The Lord is with your sister . . . and with you," Lena said, wishing there were some way she could accompany the poor woman home, but her first responsibility was to Mimi. "Try to rest now."

Rebekah nodded and reached for Lena's hand. She held it for the longest time as silent tears rolled down her wrinkled face.

And all the while, Lena breathed a prayer for the broken-hearted woman.

26

Mid-February was still a month away from spring-cleaning, but Lena was impatient to free the yard of winter's debris. "I just want to be done with it. Do ya know that feelin'?" she asked Mimi.

"*Ach*, spring'll be here quicker than we realize," Mimi replied, agreeing with Lena. "I feel it in my bones."

Lena finished slip-stitching the facing to an *Englischer*'s vest. "I hope Rebekah's holdin' up all right, traveling by herself." She glanced at the day clock on the wall. "I wonder when she gets in."

"I feel for her—just as she's startin' to recover from her husband's passing an' all," Mimi said quietly.

"She didn't say how long she'll be stayin' back home when I was over there yesterday. Do you know?"

Mimi shook her head. "Could be a while . . . if her sister lingers."

"Well, I hope it isn't as grave as that. And meanwhile, Cora Ruth has her hands full with the children. Thankfully Melvin can help some till plowin' and planting begin."

"Rebekah should be back by then."

"I hope so," Lena said, then lifted her friend up to God while she knotted the long black thread and began to make small stitches around a newly created buttonhole.

—⁘ ⁘—

What was it about the smell of wood shavings that woke up the senses? Harley wondered as he stepped inside Manny and Arden's cabinetry shop. The place was already open to the public, and two other farmers were there tossing around the idea of remodeling their wives' kitchens.

"Word's gotten out 'bout you two," Harley could hear one of them telling Arden, who looked mighty professional in a tan carpenter's apron.

Harley waved at him. "Manny around?"

"Back yonder," Arden said, pointing him toward another room, where Harley found his son-in-law bent over a sawhorse, beads of sweat standing on his brow.

Harley wandered over to greet Manny, who nodded and kept sawing. Not wanting to keep him from his work, Harley moseyed around the place, impressed by how well laid out it was, in particular the organized pegboard where hand tools hung on the nearby wall.

After a few minutes, Manny quit sawing and asked if he needed some help. It was the first he'd spoken since Harley's arrival there.

Harley simply said he'd stopped by to wish him and Arden well in their new line of work. "I realize it's been a couple weeks already, but *willkumm* to the neighborhood."

"*Denki.*" Manny looked like he was eager to get back to work, and for a moment, Harley figured that was that. But then Manny looked up again. "Tessa's happier here . . . sees her sister and the rest of the family more often."

"I'm sure your parents miss seeing ya, though."

"Oh *jah*. Mamm liked helpin' with the baby some."

Harley overlooked the latter comment, knowing that Mimi enjoyed having baby Joey around, too.

"But there's more work for me here. And honestly, I'd had it with dairy farmin'," Manny said as he wiped his forehead with the back of his hand. "Just ain't suited to it."

Harley nodded. "Some like it; some don't." He was real pleased Manny was giving him the time of day, something that had rarely happened since he'd swept Tessa off her feet and moved her away from home. For certain, those had been two dismal years for Mimi—and for him. Strong willed as Tessa had always been, Harley had hoped she might choose a young man from around here, one familiar with their church *Ordnung*. But once Manny'd caught Tessa's eye, no one but him would do. "Well, Mimi says to drop by anytime for coffee and sweets."

Manny bobbed his head.

"I've kept ya long enough."

Manny returned to work, and on Harley's way out to his horse and buggy, he saw Abram Mast. Always glad to chew the fat with an old friend, Harley waited till Abram had tied his mare to the black hitching post before calling to him. "Fancy meetin' you here." Harley chuckled as Abram came over. "Gonna sign up for a kitchen remodel?"

"Why, are *you*?" Abram grinned.

"Business is rather robust." Harley motioned with his head.

"I'd like to pick Arden's brain, but maybe I oughta drop by another time."

Harley glanced at the shop. "Are ya still thinkin' of ditchin' dairy work?"

"Actually, I may have found someone to rent the dairy and the cropland, too."

"Is that right?"

"Just kinda fell into my lap," Abram said, shaking his head. "Funny how these things work. We stew and we fret, an' then when we finally throw up our hands, the Good Lord provides."

They stood and talked further about the tendency to keep God at a distance and cling to one's own way. Then Abram said so long and headed into the shop.

Harley knew it was time to get home to finish the daily barn chores. He looked forward to telling Mimi about today's visit. *Manny seemed more comfortable around me today,* thought Harley, glad of it.

—☙ ❧—

Sunday evening, Lydia dropped by for Lena in her father's buggy as planned, since Eli had gone out of town to be at an auction bright and early Monday morning. "Nice of you to come for me," Lena said as she climbed in on the left side.

Lydia smiled as they rode off together. "Word has it this Singing will be better attended than usual 'cause of the hay-ride afterward."

"I'm sure you'll miss Eli bein' there."

"Well, it's always fun to see you, Lena Rose."

Lena smiled to herself; she appreciated that Lydia wasn't like some girls who, once they started going for steady, seemed to leave their girlfriends in the dust. "I enjoy our friendship, too," Lena said.

Lydia smiled ever so brightly.

Twilight was falling fast, and carriage lights twinkled on the back roads that ran alongside the snow-blanketed fields. From this distance, Lena thought the other buggies looked like large lightning bugs as they rolled toward the Mast farm.

"I brought my published poem along, like you asked." Lydia reached behind her and handed Lena a black folder. "You can use the flashlight if you want to read it now."

"Oh, I'd like that."

"I didn't tell ya before, but it's a love poem."

Lena wondered if perhaps Eli had inspired the poem. More curious now, she found the flashlight, switched it on, and began to read.

When she'd finished, she turned off the flashlight. One by one, the stars were appearing. "I understand why the magazine picked this poem, Lydia. It's just beautiful."

Lydia thanked her. "I was writing 'bout my Dawdi and Mammi Smucker, the sweetest couple ever. They prayed together every day." She went on to say that they had passed away within just two months of each other—to the very day and hour. "I honestly don't think Dawdi had the will to go on without her, so the Lord must've given him the desire of his heart and called him to Gloryland, too."

Thinking how dear this was, Lena wondered if James Zook felt the same way. Mimi had once remarked how very sad James was, but while he certainly had his solemn moments, he still had a lively sense of humor.

Lydia turned to look at Lena. "True love ain't so common, I think—at least the kind my grandparents had. But I do hope to have that special sort of love with Eli." Lydia sighed. "I s'pose my hopes are high, though."

Mine too, Lena thought, glad to have read Lydia's touching poem.

⸺ 𝒞𝓈 𝒞𝓈 ⸺

After the refreshment time midway through the Singing, when the young men were taking their seats on the opposite side of the long row of tables, Lena noticed several couples exchange meaningful looks. It reminded her how things had been with Hans last summer, when he'd first sought her out.

Just then, Lena realized that Arden Mast was looking her way, a concerned frown on his face. Had she forgotten to keep singing? She gave him her best smile and sang more heartily than before.

Later, during the wagon ride, Lena sat beside Lydia and her younger cousin Vera, hoping to discourage Arden from getting too near. There was really no subtle way to look to see where he had ended up on the wagon, but there was a group of young men on the back end, laughing and talking, and she was certain she'd heard his laugh amongst them. Some of the fellows were still singing gospel songs, all in unison.

Lena couldn't pick out Arden's deep voice, although she really wasn't trying to. Now and then, she entered into conversation with Lydia and Vera, who were currently looking up at the northern sky as Lydia pointed out the seven stars that made up the Big Dipper.

"Once ya locate the Big Dipper, it's easy to find the Little Dipper," Lydia was saying. "It can be harder, though, when the moon's starting to rise . . . like tonight."

Smiling, Lena told Lydia, "You should write a poem about the stars."

"That's a real *gut* idea," Vera said, still staring at the sky.

"It'd be fun to see what ya come up with," Lena urged. "You're a fine poet."

Lydia laughed merrily. "I honestly don't know 'bout that."

"Those stars are like jewels, ain't so?" Vera said, still transfixed by the glittering sky.

"They're pretty, but I'd say people are the real gems," Lydia said, giving Vera a quick little hug. "Relationships are more interesting to me."

Observing Lydia's warm interaction with Vera, Lena was glad for her friendship with Lydia. Cousin Eli was fine, but it wasn't the same as having another young woman to talk to.

─◦ ◦─

The hay wagon rolled through the night over the snow-packed field lanes that crisscrossed the various Amish farms. The air was surprisingly still, ideal for a winter's evening outdoors, although

Lena was still very thankful for her warmest mittens, made by dearest Mamma two Christmases ago. She curled her fingers tightly together inside them and slipped her thumbs out of their spots, creating even more warmth.

After a while, Vera leaned her head on Lydia's shoulder, and some of the other girls moved around, some even going to sit next to a beau, their booted feet dangling over the side of the wagon. Lena had relished the cold, stimulating air on her face at the beginning of the ride, but presently her nose began to sting, and she pulled her woolen scarf up over her face, leaving space for only her eyes.

Lydia whispered that she thought the ride was too long, and Lena put her arm around her, huddling near.

"I wore long johns—did you?" Lena whispered back.

Lydia giggled now. "Oh, wouldn't have come without 'em."

"Growin' up in Michigan, all us kids wore them through the winter."

The ride lasted for another ten minutes or so, and when they stopped back at the Mast farm, it was Arden and another fellow Lena didn't know who helped all the girls down from their wagon, shining their flashlights. Lena smiled, wondering if it was possibly an excuse for Arden to talk to her.

"Did ya have a *gut* time?" Arden asked as they went together to the stable to get Lydia's father's horse.

"*Jah*, did you?"

"It was the best part of the evening," Arden said, "being out there with so many friends."

The light of his flashlight and the nearly full moon made it easy to lead the horse back to the carriage, where Arden insisted on hitching up for Lydia, who was still nowhere to be seen. Lena guessed she might have run to the outhouse with some of the other girls.

Arden led the horse into position and backed him into the parallel shafts.

"Nice of you to do this for Lydia," Lena said.

"I don't mind."

Not more than a half minute later, Lydia came rushing over. "*Puh!* I forgot where I parked the buggy!" She was laughing as she approached. "For pity's sake." Lydia continued to laugh, shaking her head as she went to step up into the driver's seat.

Lena wondered how Lydia had gotten so lost.

"Well, have yourselves a fine week," Arden said quickly. "*Wunnerbaar-gut* to see ya, Lena Rose."

"*Gut Nacht.*" With that, Lena climbed into the buggy. It was later than usual after a Singing, and she didn't want Harley and Mimi to worry, never wanting to take their hospitality for granted.

Lifting the buggy blanket, Lena settled in for the ride home as Lydia pulled forward toward the road. Lena closed her eyes as the motion of the buggy soothed her. She felt relaxed, though a bit chilled.

"Thinking 'bout something?" Lydia asked, interrupting the peaceful silence. "Or . . . someone?"

"It was a real *gut* time tonight, *jah?*"

"The Singing . . . the wagon ride, or afterward?"

"'Specially the wagon ride," Lena said, meaning it.

"All right, then," Lydia said, sounding a bit disappointed.

"You should know I'm not one to jump from one beau to another," Lena added softly.

"Well, *nee* . . . I wasn't thinkin' that. Just wonder if Arden's someone you might enjoy spendin' time with. He sure seems to like you."

Lena shrugged. "He is nice," she said, recalling how he'd asked her to let him know about going to coffee. But he hadn't mentioned it again, and neither had she.

27

There were times when Lena questioned if she shouldn't just quit holding her breath to return home and, like Lydia had encouraged her, be content with where God had placed her.

Lena was contemplating this as she made ready for the Singing that evening, the first Sunday in March. While brushing her hair and redoing her bun, she recalled talking with Rebekah at the shared meal earlier today, after Preaching service. She had felt such relief hearing that Rebekah's sister Rachel had made a turn for the better; Rebekah believed it was partly due to their being together again, which Lena completely understood.

Looking in the mirror, she made sure all the wispy new hairs were neatly caught up, then hurried downstairs to eat supper. Lena realized just then that she was looking forward to attending Singing.

Later, as Lena rode with Cousin Harley in the family carriage, she let him know that Eli and Lydia would be bringing her home after the Singing. "I won't be out real late."

Harley went on to say that Ada and Tessa had sometimes pushed the limit on that when courted by their now husbands. "Ain't somethin' I'd ever worry 'bout . . . not with you, Lena Rose."

He gave her a glance. "Have you had any recent news from home?"

"Just that Emma is putting out more feelers to find a job for me."

"You sure are determined. And ya must be awful sorry 'bout that one fella."

"Honestly, Hans wasn't meant for me."

Harley smiled kindly. "Then I 'spect I shouldn't waste any more time feelin' sorry for ya."

"*Jah*, no need."

Harley seemed pleased. "The Lord will provide, if it's His will."

Lena sighed, but she kept mum. She knew she was supposed to trust God to do what was best for her, but it didn't stop her from spending oodles of time praying about this.

When Harley pulled into the lane leading to the large bank barn, she thanked him. "I really appreciate you and Mimi, I hope ya know."

"And we love havin' you with us." Harley's voice wavered, and he looked away.

Lena felt touched by how much he cared. "*Des gut.* Because it sure seems like you'll have me around for a while yet."

"*Jah*, and I hope for your sake it isn't too much longer. I know ya never expected to stay here this long."

She gazed at him. It still felt like she was looking at her own father . . . just years older. The resemblance was a source of comfort to her.

"Hope ya enjoy yourself tonight." Harley lifted the driving lines, and Lena felt sure that it was meant to signal her exit.

"*Denki*," she replied.

"*Du bischt willkumm.*"

Climbing out of the carriage, she waved politely, and he called to her to be careful on the slippery snow. *Always looking after me,* she thought. *Like Dat would have wanted him to.*

—◌ ◌—

Lena felt more at ease this time as the Singing commenced and she joined her voice with the others. She supposed it was because she had Lydia beside her, someone Lena would definitely keep in touch with.

During the evening refreshments, Lena Rose stayed right with Lydia, talking for a while just the two of them, then going together to visit with some of Lydia's cousins, including Vera. The younger girls were all aflutter about a couple new fellows who'd just turned sixteen, which amused Lena—she and her own girl cousins had acted much the same back home. *There's always a new batch of* Youngie *turning sixteen,* she thought, knowing that this would be of no help to her when she returned to Centreville, since she would be nineteen in late March. *Too old for the younger fellows.*

Suddenly, she heard Arden's voice before she spotted him, and when she turned around, he and a few other young men were walking toward her and Lydia and her cousins. Soon, they were all mingling, and then Arden was standing next to Lena.

"*Wie geht's,* Lena Rose?" There was that endearing smile again.

"Keepin' real busy. You?"

"Learning a lot from Manny, and getting requests for remodeling."

"Well, that's *gut* for business, I'm sure."

"Absolutely," he said, smiling. He touched her elbow lightly, leading her away from the group. "I'd still like to take ya for coffee, maybe after the Ping-Pong gathering next Saturday . . . okay with you?"

Lena's eyebrows lifted. She had not expected a renewal of this invitation.

"You look startled," Arden said, frowning thoughtfully. "Just thought we could talk for a while somewhere quiet."

She wondered what he had in mind to discuss. "Are things goin' better 'tween you and your father?"

"The reality is slowly settling in, and each day Dat's more understanding about what I'm reachin' for. I wouldn't say that he's happy 'bout it, though."

"Overall, you must be relieved."

Arden nodded. "When I'm not workin' with Manny, I still help round the farm when I can. I'll do that till Dat finds someone to take my place." He paused. "It's only right."

His words made an impression on her—whatever tensions existed between Arden and his father, it was clear that Arden was trying to do what he could to help make this news easier. And even after the parent sponsors called the youth back to the table and benches to sing a few more hymns, Arden's comments and his demeanor were foremost in Lena's mind.

After the final song—a lively rendition of "Shall We Gather at the River?"—she told Lydia in a whisper, "Arden wants to go for coffee with me next Saturday evening."

Lydia's face beamed. "This is so *gut* to hear!"

Lena shook her head. "Just havin' coffee doesn't change anything, okay?"

"All right, then." Lydia reached for her hand and squeezed it all the same. "But I'll want to hear about it sometime, *jah*?"

28

Lena attended another youth outing the following Saturday—a Ping-Pong play-off in the unfinished basement of Lydia's parents' home. As before, Arden lingered near the snack table, striking up a conversation with Lena over coffee and cookies.

Lena found it enlightening to learn more about Arden's new vocation. "Word's spreading quickly," Arden said, pleased, although he seemed humble about his woodworking skills, coming just short of saying he'd inherited the talent from his father. "I want to help others—it's important to be a good steward."

"Does Manny think the same way?" she asked while they held their coffee cups and nibbled on warm chocolate chip cookies.

"For the most part," Arden said. "Why do ya ask?"

Lena wouldn't share the few conversations she'd overheard between Harley and Mimi. "My father used to say that it's wise to partner with someone similar in attitude."

"Well, Manny and I might not see eye to eye on every jot and tittle of what we do with our personal finances, but we both want to build a strong business. Get established here locally for many years to come, Lord willing."

Lena still found it interesting that the two men were so keen on doing something other than farming—not so unusual in Centreville, but pretty much unheard of in Lancaster County. And she certainly had not missed the words *here locally*, either. Truly, Arden and Manny were working to build a business that they could pass down to their children.

———— ⌒ ⌒ ————

"Tell me more 'bout your brothers and sisters," Arden said once he and Lena Rose were seated in a small restaurant, not far from the location of the Ping-Pong gathering.

The place was rather empty, given the later-than-supper hour, and Lena assumed Arden might be glad if what he had in mind to discuss was as private as he'd seemed to indicate.

She folded her hands on her lap beneath the table. "Well, for one thing, Emma has a beau for the first time ever, which makes it hard . . . me bein' here and missing our sisterly talks. And Wilbur just started goin' to Singings. I missed his birthday, just like I missed Liz's and Verena's and Timothy's." She paused, thinking she must sound like she felt sorry for herself. "I don't mean to grumble."

He looked across the table at her, a caring expression on his face. "I can't imagine what you've endured," he said quietly.

The waitress came just then and took their order for coffee, then asked if there was anything else. Arden invited Lena to have a piece of pie.

"After all the treats earlier, I really don't need anything more," she said politely, not wanting him to spend much on her, since it wasn't really a date.

"What if we split a piece of pie?" he said, his smile encouraging her.

"It's up to you." She shrugged. "I would only have a taste or two."

"That settles it, then," he said with a glance at the waitress. "What kind will it be, Lena Rose? You choose."

She couldn't help but smile. "Coconut cream?"

"One of my favorites, too!" Arden winked at her and placed the order. After the woman left, he asked Lena, "Did you and your mother and Emma take turns cookin'?"

"Well, I helped more with sewing. With ten children, there was always someone needin' something. Then when Liz and Verena got a bit older, they sometimes took turns with Emma, making desserts and cookies." Lena wondered if Arden was curious about her cooking ability. "It was a busy, busy house, let me tell ya! And when we went out, it was a challenge squeezin' into even two carriages."

Arden tilted his head, listening.

"But really, the only time all of us had to crowd into the buggies was on Preaching Sundays. After the twins were born, and then little Chris, too, our relatives started comin' to see us on the off-Sundays from church. It was much easier that way, and Mamma and Dat appreciated not having to leave the house. Still, I kinda missed it. Dat used to let us chatter in the buggy till we turned out of the long driveway and onto the road."

"Then what?"

"He would put his fingers in his mouth and whistle sharply, which made some of us giggle. After that, we knew better than to make a peep."

Arden nodded. "That's a *gut* way to do it. My Mamm preferred us kids to be quiet in the buggy, too, at least when we were younger. Dat never seemed to mind, though—and trust me, he would've said somethin' if he had."

They talked a bit more about what they'd loved about growing up in large families; then she got off on a tangent and mentioned their family meetings. "They were originally Wilbur's idea back when he was ten or eleven. He really liked to call the meetings to order, and Dat would let him round up the other children beforehand, appointing him the speaker of the house."

Arden chuckled. "Now, *that's* funny."

"Well, the positions of president and vice president were already taken by Dat and Mamma, of course."

"These meetings . . . what sort of things were discussed?" Arden leaned back and crossed his arms, his blue-green eyes fixed on her.

"Oh, things like how much longer the girls were spending in the one and only bathroom compared to the boys, who naturally brought it up." She smiled. "And we talked about who would do which chores, too. Liz, for example, wanted to help in the barn, instead of washin' dishes. And there were times when Wilbur thought he shouldn't have to go to bed as early as the rest of us, because he didn't think he needed as much sleep."

Arden grinned, seemingly enjoying this.

"I guess you didn't have these kinds of meetings, then?" she asked.

"My parents decided most everything. There was very little input from any of us."

"Well, we only got to discuss activities and whatnot. We weren't involved in what you'd call any significant decision-makin'."

Arden drew a breath, his shoulders rising. "I hope talkin' like this isn't making ya more homesick, Lena Rose."

She shook her head. "Remembering the happy times isn't a sad thing. I don't want to forget them."

The waitress brought their coffee and the single piece of coconut cream pie, and the conversation moved on to other topics, including Rebekah Petersheim. "My Mamm thinks it's mighty kind of you to befriend her when others are a bit cautious."

Lena's skin prickled. "Why, though? Rebekah's as devout a woman as any I know."

"My parents and I have nothing against her," Arden said.

"She deserves only compassion," Lena said, though she didn't say more. Some things should only come from Rebekah's own lips.

"I like that 'bout you," Arden said softly and leaned forward. "You stick up for people. You're loyal."

She nodded, feeling pensive. "Dat and Mamma always were, too. I guess I learned it from them."

"You've been through so much . . . and you're still a strong person." Arden picked up his coffee cup and held it, looking over at her before taking a drink. Then, smiling, he said, "I've been thinking 'bout something lately . . . quite a lot, to tell the truth." He paused, his expression earnest. "This is what I wanted to talk to you about."

She wasn't sure what to expect.

"I'd like to be more than friends, if you're willin'."

She was tempted to say that it was too soon after her breakup with Hans, but she caught herself. It wasn't simply a matter of whether she was available. Lena needed to make things clear. "I'm flattered . . . but I'm determined to return to Michigan as soon as I can."

Surprisingly, Arden didn't seem fazed. "That doesn't mean I can't try to change your mind, *jah?*" He gave her the dearest smile, his eyes searching hers.

You might try, she thought, holding his gaze.

By the time they'd finished their coffee and the shared piece of coconut cream pie, the time had gotten away from them. "Goodness, I hope Cousin Harley isn't concerned," she said as Arden helped her into his shiny black courting buggy after paying the bill.

"I'll get ya right home." Arden ran around to the driver's side of the open buggy and leaped in, and they were off.

⁓ ᖇ ᖇ ⁓

As Arden directed his horse over near the mailbox on the shoulder of the road, Lena noticed the Stoltzfus farmhouse was dark except for the kitchen. He got out to help her down, holding her hand long enough to squeeze it gently. "I'll be thinkin' of ya this week, Lena Rose . . . praying, too."

She contemplated saying something pleasant back or simply thanking him, but nothing seemed appropriate. Certainly, she shouldn't encourage him, even though a part of her wanted to. It was real nice to have a fellow's attention again, especially one as good-looking and congenial as Arden Mast. "I had a *gut* time, and the pie was delicious" was her response. She waved to him and hurried up the driveway. "*Gut Nacht.*"

Just before she turned to step onto the walkway, she looked back and was surprised to see him still standing outside his courting buggy, its large red safety lights flashing. He raised his arm high to wave to her.

His words from earlier that evening echoed in her mind: *"I'd like to be more than friends."*

Never had her heart pounded so hard, clear up to her ears. Not waiting a second longer, Lena walked to the back steps and opened the door.

Harley was sitting by the upstairs window in Mimi's comfortable chair while she slept, waiting for Lena Rose. He hadn't worried, really, when she didn't arrive home as early as he had expected, but as he'd sat there praying about a number of things— one being his improving relationship with Manny Beiler—he offered a request for God to guide Lena as to her future, just as Mimi had also been fervently praying.

Now, thankfully, he could hear Lena's light footsteps on the stairs and knew she was safely home. Harley tried to imagine what it would have been like had he and Mimi ever made the trip to Michigan to see Cousin Jacob and his family. Might they have been closer . . . and might Tessa and Lena Rose have become friends?

Who's to know now? he thought as he pulled himself up from the chair to make his way to his side of the bed.

All through the rest of March, Lena continued to attend various youth outings—the evenings away helped her to feel less lonely. Lydia, it seemed, was usually with Eli, and Arden frequently sought out Lena. And while spending time talking with him was definitely something she looked forward to, the high point of each week remained the many letters Lena received from her family.

The sometimes foggy, wet mornings of March soon turned balmier, and Lena quietly celebrated her nineteenth birthday with the Stoltzfuses on Friday, March 24. Evidently a little bird had also alerted Arden, so Lena Rose had a visitor that evening who arrived with a wrapped present—a poetry book by Helen Steiner Rice—and a birthday card with a thoughtful greeting. Mimi didn't seem too surprised at Arden's arrival, as she had another placemat and dessert plate at the ready for Arden to join them for cake and ice cream.

Arden also stayed to play Dutch Blitz with all of them, including Solomon, whose spectacles kept slipping down his nose as he studied his cards. Thankfully, Solomon didn't make a big stir about Arden's being there, which only further endeared Harley's elderly uncle to Lena.

Then, when everyone retired for the night, Arden encouraged her to walk with him to the utility room, where he put on his coat and said, "I hope this is just one of many happy birthdays ahead for you, Lena Rose." He paused, and it seemed as though he wanted to say more, but instead, he reached to touch her hand before turning to head for the door.

Trying to ignore the fluttering in her stomach, Lena made her way upstairs, forcing herself to think only of her siblings, wishing they could have celebrated with her, too.

CHAPTER

29

A few days later, on a beautiful, fragrant Monday morning, after Lena had taken a short break from the sewing room to check the washing on the line, she noticed Mimi out sitting on her prayer bench, hands folded in her lap and her face turned heavenward. Lena hoped the woman was feeling better this morning.

Mimi had experienced an upset stomach over the weekend, so much so that yesterday afternoon she'd had to leave the kitchen to lie down for an hour or so. Then later, Lena had been alarmed when Mimi suddenly called out in pain from her bedroom, holding her right side as she hobbled through the kitchen to the back door, where she called for Harley, who was in the barn for milking.

"I'll go and get him," Lena had said, rushing out.

By the time Harley arrived, Lena right behind him, Mimi was sitting at the kitchen table saying she might need to see a doctor. Harley was all for it, but within a few minutes, Mimi had made a turn for the better and no longer seemed frightened. Harley suggested she take it easy and let Lena fix supper. So Mimi had been doing less since then, drinking peppermint tea and eating small amounts of chicken-and-rice soup. She'd said she felt some better after the rest and pampering her stomach.

Presently, however, Lena was keeping her eye on Mimi, who looked rather peaceful there on the prayer bench, the sunlight warming her dear face. *O Lord, grant Mimi a day free of pain, I pray.*

Lena decided to bring her sewing outdoors, where she could sit with Mimi. "How are ya feelin' now?" she asked, offering to get her something to sip on. "More tea, maybe?"

"I'll be all right," Mimi said, looking paler than normal. Her arms were folded tightly over her stomach. "I don't want ya to fuss over me."

"Not fussin' . . . I care about you." Lena spotted Harley coming this way. "Very much."

All of a sudden, Mimi gasped and clasped her chest, and a feeling of dread seized Lena—this was no stomach bug.

Harley was at his wife's side in an instant. It was clear from her moans that Mimi was in serious pain. Immediately, Harley hollered at Eli to get on one of the horses and ride "right quick" to the Grants'. "Call an ambulance. Hurry!"

With a horrified glance at his mother, Eli did as instructed without delay. In the same moment, Harley came around and lifted his wife in his arms and carried her swiftly into the house as Lena held the door for them.

Lena's heart was pounding and, feeling ever so anxious, she began to call upon the Lord for help. *Please take care of dear Mimi. Oh, please!*

⸺ ⟡ ⟡ ⸺

The emergency room was an unnerving place for all of them, particularly poor Mimi, who'd never spent a single day in a hospital and was now surrounded by doctors and nurses. One of the doctors had talked quietly with Harley, informing him that

Mimi was suffering a gallbladder attack, one severe enough to warrant emergency surgery.

Despite Harley's protests that both women needn't stay all night, Lena and Ada remained with Mimi during the long hours immediately following the invasive abdominal surgery. As for Harley himself, they urged him to return home to get some rest. "She'll need ya to be strong for her, Dat," Ada told him.

Barring any complications, Mimi would be in the hospital for three to four days, which meant Lena would need to do all she could around the house. During the daylight hours, she would cook and keep up with the sewing as much as possible before heading off to the hospital. That first evening, she and Ada and Tessa took turns sitting by Mimi, whose sisters and daughters-in-law also rallied to her side. In fact, the whole family agreed that she must have someone with her during her waking hours, hospital or no.

―⁂―

On the second afternoon following Mimi's surgery, Lena received an amazing letter from Aunt Mary Schwartz in Centreville, saying she knew of a young woman in the church district who needed a live-in mother's helper. *I believe we've found a way for you to return home, dear Lena!* Aunt Mary had written. *Remember Darlene Wickey? Well, her doctor has just ordered bed rest for the next six weeks till her second baby is due. Darlene and her husband need someone right quick to look after two-year-old Katie Ann. I took the liberty of telling her I was real sure you'd want to do this. Please write immediately and let me know.*

"Would I *want* to?" Lena said aloud, thrilled at this opportunity. *Glory be!* she thought, twirling around the kitchen. "I'm goin' home!"

Running upstairs, she pressed Aunt Mary's letter close to her chest and dashed to her stationery drawer. "Oh, this is the best news ever!"

Sitting down, she immediately wrote her answer, then pushed the letter into an envelope and addressed it. *I don't need to think twice about this!* She hoped she might borrow the buggy from Cousin Harley. *I must get to the post office before the evening mail goes.*

Just then, she remembered that Harley and Eli were milking the herd. She wouldn't bother them; she would need to wait till tomorrow's mail.

So she headed back to the kitchen, where she pulled out Mimi's cookbook to find something interesting to make for supper. As she flipped through the pages, her exhilaration faded as reality closed in. *What am I thinking?* She leaned against the counter. *Mimi needs me to keep the house running while she recuperates over the next month.*

Going to sit on the wooden bench at the long table, Lena felt the disappointment deeply, but she also knew what the Lord wanted her to do. *I'll need to write a different letter to Aunt Mary, declining and asking her to thank Darlene for thinking of me. For now, Mimi must come first. . . .*

After supper, as twilight tiptoed near, Lena strolled out to sit on Mimi's old prayer bench, a shawl wrapped around her shoulders against the springtime chill. The sounds of horses and buggies on the road out front, and people talking as they passed by, continued toward sundown as Lena sat there. She stared at the broom she'd used earlier to sweep off the walkway, having left it out by mistake. Biting her lip, she wished she could just burrow away inside the nearby potting shed, close the door, and cry without being heard.

Hadn't she prayed enough? She'd tried so hard to be patient

as her relatives and the brethren worked out a way for her to return home, and now she could not even accept the first real opportunity she'd had.

The longer Lena sat there, the more frustrated she became. Her neck muscles were in knots, as was her stomach. She had not known that a person could go from such happiness to frustration within such a short span of time.

At last, she began to pray. *O Lord, I give up. It's just not working out the way I'd planned.* She sniffled, holding back tears. *I surrender my longings for home . . . every last hope and dream of returning.* She paused for a moment, then, bowing her head in humility, she added, *If I'm to return, it will have to be up to Thee, O Lord. Amen.*

Sighing deeply, she felt a gentle breeze drift over her, like what Mimi described as the presence of the Holy Spirit. Lena felt the rigidity begin to leave her neck and shoulders, and she let her hands rest on the prayer bench on either side of her. *I'm at peace,* she thought. *Whatever happens now is God's will . . . and in His time.*

CHAPTER

30

Harley had just returned from Manny and Arden's shop, where he'd discussed the possibility of building on a smaller addition to the house for Solomon to move to eventually. Harley wanted to involve Manny as much and as early as possible, so he was getting the ball rolling with some initial conversation.

Presently, he sat down on the front porch overlooking the road and fields beyond. He thanked the Lord above for sparing his wife's life, mighty grateful the doctors had acted so quickly.

He was encouraged by Mimi's brave attempts now at becoming more mobile following the surgery—she was stiff and sore from the long incision, which impaired her ability to do the things she wanted. Still, she was far enough along to come home, and he could hardly wait for tomorrow afternoon's discharge from the hospital.

Harley had actually thought of going around the backyard to sit on his dear wife's prayer bench but didn't want to encounter anyone coming or going. He wanted a few moments of complete solitude, enjoying the sound of the birds calling as they flew back and forth amongst the trees.

He hoped Mimi would still get the rest she needed once home.

She'd inquired today for the umpteenth time about her sewing work, and Harley had been glad to let her know that Tessa planned to keep working with Lena Rose. Considering everything, Lena Rose had definitely been stretched thin. Thankfully, Lena's burden had been made easier by a good many of the womenfolk, including Lydia Smucker and her mother, Fannie, who had stopped by with prepared food. There had been almost too much food coming into the house, although they had shared it with Solomon and Eli.

Regarding Tessa and Lena, he had no inkling how they were getting along—his younger daughter had always seemed standoffish toward Lena Rose. Even so, the fact that Tessa wanted to help, as well as the fact that she'd been spending time with Mimi, was mighty encouraging.

As of yet, Manny had not come around to the house for a visit on his own, though Harley had stressed several times lately that the door was always open. Of course now, with Mimi's long recovery ahead, it would probably be a while longer. Even so, Harley knew it was only right to keep offering the hand of fellowship, attempting some sort of civil association. *A relationship more like the ones with my other in-laws*, he thought.

Stretching his arms high over his head, Harley drank in the warm, humid air and looked forward to Mimi's feeling strong once again. His loving wife had maintained her sweet spirit in spite of this painful trial. And what fierce determination she had!

He thought of Lena Rose's earnest desire to return to her siblings and realized that she, too, had that same admirable grit. Selfishly speaking, it would have been a bittersweet day for Mimi, and for him, too, if Lena had accepted the job as a mother's helper back home. Lena had shared with him about it at supper yesterday. *She turned it down to help Mimi through her recovery,* he thought, more thankful than ever for the young woman the Lord had brought into their lives.

Getting up just then, Harley walked back around the house to assess the pasture fencing. Later, he would mow the yard, a chore Mimi or Lena Rose would normally do, but with everything else Lena Rose had to do, Harley didn't mind temporarily taking on women's work. Even Solomon had offered to help with something, but his uncle wasn't in any shape to be walking behind a push mower.

Ada had mentioned coming over in the evenings when her husband was able to stay with the children. She also intended to keep Joey for Tessa on days Tessa helped with the sewing—a very good idea, given that Joey was crawling everywhere nowadays.

Witnessing his family's coming together this way gave Harley the shot in the arm he needed to keep plugging along with his farm—at least till the time was right to turn it all over to Eli. *One day, he and his bride, and their little ones, will live in this house,* Harley thought, and went to return to the farm work.

─ে৹ ৹ে─

Tessa stopped by to offer to continue helping Lena Rose with the sewing work, as she had done since her mother's hospitalization. This was a welcome surprise to Lena. *"Denki,"* she said, finding it encouraging, because during the past three days with Tessa, hardly a dozen words had been spoken.

After bidding Tessa good-bye, Lena went for a quick afternoon walk and pondered all that had happened, especially the news from home. She knew she had done right by Mimi in turning down the offer, but it didn't make things any easier.

Later that night, when Lena Rose was alone in her room, she found it hard to answer Mammi Schwartz's recent letter, which reported how downcast Chris and the rest of the family were feeling about having missed the chance to celebrate with Lena on her birthday.

My thoughtful little brother. She wondered how he would react if he heard she'd rejected an offer to live and work but a mile from where he lived with Dawdi and Mammi Schwartz. The thought made her gloomy again, and she resolved not to be the one to tell him.

Before going to bed, she opened her Bible and read for a while, hoping it would free her mind from self-pity. *Please work things out for me, Lord. For all of us.*

—⟡ ⟡—

"Can ya reach the pinking shears?" Lena asked Tessa the next morning. Friday had dawned with rain showers, and now that the sun was shining, the atmosphere felt heavy with humidity.

Tessa handed the shears to Lena. "I heard from Dat that you turned down an offer to work as a mother's helper back in Michigan."

Lena was startled that Harley had revealed this. "*Jah.*"

"Well, it took me by surprise." Tessa looked at her, eyes blinking. "You must care a lot for my Mamm."

Lena nodded. "She and your father took me in when no one else had room. I wasn't just an orphan . . . I felt homeless, to tell the truth."

Tessa was quiet for a time as she regarded Lena. "Honestly, I wasn't sure how to take it when you first arrived," she said. "And I didn't like how I felt, bein' so far removed from my hometown an' all . . . away from my family and feelin' like Mamm had replaced me in her sewing business. . . . Why, she even gave you my room."

Lena had wondered if this had been at the root of Tessa's coolness toward her. "No one could ever replace you, Tessa. I sure hope ya know."

They set to work again, talking only occasionally, but something had shifted, and Lena felt that the ice between them was broken. Things would surely work themselves out now. And she would keep doing her best to let Tessa know how essential she was to her family.

After their midmorning coffee break, Tessa asked, "Do ya think it's a *gut* idea to take on more orders, with Mamm unable to work for a few weeks yet?"

"Should we ask her, maybe?"

Tessa was quick to shake her head. "She has enough to think 'bout."

"Maybe let's just see how we do keepin' up, then."

"Well, if someone drops by with something they want Mamm to sew, I think we should just let that order wait," Tessa added. "Or if the customer is willin' to have you or me do it, that's fine."

"Sounds like a wise plan," Lena agreed, and Tessa gave her a small smile in return.

~ ⌒ ⌒ ~

That afternoon, Mimi was released from the hospital, though still a bit pale. Lena and Ada took great care to get her comfortably situated in the main level guest bedroom.

Later, Lena worked alone in the sewing room, where she thought about the things Tessa had shared from her heart. And an hour later, when the door opened and in walked Tessa to visit her mother, Lena was delighted, though not nearly as much as Mimi.

"It's nice to have you here to fuss over me," Mimi said after Tessa reached down to give her a gentle hug. "It's great to be home."

After Tessa and her mother had visited for a while, Mimi lay down for a rest, and Tessa checked in on Lena and the sewing. "I've got an hour to spare if you could use the help."

Lena gladly accepted, and as Tessa sat down in her mother's usual chair, she remarked, "You know, the days I've worked here with ya are the only ones I've ever been away from Joey," she said, looking well rested and cheerful.

"Joey's so cute," Lena said, happy for the conversation. "He puts the G in go."

"He's a handful right now, for sure." Tessa laughed.

"Oh, he'll grow up fast enough."

"You helped raise your little brothers and sisters, ain't so?" Tessa asked.

"Well, some of them, but especially Chris, my youngest sibling."

They talked about Lena's family, and then Tessa mentioned Manny's passion for cabinetmaking and remodeling work. "It's goin' amazingly well," Tessa said. "He and Arden have more customers than they ever hoped for, at least for two men just starting up." She paused a moment and glanced Lena's way. "Manny's told me that you and Arden are a couple and have been seein' a lot of each other."

Lena was a little shocked by this. "*Nee* . . . we're only friends."

Tessa gave her an odd look. "That's not what Manny thinks. He says Arden's determined to court you."

Is this what Arden's telling people? Lena wondered, realizing that more than just Manny might see their relationship that way. *Maybe I should be more careful . . . not spend so much time with him,* she thought, realizing she was on dangerous footing. But then, Lena didn't really want to stop seeing him. He was so understanding and fun to talk with; she'd miss him. Lately, she'd even found herself praying for Arden—for his new business to continue to prosper, and for his relationship with his father to improve, though Arden had said that his Dat wasn't as miffed now.

Tessa continued. "When we were dating, Manny used to tell

236

me, 'Ya don't have to have everything figured out to take the next step.'"

Lena wondered if, like Mimi, Tessa meant that God had everything planned for every person, and it was important to simply trust Him for the future. "Did what Manny tell ya help?" she asked, eager to know.

"Well, it helped me try not to worry about the details of things, *jah*. And here I am, married now and with our first baby."

Lena wished Mimi were here to weigh in on Manny's advice to Tessa. Would Mimi agree? Or would Mimi talk more about the importance of prayer in all of that?

Tessa grinned at her. "From what Manny says, Arden's a real fine fella."

Eli says the same thing, Lena thought, only smiling in return. *And I'd have to say he's right.*

CHAPTER

31

Harley was sweeping out the barn later the next morning when Manny Beiler's family buggy rolled into the driveway with Tessa and little Joey. "Well, what do ya know," Harley muttered, setting his push broom aside and opening the barn door.

He went out to welcome them, mighty pleased to see Manny carrying a fancy fruit basket all wrapped with yellow cellophane and a big gold ribbon.

"This here's for Mimi," Manny said and handed it to Harley before reaching to take Joey from Tessa, whom he helped down from the carriage. "Just thought we'd stop by an' say hullo."

"To celebrate Mamm's homecoming," Tessa added as she stepped across to the walkway that led to the back door.

Harley trailed behind with the large fruit basket, squelching a grin. *Mimi will be surprised to see her and Joey again so soon,* he thought. *And doubly pleased Manny's along.*

Lena came to the door and opened it; then when she'd greeted them and made over little Joey, she politely excused herself to see if Mimi was still resting while Tessa took the fruit basket from Harley and set it in the middle of the kitchen table.

Manny found a seat on the bench, put Joey on his lap, and

whispered in the little fellow's ear. Then Manny blew lightly on Joey's button nose, prompting giggles.

"Mighty nice of yous," Harley ventured, wishing he'd never been standoffish with Manny after he and Tessa married. *It's partly my fault he doesn't come round much*, he thought. *Tessa surely knows I was never pleased with her choice. Dummkopp, I was, and with such rigid expectations, too!*

Tessa glanced at Manny as if to encourage him to say something.

Manny lifted Joey and blew into his chubby little neck, creating a stream of cackles. "You wanna see your Mammi, don't ya?" Manny said in *Deitsch*, focusing his attention on the eight-month-old. "Here now, show Dawdi how old you're gonna be soon." Manny helped his son put up his chubby pointer finger. "There, that's right."

Soon Mimi appeared, Lena walking at her side as they came into the kitchen. *She's tuckered out*, thought Harley, going to assist her and motioning for Lena to have a seat at the table.

Manny held Joey up for Mimi, who leaned slightly to kiss her grandson's dimpled cheek. Then, seeing the fruit basket, she exclaimed, "*Ach* . . . what'd ya bring?"

"For you, Mamm," Tessa said, moving over to let Mimi sit next to her.

"What'd I do to deserve that?" Mimi shook her head, laughing. "Ain't done much of anything here lately."

"Aw, Mamm . . ." Tessa slipped an arm around her. "We're glad you're on the mend."

Mimi didn't go on like some folk might have in her condition, but she did say how she wished Joey might sit on her lap. "But I'd better wait till I'm completely healed up. Lord willin', it'll be soon." She smiled at Joey, who clapped his cute little hands just then.

Harley grinned at the boy, aware of the tender bond between Mimi and their youngest grandchild.

Manny and the family stayed awhile longer, and Tessa asked if there was anything more she could do in addition to helping with sewing projects.

"Oh, you just take care of your little one, my dear. Lena Rose will see to getting meals and such."

"Well, I'll still come over an' help wherever needed," Tessa added, offering Lena Rose a friendly smile. "Don't be shy about asking."

Harley noticed the exchange and was glad of it. *A relief,* he thought.

Eventually, Manny said he had to get back to work, so they couldn't stay very long, even though Mimi tried to convince them to linger for the noon meal. "I told Arden I'd help him wrap up a project this weekend."

"I'll see ya soon, Mamm," said Tessa as they rose from the table and said their good-byes. "Don't overdo things now as you feel better. I know how you are."

"Don't ya worry," Mimi said with a little wave. "Real nice to see all of yous," she said, looking now at Manny.

"*Jah,* come anytime," Harley said, thinking he should offer to shake hands with Manny. Then again, he didn't want to force himself where he wasn't wanted when Manny and Tessa had come without coaxing.

Next time, he thought.

Suddenly thinking the better of it, he reached toward his son-in-law and was pleasantly surprised when Manny gripped his hand in a firm handshake.

⁓ ᴄᴑ ᴑᴄ ⁓

Nearly three weeks passed, and Lena returned to attending numerous activities with *die Youngie,* including Ping-Pong, volleyball, and now, with the end of April approaching, sometimes going fishing with Arden. At last the day came when Mimi was ready to resume her sewing work, telling Harley and Lena at that Friday breakfast that she felt ready to sew for at least an hour or so, here and there. "I'm feelin' much more like my old self again. It won't be long and I'll be back to normal," she said as golden sunshine poured in through the windows Ada had scrubbed clean just that week.

Harley smiled broadly, as if buoyed by his wife's return to the regular order of things, and he thanked Lena for all she'd managed to do during the past weeks.

"Honestly, I was glad to help. I feel like Mimi's become my second Mamma," Lena admitted.

Mimi came over and gave her a hug. "Well, and if ya don't know it by now," she said, "I think of *you* as one of my daughters, Lena Rose."

A *daughter*, she thought, Mimi's words warming her heart.

—⁂⁂—

The next morning, while Lena finished washing floors in James Zook's house, he asked if she had a few minutes to chat. "Of course," she said and went to sit in the screened-in back porch with him while the floors dried. "You might've heard that Rebekah Petersheim has been comin' over to help me some," he said, his face turning a bit pink—he seemed rather guarded about sharing this.

"Oh *jah*, and such a fine cook she is." The fact was, Lena had only learned last week from Rebekah herself that the woman had been *"stopping by to visit"* James from time to time. The idea of the two formerly lonely souls spending time together had tickled Lena.

"Well, an' Rebekah's been doin' the washing for me, too . . . and some light housekeeping now and then."

Lena smiled. Rebekah hadn't told her *that*.

Still seemingly hesitant, James asked, "So what I'm getting at—if it's not too sudden—would ya mind if I had Rebekah do all the cleaning over here and whatnot?"

"Not at all." Lena would miss the man and the income, but she also felt relief that he had someone to look after him once she finally returned to Michigan, whenever that might be.

He held out his hand to shake hers. "You've been a godsend, Lena Rose."

"*Denki*, James. I've enjoyed my time here," she told him. "And Rebekah's a dear woman."

James's eyes lit up. "Ain't she, though? An' she says the nicest things 'bout *you*."

Lena didn't dare ask if James was thinking of marrying again. Most older folk their age just remained close friends. Even so, Lena had noticed all the smiles on James's face here lately.

"If you'd wanna work one more Saturday, that's fine," he was saying. "I really didn't give ya much warning."

She didn't want to complicate things, not if Rebekah was eager to help. "That's kind of ya, but it's not necessary."

"*Denki*," he said, "for understanding."

"I was real happy to help," she said, patting his wrinkled hand.

On her way home, Lena waved at a number of passersby in buggies, thankful for the warm sunshine. She felt happy for James and Rebekah, knowing from experience that friendship was a healing balm. And considering the difficulties and heartache both had experienced in losing a spouse, Lena liked to think they were being given a second season of love.

What about my own season of love? she thought suddenly. She had put the idea of courting on hold until she returned home, but truly Arden was as attentive as any beau she might hope for. He had been talking, here lately, of wanting to take her out for supper. But seeing how he looked at her, and aware of her own growing feelings for him, Lena worried that a real date might lead him to think she was ready to be his girlfriend.

Her hope had always been, and still was, to return home. *And Arden's home is here*, she thought, recalling what Eli had told her about Arden's first serious girlfriend and how he had let her go. *I can't fool myself. Things couldn't possibly be any different for us.*

32

As usual, Lena lived for each day's mail delivery. Emma's most recent letter had stated that she was still praying in earnest about Lena's return, as were all the children. *We want you home again, dearest sister!*

Lena could only imagine how much Chris and the others had grown by now, especially the younger boys. *Time is marching on,* she thought, yet she was more hopeful than she had been in weeks.

On this sunny afternoon at nearly the end of April, she ran barefoot out to the road to check the mailbox.

What she found awaiting her from Centreville was a letter from Clara, Preacher Yoder's wife. Clara relayed that their youngest daughter was moving to Berne, Indiana, to live with an elderly aunt, which meant she would be leaving her position as the teacher at the local Amish schoolhouse. And, of all things, Clara was writing to offer their daughter's room—and the teaching position—to Lena Rose. *Are you interested? The school board agrees you're the perfect choice,* Clara had written. *If so, may we hear back from you directly?*

Elated, Lena ran all the way back up the driveway, stubbing

her big toe on a pebble along the way, though that didn't slow her down. "Mimi . . . ya won't believe this!"

She arrived nearly breathless in the kitchen, where she found Mimi baking peanut blossoms to take to Rebekah Petersheim tomorrow for a birthday surprise.

"What is it?" Mimi asked, setting down the jar of peanut butter and turning around. "Is it *gut* news?"

In answer, Lena began to read the letter aloud. When she'd finished, Lena smiled. "I'm getting the desire of my heart at last . . . bein' offered *another* job back home! And this one'll last the whole school year!"

Nodding, Mimi blinked back tears.

"Are you all right?"

"I'm just so pleased," Mimi said, wiping her eyes.

Lena looked into the face of this most dear woman. "I shouldn't be quite so—"

"Honestly, it just took me by surprise," Mimi replied quickly. "I'm so glad for you."

Overjoyed, Lena took a deep breath to calm herself. She couldn't deny that she felt somewhat torn—she'd truly come to love the People here in Leacock Township.

She stared at the letter, knowing this was a miracle. *I've been asked to be a teacher like Mamma!*

Lena would be mindful, though, to be a little more sensitive and less dramatic when Harley came in later for supper. After all, he and Mimi had become her family here.

—⟋ ᢒ⟍—

"Lena Rose didn't seem all that happy 'bout that letter, did she?" Harley asked Mimi as they were getting ready to retire for the night.

"On the contrary, Harley. You should've seen her dash into

the house. *Nee*, she's thrilled to pieces, but she didn't want to make ya cry . . . like I did."

Harley snorted. "Menfolk don't weep that easily."

Mimi waved her hand at him. "For pity's sake, ya know what I mean."

He went over and wrapped his arms around the bride of his youth. "*Ich liebe dich*," he whispered.

She leaned up to kiss his cheek. "Our lives will change once Lena goes."

They had discussed this before, but then they had found solace in knowing Lena wouldn't be going any time soon. Now, though, it was all so very real. "Did she say when she'd be leaving?" he asked.

Mimi took down her waist-length hair and began to brush it. "Well, she didn't mention details. I suppose she'll learn more once she writes to accept the job."

"*Jah*," he said, going over to the bed. He raised the quilt and got in, feeling mighty weary all of a sudden.

"I'm hopin' with all my heart that Preacher Yoder and his wife will hold out the invitation till I send my answer. I'd be just sick if they didn't," Lena Rose confided to Mimi on their ride over to deliver the peanut blossoms and a birthday card to Rebekah the next day.

"Well, surely they will. You're their first choice, *jah*?" Mimi said, glancing at her right quick.

Lena nodded. "Sounds like it. It's such a wonderful opportunity that I'm having a hard time believing it's real."

"The Lord is faithful," Mimi said. "You turned down that other job offer to look after me . . . and now here's this *wunnerbaar* news." Reaching to clasp Lena's hand, Mimi said softly, "Life can be difficult, and we can't always see what's comin'." She released Lena's hand and drew a long breath. "But I've learned that by comin' to grips with that, my path ahead seems easier to follow. Does that make sense?"

Lena agreed.

"Most folk go through life wishin' things were easier . . . but, for the most part, it just ain't thataway."

"*Jah*," Lena said thoughtfully. "I've certainly learned that. And it helps to accept that it's goin' to be hard."

"Strange as that may sound, I've found it's ever so true, 'specially as the years go by." Mimi looked over at her and smiled. "With God's help and direction . . . that's where the peace comes from."

Lena could see that trust and acceptance on Mimi's face and in the way she lived her life. "My parents had that kind of peace, as well," she said softly. "And being here with you and Harley has reminded me of that."

For a long time, it was quiet in the buggy as Lena considered all that Mimi had just shared from her heart.

—⸱ ⸱—

They spent some time visiting with Rebekah, who happily sampled the peanut blossoms, then passed them around to the youngsters. Lena was pleased when little Emily came into the front room and took her by the hand. "Can we go outside?" she asked.

Rebekah nodded and laughed, saying it was all right, and Cora Ruth and Mimi seemed content to stay put.

"I have a bunny rabbit," Emily said, still clasping Lena's hand. "Dat built him a hutch on wheels."

"What's your bunny's name?" Lena asked as they walked into the barn to the raised wooden pen. She looked down at the pure white bunny, his pink little nose pushing against the screen.

"It's Nibbles." Emily giggled.

Lena laughed. "The perfect name."

Emily opened the pen and reached in to pick up Nibbles and give him to Lena Rose. "He's so soft and cute," Lena said, holding the wiggly bunny close.

Emily reached to take him, but her face turned sad just then. "Mamma says you'll be goin' home real soon."

"Aw, honey." Lena crouched down to her. "It's been too long since I've seen my brothers and sisters."

"Nibbles's brothers and sisters live somewhere else, too." Emily stroked the bunny's white head. "But he's stayin' here with me. . . ." Emily's lower lip slipped out. "Why can't *you* stay, too, Lena Rose?"

Lena hugged her, then tried to turn her attention back to the bunny, feeling nearly as sad as Emily looked.

⁓ ⁓

As soon as they returned home, Lena wrote a short letter to Clara Yoder, thanking her and her husband for the invitation, and asking them when they'd like her to arrive. *I couldn't be happier, knowing I'll see my brothers and sisters and everyone else there again. This is truly an answer to my prayers!*

She addressed the envelope and licked it shut. *How will Arden take this news?* She certainly didn't want to hurt him, yet he'd known from the start that she planned to go back home one day. Even so, Arden had come to mean much more than she'd ever intended. And because they'd shared so openly all these months, becoming closer each time they were together, she wondered if he might wish she wouldn't take the job.

"How *will* he react?" she murmured, knowing he had to hear this directly from her before word got out.

⁓ ⁓

Arden might have thought they'd just come to fish, as Lena sat with him on the grassy creek bank that evening. Her stomach in knots, Lena was determined to see this through. *When the moment's right,* she thought, hoping it wouldn't be too difficult.

Making things worse was Arden's nearness just now, and she wanted the feeling to last a little longer. The ground was soft, and she tucked her long dress beneath her legs while Arden combed through his tackle box. He turned to her and grinned. "I can't believe you put up with my fishin' hobby," he said. "Real glad ya joined me again, Lena."

She nodded, trying to squelch the impending sadness.

"You do know that the way to a man's heart is to go fishin' with him," he said, giving her a wink.

"Well, I thought it was supposed to be food."

Arden frowned a bit humorously, as if giving it some thought. "*Jah,* you're right, food's first." His laughter was cheering, and she wanted to memorize its sound.

Expertly, Arden tied a fly on the end of his line and explained that one of the best times of the day for trout fishing was just after the sun dropped below the tree line, when the mayflies appeared in swarms above the creek, knotting and mating in midair. "When they land on the surface, the trout rise out of the water to feed on them," Arden said very quietly as they continued to sit in the long, soft grass, waiting with their fishing rods—dry flies on their fly lines. "It's fun to watch."

She smiled for him, capturing each moment in her memory for always.

"Mayflies can be fickle. Sometimes they show up, and other times not," he said, then added, "Mayfly swarms are a sign of clean water. But the water temperature and the air have to be just right."

The sky was still light, but only a patch of it could be seen through the thicket of trees on either side of the clear stream. Recently, she'd taken notice of the beguiling twinkling lights at dusk as the lightning bugs came out. What joy it was when Harley and Mimi's grandchildren came over for supper, then went out to chase after them, giggling and having themselves a wonderful-good time.

A chorus of crickets and katydids were the music of twilight, there in that private haven. And Lena thought about the news she must share with Arden.

It's time, she thought, hoping she wouldn't stumble over her words.

But at just the moment she'd worked up the courage, Arden stood up and offered his hand, helping her to her feet.

"Watch now," Arden whispered, leaning closer and pointing out the first two or three mayflies as they quivered a few feet above the water. As dusk tiptoed in, dozens more mayflies joined them, tethering and hovering close to the rippling stream before unknotting and flitting away.

Following Arden's lead, she moved silently to the edge of the creek bank.

He glanced at her, gesturing with his pole as if to remind her of what he'd shown her to do. "Get ready to cast your line," he said barely above a whisper.

A thrill rushed through her as his arm brushed against hers. She nodded as Arden took his position several yards from her. And in this moment, just as she was gathering the courage to reveal her plans to return home to teach school, she realized that somewhere along the line they'd become more than friends. *What Tessa said was true. We are a couple.* She blinked back tears. *Ach, what have I done?*

Lena turned to watch the mayflies come to rest on the creek's surface. She felt anxious, her eyes fixed on the flies and the surface of the water, wondering if she could catch a fish to take home to the woman who thought of her as a daughter. *Can I?* she hoped now.

Then, in that instant, she saw the trout rippling the surface of the water, some rising above it . . . ever so many.

Quickly, she cast her line.

After they had removed the string of trout from the cold water and placed them in a bucket, Lena still hadn't gotten the nerve to tell Arden. After these many months here, wouldn't she be foolish to outright reject his offer to court her? After all, Hans hadn't looked at her the way Arden had. Yet she'd done her best to keep any feelings of romance at bay while here in Lancaster County. Until recently, Lena thought she'd succeeded . . . at least on her part.

Truth was, fishing with Arden tonight, catching his joyful glances and sensing how appreciative *he* felt, she was torn. Torn between her growing feelings for him and knowing she would *never* return to Michigan if she agreed to be his sweetheart-girl.

She sighed and was aware of the lump in her throat. Oh, but it was going to be so hard to walk away from this most wonderful friend!

Minutes rushed by, and they gathered up their belongings and the bucket of fresh trout, then headed past the dense underbrush near the creek, toward his father's meadow.

She made herself finally say, "Arden, I'm real sorry . . . but I have somethin' to tell ya."

He stopped walking, his features visible in the fading light. "You're apologizing for somethin' you haven't said?"

"My heart aches for my family. You know that." She managed to take a breath. "I'm goin' back to them."

Arden set down the fishing rods and the bucket. "Soon?"

She nodded as tears stole down her cheeks.

His eyes searched her face, and then he was reaching for her, gently consoling her and taking her into his arms. "You love your family," he whispered against her hair. "And they love you." He pulled away to look at her. "I understand *that* most of all."

And then he wrapped his arms around her again. She felt breathless, scarcely able to think of her next words, let alone enough to push Arden away as she must. Because, wrapped in his tender embrace like this, she longed to stay there, his heart beating against hers, her head on his shoulder. To step away from him seemed unthinkable . . . the last thing she wanted to do. "Arden, I . . ." She moved slightly to look into his face.

"What is it, Lena?" he asked, still holding both of her hands. "Talk to me."

"I've accepted a teaching position at the Centreville Amish schoolhouse," she said, her voice breaking. "But now . . . being here with you . . . I'm wondering if—"

"*Ach,* you need to take it," he said, to her great surprise. "Without a doubt."

Feeling confused, she looked down at their hands—the way they were entwined seemed so right. *Of course I'll take the job.*

But she needed to hear it again. "Are ya ever so sure?"

Letting go, Arden straightened and nodded his head. "I hear you're a fine teacher."

She sighed. Her work with Rebekah Petersheim had gotten out.

"God's given you a gift," he said. "This is an opportunity you can't pass up."

He's right, she thought.

Another bittersweet moment passed between them. Then, with a sad sort of smile, he picked up the fishing rods, and they fell into step on the trail.

—⟡ ⟡—

Before the mourning doves were awake and cooing near her window, Lena pushed herself out of bed the next morning to tiptoe over to light the lantern on the dresser. She gazed into the small mirror, the reality of leaving Lancaster County—and Arden Mast—dawning anew.

As the first glimmers of sunlight crept beneath the dark green window shade, she went to raise it enough to peek out at the sun's rays breaking through the clouds at the horizon line. Their brilliance spread over the vast hay fields below, and her gaze drifted down to Mimi's prayer bench. Lena realized that she had so very much to be grateful for.

A lump rose in her throat, and she turned away from the window, then pulled the shade down to get ready for another day. *Arden will carry on with his life here,* she thought, *knowing that all too soon we will be saying good-bye . . . forever.*

CHAPTER

33

It was hard to know what was going through Arden's mind when Lena Rose spotted him across the side yard that Preaching Sunday. She was waiting outdoors with Lydia and Vera and the other young women for the shared meal at noon. Arden was definitely smiling at her, though not the vibrant grin she'd become accustomed to.

Fondly, she remembered their numerous talks, especially how keenly interested he'd seemed in each of her siblings . . . the way he often asked specific questions about them. Those memories were a comfort, as was the memory of Arden's strong arms around her Tuesday evening after fishing for trout—but she dared not ponder that now.

—◌ ◌—

The arrival of May was accompanied by sweet scents of honeysuckle, bell-shaped lily of the valley, and Kousa dogwood. Lena greeted the month with enthusiasm, knowing she would soon be with her family again. That first day, Mimi started planning a family picnic for the following Saturday at the farmhouse. Lena enjoyed helping Mimi with the menu and looked forward to seeing all of the Stoltzfus children and their families.

While they sewed, Lena and Mimi talked of how much fun it would be to have the whole family on the grounds at the same time. "This rarely happens," Mimi told her.

"Maybe Manny should think about expanding your kitchen so there's more room for everyone come Christmas," Lena joked.

Mimi laughed. "Well, that won't happen." She mentioned that Harley wanted Manny and Arden to build another *Dawdi Haus* for when Eli married. "I 'spect it won't be long till my kitchen is someone else's."

Hearing Arden's name gave Lena an unexpected rush of emotion, and she was relieved when Mimi went on to other, more mundane topics of conversation related to the picnic.

This'll be my chance to thank the entire Stoltzfus family for taking me under their wings, Lena thought, pleased with the idea. She wished she might also thank Arden for being such a compassionate friend, but how? And when?

Lena went to heat up the flatiron on the wood stove, still so lost in contemplation that she actually scorched one of Cousin Harley's trousers when she went to press them. "Oh no," she groaned. "Just look what I did." Embarrassed, she showed the seared spot to Mimi. "I'll buy material and make another pair," she said, choking back tears, though her tears stemmed from more than the scorching.

"*Ach* . . . we'll patch it," Mimi said as she inspected the problem area. "Those trousers are old—no need to fret."

"But I—"

"You have a lot on your mind, don't ya, dear?" Mimi took the trousers from her and set them aside in a basket of other family mending.

"S'pose so, but nothin' compared to what you've been through this spring."

Mimi's smile was sweet and encouraging as she returned to her chair. "I'm thankful to be doin' so well now; you mustn't coddle me any longer."

Breathing a sigh of relief, Lena went and gave Mimi a little kiss on the cheek.

⁓ ⁓

The days before the picnic came and went without a word from Arden. Lena Rose knew it was part of adjusting to this new and lonely life, yet something in her wished he might have kept in touch. *Since we've been such close friends.*

Another loss, she thought while beginning to think ahead to packing. Next Tuesday she would finally depart for home.

Thankfully, Mimi was now able to work her usual hours, and Harley had mentioned that very morning that he'd noticed the spring in her step once again. But it was especially good to hear Mimi laugh. *Her laughter is a song to those around her,* Lena thought, knowing how much she would miss her.

⁓ ⁓

The men in the family had gotten up early to go fishing on the day of the picnic. Mimi and Lena took advantage of the extra time alone for some last-minute preparations, including making a large quantity of meadow tea and lemonade.

The menfolk arrived right on time for the meal of barbecued chicken, potato salad, baked beans with ham bits, and homemade applesauce with cinnamon. To top it off, there was a four-layer chocolate cake and ice cream, too.

"What would a picnic be without sweets?" Mimi said as she and Lena laid out the food on the kitchen counter. "Once everyone arrives, we'll take the serving dishes outdoors," she added. "Fewer flies thataway."

Harley and Eli had set up a number of tables in the backyard, more than Lena thought necessary, and Mimi arranged some old quilts on the lawn for the children to sit or play on. Near the back of the house, pink tulips and blue hyacinths bloomed abundantly, and mature lilac bushes marched along its sides, creating a fragrant and pretty backdrop for this first picnic of the year. It was a perfect, sunshiny Saturday.

When the family members had gathered, the men milled around talking and then claimed their spots at various tables. The young girls jumped rope, and the little boys played jacks on the back walkway, while the older school-age children darted amongst all of them, playing hide-and-seek.

Lena chatted with Tessa and Ada as they carried the many picnic items from the kitchen, taking note of all the side dishes the daughters and daughters-in-law had brought. *Goodness, we'll all be eatin' leftovers for days!* It was after she'd set down the potato salad that she noticed several more buggies arriving. Surprised to see Lydia Smucker and her parents, and then Melvin and Cora Ruth with their little ones climbing down from the back of the buggy, Lena turned to ask Tessa about it. But little Joey was fussy just then, so his mother hurried over to him, leaving Lena Rose to wonder all the more, especially when James Zook and Rebekah Petersheim drove up next, both dressed in churchgoing attire.

Are all the People coming?

Harley couldn't help but glance at Lena Rose every couple of minutes, amused by her reaction to all the supposedly unanticipated guests—each family bringing more food to share. He hurried over to greet James Zook.

"Hullo," he said, a grin on his face when he observed James help Rebekah Petersheim down from the carriage. "This was a *wunnerbaar-gut* idea you had, Rebekah."

"I'll say 'twas," James replied with a smile at Rebekah, who didn't look like she was going to abide by tradition and go help the womenfolk. Rather, she stayed right there with James, her face fairly glowing.

"You kept it a secret, *jah?*" Rebekah said, then asked if the preachers had arrived.

Harley nodded. "Haven't seen the brethren yet, but they'll be here soon. Not sure both preachers are comin'."

"Well, we couldn't have asked for a better day for this," James said, standing taller, his cane at his side. He gave Rebekah a winsome smile.

"Was thinkin' that, too," Harley said, happy to stand there making small talk and enjoying the pleasant breeze.

A few minutes later, Bishop Amos arrived with Patricia, followed by Preacher Elam with his family, and then behind them, the deacon with his wife and little ones.

"Looks like we're nearly all here," Harley said, excusing himself to walk over to welcome the ministers.

"I thought this was a *family* picnic," Lena told Eli quietly as she brought out glasses of iced mint tea for some of the older folk, including Solomon, who sat on the prayer bench with Blackie panting at his feet.

"Looks like it's that and a few more." Eli adjusted his straw hat.

"Sorry, I shouldn't have said it like that," she told Eli. "*All* of yous are my family."

Eli grinned and bobbed his head. "We think of you thataway, too, Lena Rose. We really do."

Later, when the bishop removed his straw hat and led the silent mealtime prayer, Lena folded her hands and thanked God for the bounty of picnic food before adding her gratitude for the wonderful Leacock community she was blessed to know.

Lydia, Tessa, and Ada, as well as Mimi and little Emily Ebersol, all chose to sit with Lena at a table under one of the oak trees. "Have ya ever noticed how much better food tastes when eaten outdoors?" Lydia asked after finishing a drumstick. Emily looked puzzled and asked how that could be, which brought a round of laughter to their table.

Blackbirds called from the treetops, and Blackie began to bark at them till Solomon spoke sharply to him in *Deitsch*. The German shepherd let out another muffled yip before lying back down again by the prayer bench, his eyes still on the birds.

Lena realized how much she was enjoying herself in that moment, not striving and yearning to be elsewhere with nearly every thought, like she often had since her first day here. Looking into the faces of the people around her, she realized she was finally at peace.

When they'd eaten their fill—a few of the men had thirds— Mimi invited everyone to have cake and ice cream, or any of the other tempting dessert offerings.

Lena declared she was too full but was tickled pink to spot Arden near the dessert table, although he hung back on the sidelines.

"*Ach*, ya must have a little something sweet, Lena Rose," Lydia urged, inviting her to have a look-see at the spread of goodies over yonder.

Smiling, Mimi agreed. "Doesn't hurt to have a look."

So Lena Rose went along with Lydia. "I wish every day could be a picnic sort of day," Lena said, meaning it.

"You do seem awful happy." Lydia glanced at her.

Rebekah was standing near the pies and cookies and Mimi's enticing chocolate cake. Grinning, Rebekah came over and gave Lena a hug, as sunny as a schoolgirl in love. "*Wie geht's*, Lena Rose?"

"Doin' fine, but even better because I get to see you today!"

"Ever so happy to be here." Rebekah smiled sweetly. "*Denki* again for the birthday goodies and that card. It was nice of you and Mimi to remember me."

Lena patted her hand. "We love ya."

The older woman smiled all the more and asked if Lena was going to have some dessert or just look at it.

Lena laughed. "You sound like Mimi."

At the far end of the table, Lena noticed an upside-down straw hat filled with envelopes and notes. Then it dawned on Lena: As radiant as Rebekah was looking today, this must be a spur-of-the-moment wedding, which would explain why the ministers were present. *I had no idea they were doing this!*

While they decided which dessert to choose, Lena kept mum about her suspicions. *Does Lydia know what's going on?* she thought, wondering if she might find a discreet moment to ask her.

Lena had just finished eating Mimi's delicious chocolate cake and a scoop of homemade vanilla ice cream when Harley rose, hatless, held up his hands, and looked out at the small crowd, waiting before he began to speak.

The talking died down to a murmur, then ceased altogether.

"It's nice seein' all of yous here today. We have the opportunity to honor someone who has come to mean so much to us all."

Lena smiled over at Rebekah, who smiled back at her. *How sweet to have found love after all the dear woman's been through,* she thought.

Harley continued to talk. "I'm sure ya can agree that she has become like a daughter to Mimi and me, and much more than a friend to our community. . . ."

Lena resisted the impulse to raise her eyebrows. *More like a mother, he surely means.*

Harley motioned to someone, who brought him the hat brimful with envelopes.

This is odd, Lena thought.

Then Harley turned to Lena's table and looked directly at *her.* "This here's just a small token of our love for ya, Lena Rose."

What on earth?

Harley walked over and placed the upturned straw hat in front of her. And she frowned, ever so confused.

"This'll help ya remember us," he said, a big smile on his ruddy face.

Lena was so surprised she could scarcely breathe.

"You have your friend Rebekah to thank." Harley pointed to Rebekah, who had returned to sit at the next table over with Cora Ruth and Fannie Smucker, Lydia's mother. "All of us pray you'll go with God, Lena Rose."

Touched at their loving gesture, Lena put her hand on her chest and shook her head. "I hardly know what to say. *Denki* to everyone." Lena rose and saw the large gathering . . . all of them looking her way. And Arden smiled at the perimeter, arms folded as he stood there with Eli.

She caught Harley's eye where he'd returned to sit with Aaron and his other sons. How could she forget the times he'd dropped everything to drive her places? And there was Mimi, eyes shining . . . oh, all the heart-to-heart talks they'd enjoyed! Looking then at Lydia, Lena was sincerely grateful for such a friend. *Like a close sister.*

Truly, there were so many people here she had come to care for: wise old Solomon, as his father had so astutely named him; and Preacher Elam King, whose sermon her very first Preaching service there had brought tears to Lena's eyes.

And little Levi, Aaron and Sadie Ann's youngest, sat on one of the quilts with his older sisters—the little boy who'd fallen for Solomon's Christmas story about the shrunken pony.

So many wunnerbaar-gut *friends,* she thought, her heart full.

"I'll never, ever forget your kindness to me," Lena said. "Not just today, but on all the days I've spent here in beautiful Leacock Township."

Now everyone was clapping, and Rebekah hurried over and whispered in her ear, "Look at all those cards and notes! You'll have plenty of reading material for the journey home."

Lena gave her a hug. "Ain't you somethin'!"

A line began to form then, the men coming to shake Lena's hand, and the womenfolk hugging her neck. Lydia's tears threatened to spill over, and Tessa gave Lena a gentle embrace as little Joey crawled over to Lena and wanted to be picked up. She reached down for him, cuddling Joey for a moment before he wiggled, wanting down again.

Later, when the visiting ended in time for afternoon milking, Lena helped Mimi clean up the kitchen. "Well, I have to admit you took me completely off guard with that picnic. And here I thought James and Rebekah were going to tie the knot in some informal sort of wedding!"

"You really thought that?" Mimi looked surprised as she dried her hands on the kitchen towel. "*Nee*, this was always gonna be your day, Lena Rose."

"I don't know how to repay ya."

Mimi shook her head. "That's the beauty of giving . . . and you've certainly done just that from the moment you arrived." She smiled and suggested that Lena take the brimming straw hat upstairs to read the cards in private.

Lena felt quite humbled and almost shy. "You all kept it such a secret."

"Oh, we tried." Then Mimi added, "And lest I forget, Eli offered to accompany you to the bus depot when it's time." She paused. "No rush on our end, I hope ya know."

"So nice of him, but there's no need, really." *I came here on my own; I can manage,* she thought. "I'll be sure to thank him, though."

"Let me know what ya need as far as packing . . . or whatever else."

To think she was actually leaving—Lena's head was whirling with the knowledge. Assuming Clara Yoder had kept it a secret, Lena would arrive in Centreville even before her siblings heard the news. *What a grand surprise!*

With that wondrous thought, Lena headed upstairs with Harley's full straw hat, still amazed at this lovely turn of events.

───※ ※───

Before opening the envelopes, Lena placed the hat on the bed and knelt down. Folding her hands against the bed quilt, she remembered what Solomon had said back months ago. *"No one but* Gott *knows our comin's and goin's from one day to the next."* He had also encouraged her to give her worries to the Lord, she recalled.

Uncle Solomon was right, she thought, bowing her head to give thanks.

She lingered there after her prayer was finished, pondering how often Mimi offered gratitude to God. *I'll remember to do the same.*

When she rose, she dumped the contents of the hat onto the bed—it was soon apparent that everyone had brought a card or letter.

There were pretty homemade cards from Lydia and Rebekah, and one especially thoughtful note from Tessa, who assured Lena not to worry about Mimi working alone—*I plan to sew alongside Mamm again like before I got married. Manny thinks it's a good idea, and besides, it'll be nice for Mamm—well, for both of us. But we'll miss you, Lena Rose!*

Lena wiped away a tear, thinking how far she'd come with

Tessa. Then, reaching for the next card, she recognized Arden Mast's handwriting.

Dear Lena Rose,

I hope you enjoyed your special picnic. Harley and Mimi are far better at keeping secrets than I would've suspected.

I'm already praying for your safe trip home . . . and a joyful reunion with your siblings. They'll be so happy to have you near them again! To be honest, I can't say I blame them.

May God keep you and your Michigan family in His care always.

I'm so glad I met you, Lena Rose! My only regret is that we didn't have more time together.

Sincerely yours,
Arden Mast

"I'm glad, too, Arden," she whispered. "Ever so glad." Reluctantly, she placed the note back in its envelope and put it in the drawer with his other occasional cards.

She continued reading the other farewell greetings, trying not to think too much about Arden. Even so, considering the fact that he had been so eager to court her and keep her right there in his beloved Leacock Township, she could not get over the fact that he'd not only come for the picnic, taking time off from his booming business, but had written such a nice send-off.

If only she could thank him in person . . . but she didn't dare.

34

After supper the following Monday, Lena wandered down the driveway and headed for the road, anxious to walk off some tension from packing. Tomorrow, she would at last depart for home.

She heard someone whistling a tune and turned to see Arden, his fishing pole slung over his shoulder. "Hullo," Lena said when he spotted her. "Catch anything?"

"A few, but I tossed 'em back."

"Oh?"

"Jah. Dat's been fishin' a lot lately, so Mamm's plumb tired of cleaning and cookin' fish."

"So ya went just for the fun of it?"

He nodded. "Perty much." Smiling, he stopped near the old tree that grew near the road, a shady spot where Lena had sometimes paused to read letters from home when she was too eager to wait till she got in the house. "But to tell the truth, I was hopin' to see you one last time, Lena Rose."

She didn't let on that she'd hoped so, too. "Well, I'm all packed up and ready to go," she said, trying for his sake not to sound too excited.

"Sure wish I could be a frog in the bog out there, observing your reunion with your siblings. 'Specially little Chris."

She nodded. "It's been such a long time. I can hardly wait now."

"Well, I'll be cheerin' you on from here," Arden said, and with a wink, he headed up the road.

She watched him go, and something inside her longed to run after him. Instead, she called, "*Denki* for bein' such a *gut* friend!"

"It was easy, Lena Rose," he said, turning to wave. "*You* made it easy."

"*Hatyee*," she whispered, scarcely able to speak and wishing they didn't have to part. She couldn't imagine not ever seeing him again. "So long, Arden."

⸺ ☙ ❧ ⸺

"Remember how we felt the day she came to us?" Harley asked Mimi as they stood at the end of the driveway, watching the taxicab take Lena Rose down the road.

"She was heartbroken, poor thing, yet she smiled for us," Mimi said softly; then her hand was over her mouth.

"Lena Rose is always thinkin' of others," Harley murmured as he walked with Mimi toward the front porch, where they sat, nearly dazed. He hadn't thought he'd be shedding tears over seeing the young woman off. But there he was, pulling his blue-and-white kerchief out of his trousers pocket.

"Aren't we a sight?" Mimi said, patting his knee.

"She filled up the house with joy in spite of her own sadness."

"I'll say." Mimi smiled at him. "Let's think on that, *jah*?"

"It's obvious she's excited to go home," Harley added. "Heard from Eli that Arden Mast encouraged her to go ahead with the teachin' position out there."

"Makes ya wonder."

Harley nodded, agreeing with Mimi. How would Lena's leaving affect what had seemed like a budding relationship between her and Arden?

Harley closed his eyes, taking this moment away from his field work to reminisce and to comfort Mimi. He imagined Lena Rose arriving in Centreville, running to meet that little brother of hers. He still could kick himself for never really knowing Jacob's Elizabeth and their brood. But he'd been fortunate to know Lena Rose, and if she was any indication of who the rest of them were . . . well, Jacob had been a blessed man.

"You all right, love?" Mimi asked. "You're awful quiet."

"Just thinkin', is all. You?"

Mimi patted his hand. "Manny and Tessa are bringin' supper over tonight. Ain't that nice?"

"Bringing the boy, too?" Harley chuckled.

"Oh, you—'course they are."

Harley would have liked to stay put right there, but that would have to wait till someday when he could sit with this sweet woman of his for as long as he wished. "Time to finish plantin' corn," he said, rising with a grunt.

"I have work to do, too," Mimi said.

"Why don't ya leave redding up Lena Rose's room for another day," he suggested, thinking how hard it might be to do today.

"Ada's comin' tomorrow to help with that," Mimi said as she walked into the house by way of the front door.

Harley headed back around the side, out to catch up with Eli and the field workers. *O Lord in heaven, go with Lena Rose this day . . . and for all the days of her life,* he prayed. *Bless her with Thy loving-kindness and grace.*

—⁓ ⁓—

Glad for every stop during the long overnight bus trip, Lena stretched her legs as they finally pulled into the Elkhart, Indiana, station. She hoped the driver she'd lined up to get her to Centreville would be on time. Preacher Yoder's farmhouse was close to her grandparents' *Dawdi Haus*, as well as to where Emma, Verena, and Liz were living . . . none of them far from the schoolhouse, either. Lena Rose would be walking quite a lot to visit them, and happily so. *After all the sitting and sewing,* she thought with a smile, wondering how Mimi was doing now that she was gone. And Harley, too. Her last week there had been a whirlwind as she prepared to leave.

She smiled at the memory of the "family picnic," still vivid in her mind. She gathered her things and disembarked from the bus, then went to wait in the line for her suitcases.

Centreville is just over the Indiana border, she thought, excited. *Thirty-one miles and I'll be home!*

—⁂—

It was nearing eight o'clock that morning when Lena's driver slowed to make the turn onto the familiar dirt road, the very one where Dat had first taught her to drive their horse and buggy, and the road their family had faithfully taken so many times to Preachings. How often had she and Mamma gone this way to Murk's Village Store or to the post office? The memories soared in Lena's mind, and she felt surprisingly wide-awake in spite of having spent the night on the bus.

She knew this idyllic area like the back of her hand, but seeing it again made her want to get out of the cab and walk the rest of the way to Preacher Yoder's place. Resisting the urge, she leaned into the seat and gazed out the window as they rode past the field where pumpkins were often harvested in the fall. Farther up, cattle grazed on fertile land, and at the end of one of the lanes, Lena spotted a cardboard sign with the words *Sewing and Alterations* printed in large letters. Immediately, her thoughts flew to Lancaster County and to Mimi and Harley . . . and Arden.

As they turned into Preacher Yoder's narrow dirt driveway, Lena Rose reached into her purse for her wallet to pay the driver. She could hardly wait to surprise her siblings. But right now, Lena wanted to visit with Clara Yoder, to thank her in person for this amazing opportunity, even though she'd already expressed her appreciation in a letter.

After paying for the ride, Lena carried her heavy suitcases up the walkway. Red and white geraniums filled the clay pots on either side of the wide porch steps, and a redwood swing hung at the far end of the porch. She leaned over to rub the neck of the Yoders' yellow Lab. "Remember me, ol' boy?"

Just then, Clara Yoder opened the screen door, her blue eyes lighting up. "You're here!" She showed Lena to her new room, conveniently near the kitchen and with an east-facing window. *Just like at Harley and Mimi's,* she thought.

Clara offered to cook breakfast for her, which Lena politely turned down, having nibbled on an apple and some snacks earlier. "If ya don't mind, I'd like to go and surprise my brothers and sisters—at least the ones not in school."

"Well, Wilbur's away at the RV factory, I'm sure ya know," Clara said. "He's likin' his job there. But Emma should be around. She's been baking quite a lot, talkin' about getting a job at a bakery somewhere."

"I'm not surprised," Lena said, again thanking Clara for inviting her to stay there and for thinking of her for the teaching position. "You have no idea how happy I am to be here at long last!"

Clara nodded. "The People will be glad to know you've made it back—so many have been askin' about you. My husband and I had hoped you'd arrive in time to meet with the school board to discuss the curriculum for next year, and before the annual cleanup at the schoolhouse, comin' up in July. This is ideal timing."

"Well, I hope you aren't putting yourselves out for me, Clara. I'll help around the house and pay ya room and board, too."

"We've already discussed that," Clara said. "No rent until school starts in the fall and you're getting paid."

"Are ya sure?" Lena truly wanted to pay her way, considering all the Yoders were doing for her.

"Absolutely," Clara said. "We want you to feel comfortable here. After all, you've been wanting to get home for, what, eight months now? Your sister Emma has been so sweet to keep me up-to-date."

Lena Rose thanked Clara yet again, and when she was alone in the room where she would be staying, she quickly unpacked. Going over to look at the bookcase at the far end of the room, even more spacious than Tessa's former bedroom, she let the tears of relief flow. *I'm blessed beyond measure,* she thought as she took down her hair and brushed it. She reached for the hand mirror, checking to see if her middle part was straight before braiding her hair the way the womenfolk here always did, wrapping the braids to make a bun before putting on her black head covering. *I nearly forgot how. . . .*

Going to the window, she admired its view of cropland and a green meadow already blooming with wildflowers, and she paused to thank the Lord above for this most remarkable day of days.

―⟋ ⟍―

Barefoot, Lena Rose walked out to the road and headed north. She took in the familiar sights on both sides—the rustic outbuildings, the neighbors' rain cisterns, the quaint-looking gazebos, and all the tall birdhouses. She cherished everything about being home again. *How'd I ever manage to leave?* she wondered, nearly breathless at the thought of seeing her family again.

She recalled what Clara Yoder had said about Emma's interest in baking and wondered if her sister was still making her favorite lard-laden biscuits. *"So yummy, but they go straight to my hips,"* Mamma used to say.

Lena ran around to the back of the house where her sisters had been living and rapped on the screen door. She could hear Emma talking to someone as she waited on the back porch. *Shall I sneak in?*

Emma must have spied her, because she let out a squeal. "Lena Rose!" She dashed to the back door, flung it open, and hugged Lena ever so tight. Tears came, and soon they were both sobbing with joy.

"Guess what? Liz and Verena are home from school this mornin', a half day, since they're taking an end-of-year test this afternoon," Emma said. She then called to their sisters, *"Kumme schwind!"*

Right quick, Liz flew out the screen door, followed by Verena, their eyes wide, their faces all smiles.

"Come here, all of yous!" Lena said, reaching for her younger sisters, who clung to her and Emma.

"This is the best surprise," Liz said, brushing tears from her cheeks.

Verena was nodding, seemingly speechless.

"You look like you're in a daze," Emma told Verena.

"I . . . I must be." Verena reached out to touch Lena Rose.

"That's okay, go ahead and pinch me." Lena laughed and leaned to hug her.

They invited Lena inside, asking so many questions: When had she arrived, how had she gotten there . . . and had she seen any of their brothers yet?

Standing in the middle of the large kitchen, Lena answered everything they were curious about and so much more.

"Wait'll Chris finds out you're here," Emma said, grinning and shaking her head. "I still can hardly believe this!"

"Honestly, we were startin' to wonder if you'd ever get home again," Liz said, clutching Lena's hand. "Even though we prayed you would."

"You haven't changed much at all, Lena Rose. Not one little bit," Verena said quietly, her eyes brimming with tears. "But I s'pose ya think we have."

"Well, you and Liz are taller, that's for sure. You're young women now." Lena Rose looked admiringly at the three of them. "You're so beautiful, each of you. . . . I know we shouldn't say such things, but it's the truth."

"Mamma used to whisper it to us," Liz said. "Remember?"

"I surely do." Lena extended her arms wide to embrace all of them again. "Oh, how I love you!"

⁓ ⁓

Farmers were busy in their fields, and while Lena assumed most of the plowing was done, there was plenty of planting and cultivating going on. She relished the sunshine on her face and the soft May breeze. To think summer would be here soon, with haying and the womenfolk canning vegetables and making jellies and jams.

Hoping to see her grandparents, Lena hurried on to their *Dawdi Haus* and knocked on the back door, calling out softly so as not to alarm them.

Mammi came to the door, real serious at first; then her face burst into a welcoming smile. "Well, praise be! It's you in the flesh, Lena Rose. Come in, come in!"

Lena kissed her on both cheeks, their tears mingling. "I missed ya so," she whispered, letting Mammi hold her near.

"Let me look at ya." Mammi stepped back, eyeing her as her cheeks were damp with tears. "Seems to me, you're lookin' more like your Mamma."

"Am I?" Lena pressed her hands to her face. But it was Mammi she wanted to gaze at—she looked so frail. "Is Dawdi around?"

"Nappin' like usual."

Lena asked how he was feeling, and Mammi said he was moving more slowly. "He sleeps a lot nowadays and has little energy," Mammi said as she wiped her brow with her white hankie.

Lena was concerned and wondered how they could possibly keep up with Chris. It wasn't fair to expect them to take care of such a lively youngster. *I need to find him a more suitable living arrangement*, she thought.

But she changed the topic to her school teaching job, come fall. "Had ya heard I was comin' home?"

"Well, it was your Dawdi Schwartz and Noah who put the idea in Preacher Yoder's head." Mammi laughed softly, then put her hand over her lips. "I'd better not wake Dawdi till he's had his forty winks," she whispered.

Moving into the kitchen, they talked a bit more, and Lena asked, "How's Chris doin'?"

"Well, he still pines for his siblings . . . and for you, most of all." Mammi hobbled over to the sink and poured a glass of water and took a drink. She got another glass down from the cupboard, filled it, and handed it to Lena Rose as they went to sit at the small table. "Chris said right from the start that he wished he lived at Elmer Neuenschwander's farm with his school-age brothers," Mammi said, holding her glass with both hands. "It makes your Dawdi and me awful sad for him."

"Well sure," Lena said. It made her feel sad, too.

"He's a fine young scholar, though, so no worries there," Mammi added, then offered to make Lena a ham-and-cheese sandwich. "We eat very light anymore."

"Why don't you let me make something for the three of us?" Lena asked. The reality of how much things had changed since last fall, especially in regard to her grandparents' health, weighed heavily on her. But what could she do?

CHAPTER

35

After enjoying a noon meal of sandwiches and some home-made split-pea soup with Dawdi and Mammi, Lena headed back to Preacher Yoder's place, wanting to write some quick letters before school let out—one to Mimi, and definitely one to Lydia. She found her stationery and went to sit on the chair over near the bookcase. Since there was no desk, she removed one of the books to use it as a lap desk, then considered what she wanted to share with her other family.

She penned her thoughts about the bus trip here and how wonderful it was visiting with her sisters this morning, writing first to Mimi.

Next, she wrote to Lydia, but partway down the page she stopped. It was all she could do not to ask about Arden, even though it had been such a short time since she'd encountered him on Eby Road.

She considered all the miles that separated her from Lancaster County, yet she did not regret leaving. After all, Lena's parents were buried here in Centreville, and her brothers and sisters were here, and they would eventually marry and start their own families. *Dat and Mamma's grandchildren will run and play on Michigan soil someday,* she thought.

Wistful, Lena looked out the nearby window, staring at the moving clouds and the cobalt blue sky. She thought of what she might have had with Arden, had she stayed. "I must not have loved him enough. . . ." She rose and walked to the dresser to remove his few cards. Sitting on the bed, she reread the words he'd taken the time to write even when she'd said she only wanted friendship. *He was so accepting of that and understanding about my need to be with family.*

After she had put her things back in order, Lena headed down the hall and around to the kitchen. There, she offered to help Clara roll out dough for two pies, and Clara gladly handed her a work apron.

"Thought I'd take a pie over to your Dawdi and Mammi later," Clara remarked.

"Well, that's perfect—custard is Dawdi's favorite."

"I remember your Mamma's delicious custard pie recipe," Clara said. "In fact, I memorized it some years ago."

Lena nodded. "How I miss her and Dat."

Clara smiled thoughtfully. "Undoubtedly, it will take time to get used to bein' back, yet still living apart from your siblings."

"*Jah*, feels a little like I'm walkin' in a daze," Lena admitted. "It's strange not to return to the house where we were all born and grew up." She sighed. "I keep thinking that if I just stopped by, I'd find Mamma and Dat there."

"I'm sure so." Clara beat the eggs and then added brown sugar and vanilla before carefully adding scalded milk and cream.

Lena filled one of the pie shells with the mixture, and both pies went into the cookstove that looked very much like Mimi's.

Lena assumed the two Yoder children who still lived at home would be present for supper that evening, and she looked forward to being one of several young people in the house, for a change. Lena had made plans to meet Emma after the meal to surprise

Wilbur once he was home from work. *I can only imagine his expression!* Lena thought, ever so happy.

—⌒⊙ ⊙⌒—

An hour later, Lena stood at the edge of the school yard, waiting for the closing bell to ring. Mammi Schwartz's remarks continued to echo in her head, and it pained her to think that her grandparents were in decline, and that Chris still missed his siblings. *Maybe now that I'm back, he'll be more content, knowing I'm close by.* She took heart from that. This summer, she would encourage Chris to visit her often, and of course, she'd be over frequently to do things for Dawdi and Mammi, too. She hoped to try to line up some sewing work, too, once Uncle Noah took Mamma's treadle sewing machine out of storage.

Yet it was fall and teaching that she most looked forward to. To think, she would see her school-age siblings every weekday! After being apart all this time, it would be an ideal situation.

The bell rang loudly three times, and the older scholars came bursting through the doorway. The first few boys leaped off the steps and ran through the school yard toward the road.

Lena Rose watched carefully and wondered which of her brothers she'd spot first. Inching forward, she caught herself, knowing she should hang back and try not to be in anyone's way.

Mose and Sam walked out together, so tall and slender—goodness, had they grown several inches since she'd last seen them?

When they looked her way, she raised her hand to get their attention, and just like that, they tore down the steps. "When did ya get back?" Mose asked, his face flushed, his smile big.

"This mornin', but you were in school, so I tried very hard to be patient."

Sam, the quieter of the two, kept grinning. "Chris will prob'ly cry when he sees ya," he said softly.

Mose made a face. "*Puh!* He's not a baby!"

Benjamin and Timothy jumped down the steps, then stopped in their tracks and stared. Unexpectedly, they turned around and called for Chris. "Come quick—see who's here!" Ben said, waiting for his youngest brother to shyly walk to the doorway and look out, his eyes squinting into the sunlight.

Stepping aside, Ben and Tim let Chris dash ahead, straight to Lena Rose, who greeted him exuberantly. Even he had sprouted up like a dandelion over the school year. His cheekbones were more defined, too—the baby fat gone. But he was the same darling boy she'd practically raised.

Chris stared up at her, his hand shielding his eyes. "You were gone mighty long, ain't?"

"Well, I'm home now." She refused to cry at the joy of being with all of them again.

Chris was working his lips as Ben and Tim came to stand by him, all of them beaming at Lena Rose, love on their faces. "This is the best day in a long time," Tim said quietly.

"I second that," Ben said.

"It's *gut* to see ya, Lena Rose," Chris said, walking beside her as together they headed across the school yard for the road.

"Chris thought you'd never get home," Mose said, swinging his lunch bucket.

"We *all* thought that," Ben said, poking Mose and laughing.

"*I* knew she'd come back," Chris said as he looked up at her. "I really did." His voice broke a little, and he snapped his suspenders.

"Let's walk Chris over to Dawdi and Mammi's," Mose suggested, eyebrows high.

"*Jah.* Dawdi should be wide-awake after his nap," Chris said. "And Mammi will give us all a snack."

Lena couldn't think of a better way to spend the afternoon. And there was still one more wonderful sibling to greet!

I'm back where I belong, she thought, keeping up with her energetic brothers, their matching straw hats bobbing on blond heads as they walked, the twins leading the way.

———

The hoped-for reunion with Wilbur didn't take place after supper that evening because he'd run an errand to the Truckenmiller hardware store, and the family he lived with said they weren't sure when he was due back. Lena Rose and Emma had walked over there together, passing greening wheat and barley fields, but instead of saying they'd return later, Lena left a note for Wilbur, telling him that she was in Centreville and would love to see him when it suited.

So they headed to where Emma lived, slowing their pace, and Emma mentioned that Hans Bontrager was engaged to be married this November. "I thought you might wanna know."

"Such a relief," Lena said, and it was. She was happy Hans had found a good match. "And you're still seein' his brother, Ammon? Any updates?"

"We're fairly serious . . . though I hope it doesn't make ya feel awkward."

"*Nee,* you're free to date who you want to, no matter who Ammon's related to."

Emma blushed. "He's so *gut* to me."

"That's *wunnerbaar,* sister. Truly."

As she and Emma walked, some folk waved and others called out a *willkumm* to Lena Rose.

"How's it feel to be back?" Emma asked.

"Honestly, I'm afraid I'll wake up tomorrow, and it'll all be a dream."

Emma frowned. "You yearned so to be home. You wrote so many letters!"

"That's putting it lightly." Lena laughed; it was wonderful to have this time alone with Emma. It seemed as if they were picking up right where they'd left off.

"Will ya keep in touch with Dat's cousins back in Lancaster County?" Emma asked out of the blue. "You seemed so fond of Cousin Mimi . . . and your friend Lydia Smucker, too."

"I've already written them both—can ya believe it?"

Emma seemed to be thinking about something else. And after a little while, she asked, "What about your friend . . . Arden Mast?"

Lena was surprised she brought him up.

"Is there anythin' you wanna tell me?" Emma smiled, the wisps of new hair at her temples fluttering in the breeze.

"Well, ain't you nosy?" Lena laughed.

"Ah . . . so you still like him?"

Lena sighed. "It's all over between us, Emma."

"But that's not what I asked."

I do like Arden, very much. Lena sighed inwardly. *But we weren't meant to be.*

⟶ ℭ ℭ ⟵

Once Lena returned to the Yoders', she and Clara sat out on the front porch at sunset to watch the horses and buggies go by. Clara kept her entertained with stories of her grandchildren's antics, and Lena kept hoping Wilbur might stop over. "I got another letter from Lillian yesterday," Clara said now, mentioning her youngest daughter. "She seems to be enjoying it out in Berne. She wonders how the substitute teacher is doin' here."

"It's hard moving to a new place," Lena said, remembering her first days in Pennsylvania. "Is the dialect the same there as here?"

"Not sure. She hasn't mentioned any difference."

Nodding, Lena Rose noticed an open carriage coming this way, and when she looked closer, she saw that it was Wilbur. "Oh,

Clara, will ya excuse me?" she said, rising quickly out of her chair and bounding down the steps and out to the road.

"Hop in," Wilbur said, grinning from ear to ear. "I want ya to ride in my fine black buggy."

She stepped right in, and off they went. "I s'pose ya got my note."

"Well, I didn't inhale my supper for nothin'." He went on to ask a lot of the same questions Emma and the others had earlier today.

Lena filled him in on her life. "How about you? What's goin' on in yours?"

Wilbur's straw hat had slid back, showing his thick bangs. "The factory where I work is short on employees right now, so I've been workin' longer hours and getting overtime pay, which'll help me save up for a place of my own."

Lena was impressed with his maturity. She caught the scent of rain in the air.

Wilbur must have noticed it, too. "I have a big umbrella, in case you're wonderin'."

"You're all prepared," she said, thankful to be riding with him. "Any particular reason?"

He glanced at her, a smile creeping across his face. "I've got my eye on a girl but haven't asked her out just yet. If I get up the nerve, maybe I'll introduce ya."

"*Ach*, you'd better!" she said, laughing.

"She's real nice . . . reminds me of you, Lena Rose."

"So . . . does this young lady have a name?"

"Not sayin' just yet." His chuckle made her smile. *Ah, this brother of mine!* she thought, wondering if he and Emma might just marry before she did.

But she pushed the thought away. What mattered right now was enjoying this splendid ride around Centreville in Wilbur's handsome courting carriage.

36

The next weeks intermingled work and play. Lena helped Clara in the kitchen garden or with indoor cleaning, as well as spent time with Chris, who liked to see her every day. So she put him to work alongside her, helping to weed or plant or hoe.

Chris had become more talkative, and it felt so good to hear him express his thoughts on everything from cleaning Tubby Tabby's litter box to what kind of farmer he might be someday. Sometimes, he wanted to talk about the Bible verses Dawdi Schwartz had read after supper the night before. And through it all, Lena soaked up his attention—she'd missed so much during his first year of school that she was thankful to God for this time to catch up.

There were times when Lena missed seeing Lydia Smucker. Lydia's first letter had indicated that things were very different without Lena around. But as the days flew by, Lena could sense that her friend was adjusting to the distance between them.

Lydia also hinted that she and Eli were talking about tying the knot this wedding season, if all continued to go well in his plan to take over the family farm. *In fact, Manny and Arden will start building a smaller* Dawdi Haus *for Solomon in just a few days,* Lydia had written.

"Sounds like Lydia will be a bride come fall," Lena murmured, happy for her friend.

But as much as Lena missed Lydia, not being able to talk with Arden anymore had been the hardest. She'd even started a letter to him, but after writing two pages, she realized it was a mistake and tore it into small pieces, making sure no one could read what her heart had dictated.

There were nights, however, when she dreamed that she and Arden were out riding in his courting carriage or ice-skating . . . always laughing and having a lovely time. When she awakened, a sad, heavy feeling would fall over her, and she would miss him all the more. It was strange, really, because she had never dreamed about him while in Leacock Township. Why now?

Even so, Arden was many miles away, and she was nicely settled here. Besides, he must be totally focused on his work in the area he so fondly called home.

⁓ ⌁ ⁓

One mid-June afternoon, Chris was sitting out at a table in the Yoders' yard, turning the crank on the ice-cream maker. He looked up at Lena Rose. "Do ya think I might ever live with you again?"

The question was legitimate, but she had no answer, not when she was staying at Preacher Yoder's crowded house. "What if we pray about it?" she suggested.

"Just you and me?"

"*Jah.* I'll pray first thing each mornin' . . . and you can, too."

Chris's face shone with trust. "Mammi Schwartz says God can see our hearts."

"And Mammi's right."

"Then I'll ask God 'bout it," he said, turning the crank all the harder.

Oh, how she loved this boy! And she did her very best to show it by taking time for him every single day.

—◦ ◦—

The Amish school board, consisting of four fathers, called annually for a community workday to clean the interior of the schoolhouse, paint the exterior, and in general redd up the play yard and the boys' and girls' outhouses. Lena Rose and her siblings were on hand to help, including Emma, who reintroduced Lena to her beau, Ammon Bontrager. Lena was pleased that Ammon was just as cordial as she remembered.

But it was Hans who went out of his way to find Lena and talk to her. "Congratulations on your teachin' job," he said, as pleasant as ever.

"*Denki.*" She was glad there was apparently no animosity between them. "And I've heard you're engaged. I'm real happy for you, Hans."

He nodded and thanked her. "Hope you can come to the wedding. It'll be at the end of November, close to Thanksgiving."

As she later recalled their encounter, she felt a sense of peace. Seeing Hans again, she felt certain that splitting up had been the right choice. There hadn't been the spark she'd felt with Arden, or the same close connection, either.

—◦ ◦—

During the hot, sticky month of August, Lena was invited twice to go riding with one of Wilbur's close friends, Mark Miller, who had been politely vying for her attention. And though he was very nice and she trusted Wilbur's opinion of him, Lena felt she should let Mark know that she'd put dating on the back burner. She shared this confidentially with Emma, saying she didn't want to waste anyone's time.

"Why do you feel that way?" her sister asked, her expression concerned.

Lena simply shrugged, not wanting to say outright that her heart was still linked to Arden, and therefore it wasn't fair for her to date any young man. And because Lena didn't see how she could get over Arden, she wondered if she might be destined to be an *alt Maidel* schoolteacher. She wouldn't be the first woman to remain unmarried, she knew, recalling one of the teacher-friends Mamma had known in Indiana—happy as a schoolgirl in her singleness, surrounded by her adoring scholars.

I need to pray about this, Lena thought, knowing Mimi would urge her to do exactly that.

⸙

Summertime bounty led to picnics with family, canning bees, and work frolics. While shelling pole beans or cutting sweet corn off the cob with Clara and her daughter Abby and several other womenfolk—with help from Chris, who carried the bowls into the house—Lena occasionally caught herself imagining what Arden was busy doing. Was he thinking of her? Oddly, such thoughts were becoming more frequent, which was surprising because she hadn't had any interaction with him since leaving Leacock Township. Nevertheless, he was in the midst of many of her daily thoughts. And the longer she was away, the more she realized how much she loved him. But it was too late now.

Arden has his life there, and I have mine here.

⸙

The closer the time came for school to start, the more hours Lena spent studying and preparing to teach the curriculum approved by the Amish school board. The *McGuffey Readers* were still the reader of choice for grades one through six, as was the German Bible and the *Ausbund* hymnal, which helped the younger children learn to read and understand the German used during Preachings.

Lena was expected to emphasize working hard over getting good grades, and the board also instructed her not to display perfect spelling tests, so as to downplay competition and pridefulness amongst the students.

She enjoyed showing some of the second-grade arithmetic lessons to Chris.

"I'm ready to begin," he told her one morning as they walked together from Dawdi and Mammi Schwartz's house to the Yoders'.

Seeing how motivated he was brightened Lena's days. Chris had also offered to help her make autumn leaves and pumpkins for the school bulletin board.

"I'll wash the blackboards for ya, too," he said. "Whatever ya need, I'll do it, Lena Rose."

She wanted to tousle his hair but had to remind herself that he was going into second grade and was no longer a little boy. "Dat would be so proud of ya," she said, "helpful as you are."

"Do ya think Dat and Mamma know we're together again?" he asked, looking up at her. "Does God let them know things like that, maybe?"

Lena smiled. *Such a thinker!* "Well, whatever happens after people die, I'm very sure it is *wunnerbaar* for those who walked with the Lord. And if it's important for Dat and Mamma to know something about us here on earth, then our heavenly Father surely has a way of letting them know. You can trust His plan to take care of us."

Chris seemed to ponder that. Then he asked, "Does God know everything before it happens?"

"The Good Book says so."

He nodded. "Well then, it's true."

A pony cart was coming down the road toward them just then, and Chris asked if he might ever have a pony and a cart of his own. "It'd take me just a few minutes to get around to see everyone thataway."

"Now you're talkin'!"

Chris laughed and picked up his pace.

Lena loved these windows into her little brother's mind. She'd sometimes wondered what Chris and her other siblings would think of Arden, if they'd known him. Would they have liked him?

"Can I sit in the front row at school?" Chris's question broke into her thoughts.

"Goodness, you must be itchin' to start today, ain't?"

He nodded enthusiastically. "And can I ring the school bell, too?"

"Well, you'd have to get there extra early. And once the cooler days come, you can help build the fire in the wood stove. How's that?"

"Guess I can just go to bed earlier, like Dawdi," he said.

Again, Lena Rose smiled. At times she wondered if Chris was trying to make up for lost time with all his talk. She just hoped he wasn't spending *all* his time with her instead of seeing his brothers and doing things every Amish boy enjoyed in the summer, like climbing trees, rolling down grassy hills, and helping around the barn. Should she talk with Dawdi Schwartz or Preacher Yoder about getting him more involved with some of the nearby farmers?

It's one thing for a little boy to shadow his big sister, but as Chris grows up, is it a good idea?

CHAPTER

37

On the last Monday in August, Lena Rose stopped at Dawdi and Mammi's to get Chris, who still planned to help her before school, even though she'd already spent days getting the classroom ready for this first day.

She had awakened with the knowledge that it was close to the one-year anniversary of her parents' passing, and for that reason, she was grateful to have so much going on during this first day of school.

At eight-thirty sharp, Chris pulled the rope to ring the bell, which brought the shiny-faced scholars scurrying into the one-room schoolhouse, where they put away their lunches and looked for their names on the wooden desks.

Lena didn't need to introduce herself, but she did anyway, saying how honored she was to be their teacher this year. Then they started the day with three songs of praise, and afterward, recited the Lord's Prayer—all in *Deitsch*—before she read aloud from the Bible the story of baby Moses.

Later, after Lena had gone over the school rules for the benefit of the newest scholars, she assigned the writing of numerals from one to five to the first graders. She then gave the second graders an easy arithmetic assignment. All the while, Chris and her other siblings wore a perpetual smile on their faces, eyes alert as they picked up their pencils and got to work.

When she called the third graders to the front bench to read aloud, the rest of the scholars—the fourth through eighth graders—took a short quiz until it was their turn.

At last, it was time for morning recess. The children filed outside, talking happily amongst themselves. The younger girls had a jump rope, and Lena held one end while the girls chanted their sing-songy rhymes and took turns jumping.

She was relieved to see Chris playing ball with a number of the boys his age—two of them his brothers, and three cousins—but now and then, she noticed he would look her way. It made her wonder if he was still worried to let her out of his sight, as he had been at the start of summer, after their long separation.

Lena was delighted late that afternoon to receive letters from Mimi, Lydia . . . and the first one from Rebekah Petersheim. She began with Mimi's and was delighted to discover that Tessa was expecting a baby in late January. Mimi sounded so pleased, and she also mentioned that this time of having Tessa work with her had been a blessing in many ways.

> *Harley and Manny are getting along well, too. They've even planned a few hunting trips this fall.*
>
> *But the biggest change will be our move into Solomon's current Dawdi Haus, and Solomon into the one that Manny has worked so hard on. It's all completed, and sometime early this fall, we'll all begin the move. That will leave time to make some renovations to the main farmhouse for the young newlyweds.*

Lena smiled to think of Lydia and Eli moving into the spacious farmhouse, and she wished she could see the fine workmanship of the addition that must have taken Manny and Arden many weeks.

Setting aside Mimi's letter, Lena picked up Rebekah's, which primarily focused on the activities she and James Zook were doing during these last warm days of late summer. Lena could picture the older couple taking walks around James's farmhouse or riding in the enclosed family buggy, James holding the reins. Rebekah had written so fondly of James that Lena wondered if they might indeed be thinking of marriage. *Falling in love has evidently perked him up,* Lena thought.

Lydia's letter was the final one. She'd written about tending the market stand with her mother and having run into Arden Mast, who was with one of his sisters. Lydia had talked with Arden, but she didn't say what about, which struck Lena as rather cryptic. In fact, Lena read the letter a second time to see if she'd missed something.

The mere mention of Arden renewed Lena's curiosity about him—something that had quieted a bit as she focused on making preparations for the first day of school. *I won't ask her point-blank when I write, but it'd be nice to know what they talked about.* Lena set the letters aside, feeling very much like a part of her was still back in Lancaster County.

⸺ ❦ ⸺

By the middle of that first week of school, Lena's energy was flagging, and she realized she needed to make an effort to go to bed earlier at night. Her teaching and her siblings should be her priorities now, even though she sometimes still toyed with writing a short letter to Arden. *What would he think of that?* she wondered. *Would he consider it forward?*

Lena contemplated this for a few days until finally, on Labor Day, after a picnic with the entire church district, she sat down and wrote the letter she had been formulating for so long in her mind.

> *Dear Arden,*
>
> *How are you? How is your business with Manny coming along?*
>
> *I know it's been a while since we last saw each other, but I wanted to let you know how thankful I am that you encouraged me to take the opportunity to teach here. At the time, I was impressed that you'd urge me on like that, but I'm even more impressed now at your insight. It's not something every friend would have done.*
>
> *I'm not writing to ask anything of you. There are just so many happy memories of our times together. It hasn't been easy to forget them . . . or you.*
>
> *My brothers and sisters are a great joy to me, just as you knew they would be, and my schoolhouse full of scholars keeps me ever so busy. And I often think of Mamma, who taught me so many things; I'm not sure I'll ever fully comprehend how much I owe to her and Dat, or to people like you and Lydia and the Stoltzfuses. God has truly blessed me with the people He has brought into my life.*
>
> *Still your friend,*
> *Lena Rose Schwartz*

Before she could rethink this, Lena folded the letter and placed it in an envelope, addressed it, and sealed it. Tomorrow, she would mail it with a prayer that Arden would receive it in the spirit in which it was sent.

More than three weeks passed with no reply from Arden. Lena assumed he was either too busy or had been offended by her boldness in writing an unsolicited letter. As the days came and went, she felt increasingly bewildered, then embarrassed. *Was I wrong to write?* she thought, all the more miserable for having taken the risk.

Finally, one Saturday morning in late September, she sought out Emma for a long walk. "I did a peculiar thing," she confessed, pouring out her heart about Arden . . . and the letter.

"You *wrote* to him?" Emma was not so much shocked as gleeful. "That's great! I wondered if you'd have the courage."

Lena felt somewhat taken aback. "Why do you say that?"

"Well, when a girl loves—er, I mean, really *likes* a fella—it's best that he knows it, *jah?*"

Lena didn't know whether to laugh or not. But when she looked at Emma, she could see that her sister was absolutely sincere. "Maybe the letter got lost in the mail," she suggested.

Emma shook her head. "He's prob'ly just pondering things."

"Or maybe he's too astonished."

"Well, he might be surprised, but more than likely it's because you've come around at last." Emma paused as though considering what to say next. "Are ya thinkin' of going back there, so he can court ya?"

Now Lena was the one who was shocked. "*Nee,* I'm here, where I ought to be."

"Just checkin'." Emma leaned down to pick up a pretty white pebble. "You do know that at some point, years from now, all of us kids will prob'ly be married and have families of our own."

Jah, *and will I be alone?* Lena wondered. She tried to laugh it off. "If I'm still single by then, Emma, maybe you can build a *Dawdi Haus* for me to live in."

295

"That's silly. You'll marry—I'm sure of it." Her sister tossed the pebble high into the air and caught it.

"How can ya talk so?"

"You wait an' see." Emma grinned and reached for Lena's hand.

"I'm glad we can share face-to-face like this."

Emma agreed. "And while we're sharing, I want to ask if you'd be in Ammon's and my wedding a year from this November."

"Aw . . . I'd love to." Lena looked out across the meadow, where wildflowers still bloomed purple and red even during this golden season. She realized now that all the talk from Emma about Lena's getting married someday was really a way to work up to saying that *Emma* was. "I'm not surprised, since ya love each other," Lena told her.

"We do," Emma said softly.

Lena turned to give her an embrace. "Somehow in the heavenly order of things, Mamma and Dat must know how happy you are."

38

October brought cooler weather, and menfolk donned their black felt hats, while womenfolk took their long black woolen shawls out of their cedar chests to wear on Preaching Sundays.

As the temperatures dropped and wedding season neared, Lena began to feel increasingly lonely even though her dear family and old friends surrounded her. To compensate, she threw herself into planning the school Christmas play, although it was still two months away.

Always planning ahead, she thought while sitting at her desk. The last child had left the schoolhouse, and she had already washed the blackboard herself, since Chris had gone to play with the twins and Ben and Tim at the Neuenschwanders'.

Looking through her *Tips for Teachers* handbook, she scanned through some suggested gifts for children to make for their parents. Her eyes fell on the instructions for making letter holders. *Ideal for the younger girls to give their mothers*, she thought, knowing that many of the Amishwomen in the area were avid writers of circle letters.

Hearing footsteps outside, she assumed it was one of the children's parents coming to visit. Here lately, she'd had two mothers drop by with homemade goodies as a thank-you for a strong start to the school year. The sweet gesture had made her smile, and as the door opened, Lena glanced up. The light behind the man entering made it impossible to see whose father this was.

She rose from her desk and walked around it to greet him.

"Hullo, Lena Rose."

She recognized that voice at the same moment she recognized his handsome face. *Mercy's sake!*

Arden removed his straw hat. "Looks like you're busy," he said, his manner tentative.

"*Nee*, not that busy," she replied, trying to keep her wits about her. *Am I dreaming?*

He glanced about the room, nodding at the bulletin board behind her desk. "Your classroom looks *wunnerbaar!*"

Lena followed his gaze. "Chris and I worked on it together."

Taking in the sight of him—tall, handsome, his striking blue-green eyes—she recalled the day she realized she'd fallen in love with him. Fly fishing at twilight, of all things! And she had not forgotten how mysteriously he'd appeared at the Gordonville Book Store, as if he had stepped in just to seek her out.

"Wait a minute," she said, narrowing her eyes. "This can't be a coincidence! You didn't just *happen* to show up here, did ya?"

Arden was grinning, as though also remembering what she'd said at the bookstore.

"*Are* you following me?" she asked.

"*Jah*, as a matter of fact, I am." He was chuckling now. "And if ya don't mind, I'd like to stay around for a while . . . spend some time with you, Lena Rose."

She was dumbfounded. "What about your—"

"During the weeks and months after ya left," he said, stepping closer, "I began to realize something."

She held her breath.

"Honestly, Leacock Township didn't seem very much like home anymore. Sure, I loved everything about it, but . . ." He paused.

She bit her lip, measuring the moment and her own feelings.

"You see . . . my home is with *you*, Lena Rose."

Her heart swelled with love for this unpredictable man. Oh, if only she could say the right words, words that showed her appreciation for his long journey here. Yet she must be calm, too, though her heart would not permit it, drumming as it was.

He was close enough to touch. "*Ach*, how I missed you," he said, eyes bright.

She found herself moving closer to him as Arden reached for her hands. "I'm thinkin' of renting a place near the RV factory in Middlebury, Indiana, not far from here," he said. "I've heard there are openings for employment in the cabinetry department." He looked quite serious. "And while I'm here . . ."

"*Jah?*" she asked, ever so hopeful.

"I'd like to court ya."

It was the second time he'd asked, and now she did not hesitate. "I would love that," she said, smiling up at him. And, ever so curious about what he'd just said, she asked, "How'd ya hear about the openings?"

Arden led her outside, where they stood on the schoolhouse porch, watching a shower of colorful swirling leaves as breezes trembled the trees. There, he unraveled the news she'd somehow missed: Emma had written as much in a long letter to Eli. "In a roundabout way, you've got yourself a matchmaker for a sister," he said, adding earnestly, "I'm lookin' forward to thanking her someday . . . and to meeting *all* your siblings, too."

Lena couldn't help but laugh. "That Emma. I should've suspected she'd get up to somethin' like this!"

The autumn days that followed became some of Lena's happiest as she looked forward to spending time with Arden. That first weekend, he was able to get a driver to drop him off at Preacher Yoder's house, where he embarked on his ambitious plan to meet all of Lena's brothers and sisters, starting with Chris.

As they walked to see Chris and Lena's grandparents, Arden told her how hard it was not to reach for her hand. "It's surely known that we're a serious couple now," he said with a hopeful smile at her.

"True, but I never see any other couples holding hands in the daylight," Lena told him.

Arden sighed and said he guessed he'd have to stick around till after nightfall for sure, then, and she understood what he was hinting at.

"By the way, Emma wants us to double-date with her and Ammon real soon. All right with you?"

"That'd be perfect, 'cause I have somethin' to tell Emma, actually," he said.

"Oh?"

"You'll see." He winked at her.

When the next Sunday came, Arden returned to Centreville for the Preaching service and sat with Wilbur on the side with the menfolk. Lena was glad to see him getting better acquainted with Wilbur at that evening's Singing. But the best moment was when Arden shook Emma's hand as she entered the barn.

"Thank you for getting word to me about the openings at the RV factory," he said.

"It was the least I could do," Emma said, glancing at Lena with that twinkle in her eye, as if to add, *"For Lena Rose."*

Later, while they both sipped some cider, Emma confided to Lena how much she liked Arden. "He'll fit well into our family when the time comes." Lena blushed happily and agreed, nudging her sister to look across the haymow, where Arden was talking and laughing with Wilbur. Clearly, both of them were enjoying each other's company.

That night, Lena was thrilled to sit beside Arden in the second seat of Ammon's new courting buggy. Arden reached for her hand, and for a moment, she thought her heart had flipped upside down.

"Wilbur has a great sense of humor," Arden said.

"Didn't I tell ya? He gets it from Dat."

"That's for sure," Emma said, glancing back at them from next to Ammon in the front seat.

Lena was surprised her sister was listening in, but she didn't mind. She had no secrets from Emma. *At least not anymore*, she thought, looking fondly at the man beside her.

"Wilbur wants me to go hunting with him before Thanksgiving," Arden said. "Maybe we'll each bag a turkey."

"Like you and Eli last year, remember?" Lena said, conscious of how close she was to Arden, there in the darkness of the open buggy, the stars their only light.

"I haven't forgotten," Arden whispered, leaning closer and kissing her cheek.

Lena hadn't expected it and smiled at him, wondering if he was going to kiss her on the lips, too. But then he released her hand and slipped his arm around her, and they rode that way until they reached Preacher Yoder's house, where Arden walked her to the back door and said good-night. "My ride will be here soon, but I'll see ya again next week."

He reached for both of her hands. "Until then, I'll write to you. Maybe every day."

She nodded. "I'll look forward to it."

"That's not too often, is it?" he asked, grinning.

Never, she thought and laughed softly.

He kissed her cheek again and walked slowly backward, his gaze still on her as she waved and reluctantly made her way inside.

—◌⁖◌—

As Thanksgiving Day approached, Lena could think of no better occasion for all of her family to spend time with Arden. So far, Emma and Wilbur had kept a lid on her and Arden's courtship, but Lena Rose was starting to feel like she might burst with joy, or so she told Emma as they walked together on a Saturday morning.

"I think Verena and Liz and the younger boys might be a little surprised, but they already like Arden," Emma reassured her.

So the next day, an off-Sunday from Preaching, Lena went to visit Aunt Mary Schwartz and sat down with her in the cozy kitchen to have coffee and sticky buns. "I've been wanting to tell ya somethin' real special, *Aendi*."

Aunt Mary set down her sticky bun. "Oh?"

"I have a serious beau." Lena explained that she'd known Arden as a good friend while living in Lancaster County. "He's been courting me since last month—not long, really—just since movin' to Indiana, where he works at the same RV factory where Dat worked."

Aunt Mary's eyes welled up with tears. "Such lovely news."

Lena reached for her hand. "I'm relieved you feel that way."

"You've seemed ever so happy lately," Aunt Mary replied softly. "Honestly, it's wondered me."

"To think Arden works in the exact same department where Dat was the head."

"Isn't that somethin'?" Mary pulled a hankie from her dress sleeve and dried her eyes. "Does this fella love ya, Lena Rose?"

"Enough to leave behind his entire family and a successful

business back in Lancaster County . . . *jah*. I can hardly think of what he's giving up for me without getting a lump in my throat. It must be the hand of the Lord, that's all I can say."

"Aw . . . 'tis *gut*." Aunt Mary patted her eyes with the hankie again.

"I have an idea." And Lena began to share her hope of gathering all her siblings in one location, as well as Dawdi and Mammi Schwartz, in order for them to get better acquainted with her beau on Thanksgiving Day. "What do ya think?"

"Well, let's do it right here in this kitchen," Aunt Mary suggested. "Wouldn't that be ideal?"

"Only if my sisters and I can help with the cookin'."

Aunt Mary smiled. "We'll just see about that."

"*Ach*, I can't have ya cookin' all morning over the hot stove. Won't ya let my sisters and me pitch in?"

Aunt Mary was quiet for several moments, an endearing expression on her face. "Honestly, since I wasn't able to offer a home to any of yous when your parents died, this is what I'd like to do for you and your brothers and sisters."

"Are ya sure?" Lena didn't want her aunt to do this all on her own. "Let Emma bake some pies, at least. She'll be awful disappointed if she can't bring *something*."

"All right, then, but only Emma." Aunt Mary chuckled. She certainly liked being in control of her kitchen and her menu.

They lingered, quietly talking and drinking black coffee while nibbling on sticky buns. Now and then, Lena glanced out at the featherlight snowflakes dusting the ground.

"Your *Onkel* Noah will be real glad to hear all this," Aunt Mary said as she sipped her coffee. "He's been prayin' you wouldn't end up without the love of a husband, teaching school for years and years. And now just look at ya."

"But I *love* teaching. I hope to ask the school board if they'll let me stay on once I'm married, at least till I have children of my own. I know that's unheard of, but I still can hope."

"Time will tell."

As comfortable as she felt with Aunt Mary just now, Lena decided to reveal more. "Arden hasn't officially proposed yet, but he's been droppin' hints about getting married in a year or so. That should give him more time to accumulate some 'real *gut* money,' as he says. And time for us to find a house to buy or rent, since right now he's livin' in a small apartment near the factory."

"I won't breathe a word." Aunt Mary was beaming, her eyes shining with tears again. "And if you'd like to have the wedding dinner here, that'd be just fine, too."

Hearing this, Lena scarcely knew what to think. "I never would've asked."

"Well, see? Now ya don't have to."

They had a hearty laugh, and this time Aunt Mary was the one to reach over and clasp Lena's hand. "I couldn't be happier for ya, Lena."

Lena embraced the love she felt from her dear aunt. "You know, after Dat and Mamma died, I wondered if I'd ever feel such joy again."

Aunt Mary nodded and smiled. "Your uncle Noah will want to give his blessing, at some point . . . in your father's stead."

"Oh, I really think he'll like Arden as much as you will."

Aunt Mary raised her eyebrows and smiled thoughtfully. "From the look on your sweet face this minute, I believe we surely will."

Lena thought about Uncle Noah's blessing in Dat's stead. *The dearest words.* Her heart was ever so full as she headed on foot to the Yoders' farm. *A year from now, Lord willing, I'll be making my home with my darling!*

39

Late Thanksgiving morning, Preacher Yoder loaned Arden his enclosed carriage, and he and Lena headed over to Uncle Noah's. "So nice of the preacher, *jah*?" Lena said, knowing that Arden had already had a man-to-man talk with him about their courting, since Arden was from out of state. According to Clara, her husband had enthusiastically approved.

"Preacher Yoder seems mighty encouraging," Arden said with a grin as they headed over to Uncle Noah's farm. "It's wise to have at least one preacher on your side."

Lena smiled. "Tell me how Mimi seemed to you before ya left home."

"As content with her life and her sewing as when you were there, seems to me."

"Does Tessa work with her quite a lot, then?" Lena hoped the two of them were getting along at least as well as they had before Tessa married Manny.

"Far as I know from my Mamm, she's over there three times a week."

"That was my one worry when I left, but I should have known it would come out all right."

Arden, who was sitting tall on the driver's side of the family carriage, glanced at her. "No doubt the People back in Leacock are still talking 'bout the sweet girl from Michigan who changed their lives."

"Now, Arden . . ."

"*Nee*, really—you should hear what they say."

Blushing now, Lena wished he wouldn't go on so. "I hope to keep in touch with as many of them as possible."

"Oh, trust me. You have a ready-made circle letter group anxious to hear how you're doin'."

"Do any of them know we're courting?"

He paused, then smiled broadly. "A fella can't keep secrets from his kinfolk, now, can he?"

Lena's heart beat more quickly. "So everyone knows?"

"Manny first of all. And of course I told Eli and Lydia, too. Or do you think I didn't have to say *why* I wanted to move way out here?" His eyes twinkled, and he told her that Lydia had known he was coming. "I told her at market," he said.

She laughed. "I wondered. She was so secretive in her letter about that market day."

Arden reached for her hand and raised it to his lips. "She's all for it, as is my family."

What a wonderful Thanksgiving! she thought, snuggling close to Arden.

⸺᠃᠃⸺

Soon after she and Arden arrived, Lena had a chance to introduce him to Uncle Noah privately, before Wilbur came in his open carriage with Chris and the grandparents, whom he helped inside.

The twins arrived with Timothy and Benjamin around that time, as well, soon to be followed by Emma, Liz, and Verena.

306

Uncle Noah stood shaking hands and greeting all of them warmly, and then Aunt Mary suggested the men and boys take seats at the table while she and the girls brought over the hot turkey on a big oval platter, along with all the mouthwatering side dishes for the feast.

Lena smiled at Chris, touched to see that he was saving her a spot next to him at the table. And later, once everyone was seated and they all bowed their heads to ask the blessing, Lena found she was sitting between Chris and Arden.

Uncle Noah led the silent prayer, bowing his head longer than usual. Was he thanking God for bringing Arden their way? Certainly that was near the top of the list of Lena's thank-yous.

As Lena was sure he would, Arden took great interest in talking with each one while the food was being passed around the long table.

Chris paid close attention to Arden, as well, not picking up his fork to eat just yet and glancing at Lena Rose a couple of times. *He knows something's up!*

Aunt Mary's generous spread of food was as delectable as Lena had remembered, and when Emma's cherry pies were sliced and served, Liz and Verena sighed and looked at each other as if wondering how they were going to make room for dessert.

Naturally, none of their brothers seemed to have a problem with that, and all of them were as eager as Uncle Noah to dive into a piece of cherry pie piled high with homemade whipped cream.

Arden, for his part, made a show of leaning back in his chair and patting his stomach.

Uncle Noah must have noticed, because he nodded his head and said, "Thanksgiving comes but once a year, remember."

"Well, if I could just go and pitch some hay, maybe I'd make some room for Emma's dessert."

"Oh now . . . eat yourself full," Aunt Mary said as she cut an extra-big piece for Arden, which Lena and Arden ended up sharing.

Arden let her have the last bite, then returned his attention to those gathered around the table. "Once upon a time, Lena Rose and I shared a very generous slice of coconut cream pie," he said, surprising her. "And, to tell the truth, I knew that very evening that Lena was the girl for me."

Lena's breath caught in her throat. *Why's he saying this?*

Arden put down his fork and turned toward Lena, and she wondered what else he was going to say.

"Lena Rose, I'd like to ask ya somethin' mighty important, right here in the presence of your beloved family."

He looked at her, eyes smiling. "Will you be my bride, my dearest friend . . . and my sweetheart for life?"

Lena looked around at her brothers and sisters, all of whom were quite deliberately nodding their heads. Then, smiling back at Arden, Lena happily said, "I will . . . *jah.*"

Wilbur began to applaud, and right away everyone else joined in. A couple of the younger boys were cheering. Honestly, Lena thought it was the sweetest way for a man to propose. In fact, it was the only way Arden had wanted to do so, he told Lena on the ride back to Preacher Yoder's with Chris, who'd asked to come, too.

"I wish Dat and Mamma could've been there," Chris said as the carriage rumbled along.

Lena agreed. "Well, I really wonder if Arden would've proposed quite like that if they were still alive."

Arden shook his head. "*Nee* . . . it's because your parents aren't around that I wanted the rest of your family to be in agreement."

Chris said no more, and his silence seemed to indicate that he understood.

BEVERLY LEWIS

After they arrived at Dawdi and Mammi's, Chris clambered out of the carriage, and she and Arden watched him run up the lane, turn and wave, and then scamper around the back of the house.

"I like your family," Arden said quietly.

Lena had never felt more content. "I'm not surprised you feel that way." Nor could she deny the strong pull she felt toward him as Arden drew her near. There, in the darkness of the preacher's carriage, her darling's lips found hers, and oh, how she loved being close to him this way as they sealed their love with a kiss.

"You know," she said as he caressed her cheek, "my father wrote some postcards to Mamma long before I was born—before they were wed. I have them now, and there's one line in particular that I haven't forgotten."

Arden moved back to look into her eyes. "Tell me."

Then she quoted the line that had so inspired her. "'May God keep you in His care till we're together again, in His time.' In that line, Dat revealed how much trust he put in the Lord for his courtship with Mamma . . . and for the timing for their marriage. And then to think you signed your farewell note to me in nearly the same way," she added. Now the tears were coming, and it was impossible to stop them.

"Trusting in God's plan isn't always easy, 'specially when the way isn't clear." Arden embraced her again. "Ach, did I ever have to learn that lesson, starting the minute you moved away from Leacock Township . . . letting ya go as I did."

Lena brushed away her tears. "You mean ya had no idea we'd be together like this?"

"Lena Rose," he whispered, "meetin' you and knowin' how much you longed for your family here . . . well, it was the hardest thing for me to say good-bye that day on the road."

She remembered the agonizing farewell. "Want to know a secret?" she asked.

"Well, did ya want to run an' catch up with me, just maybe?" he teased, but then just as quickly, she could see that he was completely serious.

"It was all I could do not to, *jah*. How'd ya know?"

"I wanted to do the same thing," he confessed, reaching for her hand. "I love you, Lena Rose."

"I love you, too." *More than you might guess.* "Good things *do* come out of deep sorrow and great loss . . . at least in time," she said, her heart filled with gratitude.

Arden glanced out at the sky filled with stars, then back at her. "The two of us together like this is proof, *jah*?"

Epilogue

The weekend after Thanksgiving, Arden and I were on our way over to the Neuenschwanders' with Chris to sled with the other boys. The air was so crisp that we could see the horse's breath, like a small billowy cloud against the cold.

Arden looked at Chris, who was wearing his warmest coat, snow pants, and mittens. "Are ya helpin' your Dawdi and Mammi these days?" Arden asked.

Chris nodded thoughtfully. "Doin' my best."

"*Des gut.*"

Chris glanced at me. "Mammi says I have more energy than *two* boys!"

I smiled at Arden's amused expression.

"Well," Arden said, "I haven't talked this over with your sister here, but once we tie the knot next year, we'll be renting a house." He caught my eye. "One with plenty-a space."

Chris listened, eyebrows rising.

Arden continued. "And I was thinking . . ."

Oh goodness, I could practically feel Chris's growing excitement.

"*Jah?*" he said, leaning forward.

"Would ya like to come live with us?" Arden asked.

Chris popped right out of his seat, a grin clear across his rosy cheeks. "That's just what I was hopin' for!"

Winking at me, Arden smiled. "What do ya say, Lena Rose?"

Chris and I had prayed about this, I recalled, but I never expected it would be with Arden, back when. Oh, the love I felt for this man! "It's a *wunnerbaar-gut* idea," I agreed.

Chris reached over to shake Arden's hand; then he hugged my neck. "This is the best news ever!" he said. "But won't Mammi and Dawdi Schwartz be sad?" He suddenly looked pensive, his mouth curving down.

"Well, remember, you'll be with them for another year yet," I told him.

Chris nodded slowly. "And Dawdi's not real strong anymore, so he and Mammi might be ready to have a quieter house," he added.

"I'm thinkin' you're prob'ly right," I said, placing a hand on his shoulder. "Such a wise boy you are."

"Am I as wise as you, Lena Rose?"

I had to laugh. "What do ya mean?"

Chris was looking at Arden and grinning again. "'Cause ya picked a mighty fine beau."

"Truth be told, the Good Lord did the pickin'," I said. "And when ya say your prayers tonight, be sure to thank our heavenly Father for bringin' Arden into our lives, all right?"

Chris bobbed his head and grew quiet, and I could tell he was thinking hard about something. "Do ya remember after Dat and Mamma died, when I said I'd obey whatever ya said?"

"I never forgot."

"Well, Arden, I'll be just as obedient for you, too," declared Chris now. "And hard-workin'."

Arden was nodding, grinning now. "You know, I really have

the best end of the deal, getting to live with my new younger brother."

Chris beamed at that, and I patted his knee. "We're going to have fun bein' a family together," I said, certain it was true.

Sitting there between Arden in the driver's seat and my precious little brother, I thought, *I never could've planned such a day.* I recalled what my mother had often said to me, *"Always remember Who holds your future."*

"Dearest Mamma," I whispered as I glanced toward the sky.

My heart knew that all the dear ones God had placed in my path had been part of His beautiful plan, one that had brought me to this remarkable season of thanksgiving . . . and led me home.

Note from the Author

At times, I am surprised at the way God brings my research assistants across my path, especially those heralding from Amish communities outside of Lancaster County, Pennsylvania, where I grew up. For instance, from the first call to a Centreville, Michigan, phone shanty in the middle of a cornfield, I was blessed to begin a special friendship with a wonderful Amish couple eager to share their lives and the answers to my questions. Later, additional research assistants helped me in uncovering Amish practices in St. Joseph County, Michigan, and Elkhart County, Indiana, during the 1970s. Among them are Mel Riegsecker, Wilbur Bontrager, John MacDonald, Erik Wesner, Liz Miller Carmel, her father, and her Michigan Amish cousin, and the good folk at Nottawa Fruit Farm. Thank you all!

My sincere appreciation also goes to Cynthia Marquet, curator of the Ressler Mill Foundation. Cynthia read sections of the manuscript pertaining to the historic water-powered gristmill found on the banks of Mill Creek in Upper Leacock Township. Recently, I was honored to be given a private tour of the Mascot Roller Mills.

Henner's Lydia, by 1950 Newbery Medal winner Marguerite de Angeli, has been a treasured book in my personal library for decades and was a favorite story of my own children.

And of course I cannot thank my husband, Dave, enough; he is so involved in all the brainstorming and the proofing of each novel I write. We are the best partners!

My insightful and ever-supportive editors, David Horton and Rochelle Glöege, also play an enormous role in getting my stories ready for you, dear reader-friend, as does their wonderful editorial staff. To each one, I offer my enthusiastic gratitude.

My Bethany House prayer partners are among those precious people who have committed to praying for me. They are truly the mainstay of everything I write. May God bless you abundantly in every way.

Soli Deo Gloria—to the glory of God alone!

Beverly Lewis, born in the heart of Pennsylvania Dutch country, is the *New York Times* bestselling author of more than one hundred books. Her stories have been published in twelve languages worldwide. A keen interest in her mother's Plain heritage has inspired Beverly to write many Amish-related novels, beginning with *The Shunning,* which has sold more than one million copies and is an Original Hallmark Channel movie. In 2007 *The Brethren* was honored with a Christy Award.

Beverly has been interviewed by both national and international media, including *Time* magazine, the Associated Press, and the BBC. She lives with her husband, David, in Colorado.

Visit her website at www.beverlylewis.com or www.facebook.com/officialbeverlylewis for more information.

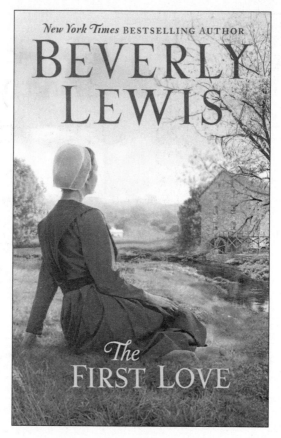

The First Love

The Next Novel from Beverly Lewis

Available Fall 2018

Sign Up for Beverly's Newsletter!

Keep up to date with
Beverly's news on
book releases and events by
signing up for her email list at
beverlylewis.com.

More from Beverly Lewis!

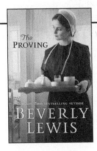

Having left the Amish life for the English world, Mandy Dienner is shocked when she learns she has inherited Lancaster County's most popular Amish bed-and-breakfast. The catch is she has to run it herself for one year. Reluctantly, Mandy accepts the challenge, no matter that it means facing the family she left behind—or that the inn's clientele expect an *Amish* hostess.

The Proving

Also from Beverly Lewis

Visit beverlylewis.com for a full list of her books.

When a young Amish woman takes a summer job as a nanny in beautiful Cape May, she forms an unexpected bond with a handsome Mennonite. Has she been too hasty with her promises, or will she only find what her heart is longing for back home?

The Ebb Tide

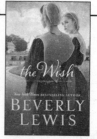

When a young Amish woman sets out on a mission to persuade a friend to return to the Amish church, will her dearest wish lead to her own undoing?

The Wish

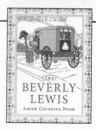

Experience the tranquil, homespun world of the Amish of Lancaster County, the setting of Beverly Lewis's many bestselling novels. This inspiring coloring book is filled with artful depictions of Amish life, including quilting bees, buggy rides, farm scenes, and more. As you color the charming images, you'll be blessed by gems of Amish wisdom and Scripture.

The Beverly Lewis Amish Coloring Book

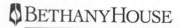
BETHANYHOUSE